GLOW UP
LARA
BLOOM

Books by Dee Benson

Glow Up, Lara Bloom
Work It, Lara Bloom

GLOW UP LARA BLOOM

DEE BENSON

HOT
KEY
BOOKS

First published in Great Britain in 2023 by
HOT KEY BOOKS
4th Floor, Victoria House, Bloomsbury Square, London WC1B 4DA
Owned by Bonnier Books, Sveavägen 56, Stockholm, Sweden
bonnierbooks.co.uk/HotKeyBooks

This is a work of fiction. Names, places, events and incidents are either
the products of the author's imagination or used fictitiously. Any resemblance
to actual persons, living or dead, is purely coincidental.

A CIP catalogue record for this book is available from the British Library.

ISBN: 978-1-4714-1291-2
Also available as an ebook and in audio

4

Typeset by Envy Design Ltd
Printed and bound in Great Britain by Clays Ltd, Elcograf S.p.A.

Hot Key Books is an imprint of Bonnier Books UK
bonnierbooks.co.uk

For Yomi,
who has always believed

&

for Rhema and Esther,
my queens

1

Dear Diary, This
Is Goodbye

Thursday 30 August, 1 p.m.

I am never *EVER* journaling again!!!

I know what you're thinking: if you're never journaling again, why are you journaling right now?

Well, this is the last entry I will ever write. Because before I stop journaling forever, I must explain exactly how my *ANNOYING BIG BROTHER*, Danny, has taken tormenting me to a whole new level!

This diary came with a lock and key. It contains my *BIGGEST SECRETS* and lots of *CONFIDENTIAL INFORMATION*. But guess what??? Danny managed to break into it while I was in the shower this morning, getting ready to meet up with my friends at the park, and he found out that it was me who broke his watch. I didn't do it on purpose. It was an ACCIDENT. But I didn't want to tell him because he's such a moaner.

What's worse, while Danny was rifling through my journal — like he had every right to read my INNERMOST THOUGHTS — he read other entries apart from the one about his watch, and he found out that I used to have a crush on his friend Alex.

That's when the BLACKMAIL began ☹

It's his turn to do the chores today: dishes, dusting, vacuuming, the works. (I know, our parents are TYRANNICAL OVERLORDS!) And guess what he said???

'FROM NOW ON, YOU'RE DOING MY CHORES OR I'M TELLING ALEX HOW MUCH YOU LOVE HIM!'

Since I would spontaneously combust if Alex ever found out that I used to have a crush on him, I'm pretty much at Danny's mercy forever!!!

The worst thing was, I had only fifteen minutes until I was supposed to meet my friends at the park. We'd planned to meet at noon, and I was really looking forward to it. But with Danny threatening to RUIN MY LIFE, I had to drop everything and do his chores.

My friend Anaya texted me, reminding me not to be late, but I knew there was no way I would be able to get there in time.

Nala, my cuddly grey cat, kept purring mournfully as I did the dishes. She can always tell when I'm in emotional distress, and she's the only member of my family that I truly get along with.

Half an hour later, as I was vacuuming the stairs, Anaya texted me again, saying: Where are you??? Kayleigh bought you an ice cream and it's pretty much melted now. Btw Becky says she has a new crush 😍

Great. My friends were at the park eating ice creams and trading major gossip while I was doing chores for my big brother from hell!

I sent her a quick reply: I'll be there soon. Sorry!

But it was still another twenty minutes before I was done, because Danny started pointing out all the spots I'd missed when dusting. Then, just to make my misery complete, he made me tidy his room, which was a stinky mess. I had to sort through his heaps of dirty T-shirts, underpants and smelly socks. There was even a slice of MOULDY PIZZA in there.

That was the last straw.

I'm now an hour late to meet up with my friends, and I'm so stressed out I'm just sitting here in my room trying not to have a total meltdown.

If I'm ever tempted to journal again, I'll see this entry and remember that it isn't worth it!

Anaya: WHERE ARE YOU? We've been waiting for over an hour!!

Me: Just leaving home now. It's a long story, but Danny read my journal.

Anaya: 😱😱😱 How much of it did he read?

Me: The worst parts. He found out I used to like Alex and said I had to do his chores or he's going to tell him. That's why I'm running late.

Anaya: Ouch 😩😩

Me: I know. I'm never journaling again.

Anaya: Really? How will you survive without journaling? You're addicted.

Me: Well, it's not safe. I can't have Danny finding out any more of my secrets.

Anaya: I think I have a solution. Give me a sec xx

Anaya: Okay, I have a solution.

Me: What is it???

Anaya: Check out *www.journalpixie.com*. You can thank me when you get here xoxo

Thursday 30 August, 1.25 p.m.

Anaya just gave me a GENIUS idea! I've been stuck in the Dark Ages this whole time when journaling software exists! I can write anything I want – just not in a diary where any old person can read it!!

I know it's been barely half an hour since I swore off journaling forever, but this changes everything.

So, hello, journaling app. I already prefer you to all the diaries I've had in the past. So safe and secure on my phone. Plus, you can use emojis 😁😔😊🐼🍃, and you can choose from lots of different fonts.

This one is called Faerie Princess.

This one is Unicorn. Cute!

```
This one is Courier. Tell me, has there
ever been a more BORING font than Courier???
```

❋〰〉◆ ↗□■◆ 〉◆ ♏〽♋●●♍♌ ◆〉■〽♌♌〉■〽◆◆◈

That font ⇈ is called Wingdings 😵. I suppose I could use that for extra security, but since I won't be able to read it myself, I'm settling for this one. It's called Cuckoo, which, for some reason, I'm finding pretty hilarious right now.

There's an option to publish your entries, which is

odd. I don't know why anyone would want to do that. Isn't that a blog, not a journal? Journals are for SECRETS. Why would anyone even be interested in reading someone else's journal, unless they're a diabolical big brother looking for juicy information with which to blackmail his unsuspecting little sister?!?!?

Even though I'm going to be stuck doing Danny's chores for a while, at least I can still journal, which means I won't have to bottle up all my feelings. I have an outlet for my fully justified RAGE and won't resort to STRANGLING DANNY IN HIS SLEEP.

2.15 p.m.

By the time I finally made it to our spot in the park (by the fountain), I was an hour and a half late!! Anaya must have already told Kayleigh and Becky about what happened because neither of them gave me any grief for being late. Just as well, because I still felt ready to EXPLODE.

Anaya immediately stood up from the low wall that runs around the fountain and said, 'Take a deep breath.'

I tried, but my breaths were coming in quick, shallow gasps, and I desperately wanted to scream.

'Her eye's twitching,' Becky said. 'That's how you know things are bad.'

To my horror, it was. My right eye was twitching so hard like it was going to POP RIGHT OFF MY FACE.

'How on earth did Danny get into your journal?' Kayleigh asked. 'You're always so careful.'

Somehow, I managed to speak. I told them, from the beginning, all about Danny and his sinister, spying, diary-reading ways! As they listened, their faces contorted with varying degrees of horror, which was very satisfying and made me feel much better.

'Tell your parents,' Kayleigh suggested. 'Let them threaten to ground him if he tells Alex that you had a crush on him. That should sort it.'

Kayleigh has four older sisters, so she's had to learn how to get her voice heard. The only problem with this advice is Danny was ten steps ahead! He didn't just read my journal entries about his watch and my old crush on Alex, but he also read a rant I wrote about Mum and Dad the other week when they grounded me in the MIDDLE OF THE SUMMER HOLIDAYS!!

Side note: I *told* you my parents are tyrannical overlords. I got grounded for TWO WHOLE DAYS when they found out I hadn't done any of my holiday homework.

Another side note: Can I just say that summer holiday homework is a ridiculous idea? It's right up there with chocolate teapots and marshmallow scissors.

First of all, if teachers can't teach us everything we need to know in all the *many* months we spend in school each year, they need to have a serious chat with themselves.

Second of all, it's called a school holiday for a reason.

I just googled the official dictionary definition of the word 'holiday' and it's 'an extended period of leisure and recreation, especially one spent away from home or in travelling'. What part of that definition says work is involved? None!

Anyway, my journal rant about Mum and Dad included words like KILLJOYS, ANNOYING TYRANTS and EVIL DICTATORS. And Danny warned me that if I tell our parents about him blackmailing me into doing his chores, he's going to tell them about that rant.

I'm totally SCREWED!

After I explained this to my friends, Becky gave a low whistle. 'OMG, Lara,' she said, 'you're basically Danny's personal Cinderella now. But fairy godmothers do exist. Maybe one will show up and whisk you away to freedom.'

I think she was trying to make me smile, but after the mouldy pizza I had to scoop up in Danny's room, I don't think I'll be seeing the humour in anything for a while (except maybe Cuckoo font, ha ha).

Anyway, I'd better put my phone away before my friends start moaning about me journaling all the time when we're supposed to be hanging out.

I'm so glad I can journal on my phone now though. I won't have to lug a book around like an oddpot who would rather write in her diary than talk to actual people. Not that looking like an oddpot has ever bothered me before. You kind of get used to it when you're . . . well, me.

2.45 p.m.

Speaking of oddpots, Richard Skelley just walked past. He's this boy in the year above at school. At first glance, he looks pretty cool with his long-ish, black rock-star hair and eyeliner. I'll get to why he's weird in a minute, but at the sight of him, Becky almost had a heart attack. You know that hot gossip about her new crush? It's him. RICHARD SKELLEY, OF ALL PEOPLE!!

I just had to dig out my phone and tell you all about it, dear App. (Hmm, 'dear App' doesn't have the same ring as 'dear Diary'!!)

Anyway, Anaya told her she can do better.

She's right too. Richard Skelley is so bizarre. Last year, I had the misfortune of witnessing him run down the hallway outside the lunch room, farting with every step. He must have released, like, SEVEN FARTS. I had no idea someone could have that much gas built up inside them. And if they did, why release it so loudly and proudly??

'You'll need a gas mask,' Kayleigh told Becky, cackling with laughter.

'Well, she's survived the animal shelter all summer without a gas mask,' Anaya said.

True. Becky's parents made her volunteer this summer. It's 'character-building', they said. (I didn't tell my parents in case they got any ideas.) The shelter had some ex-racehorses, and whenever we met up with Becky after a shift, she stank of manure. 💩 💩

(Kayleigh just noticed me journaling and went, 'You're going to get even more addicted to journaling now that you have an app.' I didn't deny it, because I think she's right. I LOVE this app already ♡)

'I'm so glad my volunteering has turned into paid work this summer,' Anaya said.

Her so-called 'volunteering' is just helping out at her mum's café, where she gets to eat paninis, drink smoothies and have all the customers exclaim over how pretty and well-mannered she is.

'Mum thought I should be fine with only getting tips, just because there's no minimum wage for fourteen-year-olds,' Anaya said. 'Well, I've had enough of helping out practically for free. I was on Google all yesterday evening, reading about it, and I tried to convince her this morning to pay me the minimum wage for sixteen-year-olds.'

'She's going to pay you?' Kayleigh asked.

Anaya nodded. 'But she said it'll be one pound less per hour than what sixteen-year-olds get.'

'That's still good,' I said. (See? I can journal *and* contribute to conversations at the same time ☺)

'Yeah, well, she's going to put it in my bank account so I can't blow it all at once,' Anaya said with a scowl.

It's good to know it's not just my parents who always find a way to suck the fun out of everything.

Anyway, we were trying to have a civilised conversation – you know, like mature teenagers – when Kayleigh randomly went, 'Watch this!' and started dancing.

'Uh, what are you doing?' I asked.

'I've been watching this dance tutorial on YouTube. It's so fun. There's a part where you need a partner, but I just use trees.' She ran over to a nearby tree and started to dance around it. Anaya burst out laughing, but I was just mortified on Kayleigh's behalf.

This whole time, Becky was silent. I bet she was thinking about Richard.

Richard would probably be chuffed if he found out that Becky likes him. She's pretty in an I-didn't-make-much-effort kind of way. And her straight black hair is really long these days, ever since she decided to grow it. She flicks it around constantly. I know because of all the times I've narrowly missed getting whacked in the face by it.

All my friends are pretty, actually. Anaya has dark, curly hair and flawless light brown skin, and Kayleigh is all blonde hair and hazel eyes. Then there's me. Plain as a pole! It's bad enough being ordinary, but I look even more ordinary than I am because my friends are so pretty.

Anaya and me were friends first, before we became a quartet. We started hanging out two months into Year 7 after I tried to sit next to her in an art lesson and knocked over a whole tray of paints. (I know. I'm a WALKING CATASTROPHE!) The paint splatted all over us both and everyone started laughing. I didn't even know Anaya's name at the time, and I thought she was going to be really annoyed, but she just stared at me in shock for a few moments then burst into laughter.

A few weeks later, Anaya and I played doubles tennis against Kayleigh and Becky in PE. It was so good to find two girls who were as wild as us. The four of us have been inseparable ever since.

Anyway, Becky froze into a statue at Richard's presence, even though he was making loud SHEEP NOISES with a bunch of people on the other side of the fountain and hadn't even noticed us. Then she got up and walked away really fast.

Me and Anaya rolled our eyes and followed her. Kayleigh stopped dancing and ran to catch up.

Becky is shy like that. If she has a crush on someone, she can never be around them, so how is her crush supposed to get a chance to, y'know, realise she exists?

To be honest, though, I'm not much better. When I have a crush I avoid them like the plague. But I have an excuse: I'm not a total stunner like Becky is. I'm so glad I don't have any crushes at the moment. Having a crush is nerve-racking – especially when you know for a fact that there's no way they would ever like you back. Everyone I've ever crushed on would probably laugh in my face if they found out.

Anyway, I wasn't impressed that we had to leave the fountain area. It's really hot today and the spray from the fountain was nice and cooling. Even worse, Becky was speed-walking towards these steps and Anaya and Kayleigh immediately reached for my hands, like I'm some OLD LADY.

I glared at them both, but that just made them laugh. Ever since the time I fell down a whole bunch of stairs at Anfield Stadium, they think it's funny to 'assist' me whenever we come across stairs in day-to-day life.

Believe me, there have been many embarrassing moments in my life, but that fall was one of the worst. I'll never forget it, and I'll never live it down.

Since it was so incredibly TRAUMATIC, it deserves a heading:

The Most Embarrassing Moment of My Life

Last year, I went to watch a charity match that the Liverpool women's football team was playing against the Everton women's team. I was a few minutes late, so I had to fight my way to my seat. On the way, I managed to trip over someone's foot and FALL DOWN THE STANDS!!

I went bouncing down the steps of Anfield Stadium. Each bounce sent flashes of pain through my whole body and I only stopped falling because I ran out of stairs to fall down. Mum said she tried to catch me. I don't believe her. She was busy gabbing to Anaya's mum. Anaya said she tried to help but I was going too fast, then people got in her way.

Anyway, after I managed to pick myself up, guess what happened next? A ball appeared from nowhere and was flying right at me!

That's right. One of the Everton women had cleared a corner kick and blasted the ball straight at my head. It almost knocked me out. In fact, I think I did conk out for a few seconds. All I remember is a *THWACK!*, a blast of pain through my skull and a ringing sound in my ears.

Then there was nothing for what could either have been a few seconds or a few millennia (Anaya said it was just a few seconds). When my brain switched back on, the first thing I felt was the pain in my nose and neck. And then . . . the cool air on my left bum cheek. That's when I realised I was lying on the ground, face down, denim skirt around my waist.

Instead of covering my modesty like a skirt is supposed to, it was AROUND MY WAIST.

Everyone could see my knickers!

And it was this old green pair with a big hole on the left bum cheek. Hence why I could feel a breeze on my bum.

After that, I wanted to die. And writing about it now makes me want to die all over again.

Seriously, without a doubt, I have the WORST life in the whole world!

4 p.m.

After our hasty exit from the fountain area, we wandered around the park for a bit until we found ourselves in the jungle gym. It was empty for once.

I tried to sit on one of the swings on the side and somehow landed on the ground. I must have pushed the seat back as I tried to sit, because then it swung forward and WHACKED THE BACK OF MY HEAD!

My friends, to their credit, didn't laugh. Anaya just helped me to my feet and held the seat still while I sat on it.

'Thanks,' I muttered, my face hot with embarrassment. I could hear Dad's voice in my head: *You never pay attention, Lara!*

'Are you guys ready for school?' Kayleigh asked.

'Ready or not, school is starting,' I muttered, suddenly all morose.

'No need to sound so depressed about it,' Kayleigh replied, leaning against one of the jungle gym poles.

(If that was me trying to lean against a pole, I would have miscalculated its position and fallen flat on my back!)

'I'm actually looking forward to school,' Becky said. 'The animal shelter has been fun, but I've had enough of it now.'

I sighed. I hate school. I'd rather not waste any brain space thinking about it until Monday, when I absolutely have to.

School would be great if it was just my friends and the girls' football team. But no, there's also lots of hard work, annoying teachers and stuck-up people who look down their nose at you just because they're popular and you're not. There aren't even any cute boys. They're all gross and think they're hilarious when they're about as funny as a slow internet connection.

But Kayleigh is so excited for the new school year, she's even 'setting goals'. Basically to 'build good study habits' so she'll hardly have to study when our GCSEs roll around in Year 11. I can't believe she's planning that far ahead. We're only just starting Year 10. Anaya, however, was impressed and said she would do the same.

I'm not a bad student. I'm actually doing okay in most of my subjects. But Kayleigh and Anaya love to 'excel'. Personally, so long as I pass any tests we're given, I'm not too fussed about how well I do. English literature is probably the least annoying subject, followed by history. Mainly because they're not too much hassle and I've discovered I'm good at writing long, waffly essays. Everyone hates maths, me included, but I'm actually okay at it.

'What's *your* goal for Year 10, Lara?' Kayleigh asked, yanking me from my thoughts.

I snorted. She knew full well that I wouldn't have any 'goals'.

Thankfully, Becky saved me from having to respond by saying, 'My goal is to basically become Esme Bucci.'

None of us could refrain from rolling our eyes. Esme Bucci is this sixteen-year-old, annoyingly gorgeous girl who is famous online for her make-up tutorials. Becky is obsessed with watching them.

She took out her phone and showed us Esme's latest video: BACK TO SCHOOL PREPARATIONS | *Hair, Brows, Lashes, Nails.*

'Lashes?' Anaya asked. 'Let's see.'

'Who wears false eyelashes to school?' I asked, bewildered.

'HI, GUYS!' came Esme Bucci's syrupy, cheerful and very high-pitched voice from Becky's phone.

We ended up watching her whole 'Back to School' series. It was six videos that lasted for SEVENTEEN (!!) minutes altogether, but we were gripped, fascinated by the lengths she was going to, from getting a manicure to stocking up on pretty pink stationery that matched her nails. Pink, she said, was her 'colour of the term'.

(Oops, Kayleigh just scowled at me then said to Anaya, 'Now that Lara has a journaling app, we're never going to be able to have a proper conversation with her ever again!')

At the end of the videos, Kayleigh said, all snooty, 'You don't need to *get* ready for school when you *stay* ready.'

'What's that supposed to mean?' Becky asked.

'Well, at the beginning of the holidays I said we should have a glow up, and none of you were interested.

But now, with a new crush and four days until school starts, you want to reinvent your whole life and become Esme Bucci!'

Anaya and I exchanged a look. Kayleigh has been talking about having a 'glow up' *all* summer. According to her, a glow up is when you transform yourself and become a better version of you. It sounded like fun when she first mentioned it, but then she said, 'We really need to have a productive summer, girls', and that made it sound less like fun and more like work. And since I basically wanted to be as unproductive as possible over the summer, I said no. Then Becky and Anaya said no too.

I did feel a bit bad for not being supportive, but I'm *really* not interested in glowing up. I know what Kayleigh is like. She likes to 'research' stuff, learn new things and read wise quotes online. Which is WORK!!! Between holiday homework and chores, I figured I had enough boredom-inducing stuff on my plate.

I'm so glad we no longer have to write 'How I spent my summer holiday' essays like we did in primary school. I spent this summer playing football, watching Marvel movies and wishing I was Zendaya. Nothing there to impress a teacher.

'Having a glow up is better than trying to give yourself a quick makeover,' Kayleigh said. 'Makeovers are superficial, but with a glow up, you transform yourself from the inside out and become a better version of yourself.'

(See? I *knew* she was going to say that.)

Something you need to know about Kayleigh is that when she decides to do something, she goes ALL IN. And the whole world has to stop and do it with her.

Now, I know I'm clumsy and kind of prone to bad luck, so becoming 'the best version of myself' *does* appeal. But I'm not sure about this whole glow up thing, simply because it's Kayleigh suggesting it. I just can't trust a girl who once dipped her hair in camel's urine on holiday in Dubai. She said that in ancient times, women used to do it to make their hair shiny. Um, what happened to hairspray? Hair oils? Deep-conditioning hair masks? Anything but CAMEL'S PEE!!

With that in mind, when Kayleigh said, 'So are you in on the glow up now?' I gave her a fast 'NO'.

'Is dancing with trees part of your glow up?' Anaya asked.

'No,' Kayleigh said. 'That was just a bit of fun. You won't have to dance.'

'It's still a no from me,' I said.

Anaya and Becky also declined. They don't trust Kayleigh much either.

'I'll glow up by myself, then,' Kayleigh said huffily.

'Time for our Summer Selfie,' Anaya said, changing the subject.

Every summer, just before we go back to school, we take a group picture. As usual, I pulled a silly face, cross-eyed with my tongue out 😜. Kayleigh started laughing. She never stays annoyed for long. None of my friends do. They're totally awesome.

7.10 p.m.

I just got back from hanging out with my friends, and I overheard Mum and Dad gushing about how great a job Danny has done with his chores today. They even said he can stay out an hour later tomorrow evening as a reward!

A reward for chores that *I* did!

I THINK I'M GOING TO PUKE!!!!!

8.18 p.m.

I just realised that I *do* have a goal for the coming school year! It's not a schoolwork-related goal, but it's still very important. You see, I'm the captain of the girls' football team. Now, people make all kinds of assumptions when they find out you like football, as a girl.

Assumption 1: *You must be a tomboy.*
No.
I'm not.
I'm just a girl who happens to like playing football. There are tomboys, girly girls and everything in-between on the team. Football is for any girl who wants to play it!

Assumption 2: *You can't be any good at it.*
HA! The Schoolgirls' Football League includes schools from all over the city, but *I* have been the top goal-scorer for two years straight so . . . yeah. I can't be that bad at it 😄.

Assumption 3: *You're only the top goal-scorer because the other girls are rubbish. You're just the best of a BAD BUNCH!!!*
ACTUALLY, we played against the boys last year. Since there are lots of boys' teams in our school and only one girls' team, the teachers put all the boys' names in a hat and chose their players at random. And guess what? We beat them 2–1. So if we're rubbish, they're even MORE rubbish!!

So, my goal for this year is to score actual goals. The girls' football team has been in SPECTACULAR form. We haven't lost a single match in almost THREE YEARS! We've had plenty of draws, and almost as many wins, but we have remained unbeaten since halfway through my Year 7.

We didn't set out to do this. In fact, when I first joined the team, we had some brutal defeats. Then Miss Simpson, our evil coach/PE teacher, joined the school, and we started losing less. (For the record, I don't mind her evilness one bit, since it works.) Then we started winning sometimes too. We ended that season with TWENTY matches unbeaten in a row.

We tried to keep it up the next year and actually managed it, which is incredible, considering that there are thirty-eight matches in a season. We didn't lose a single one. Then we almost lost our unbeaten streak last year because Zoe, the old team captain, was now in Year 11 and had to stop playing because of her GCSEs. All the amazing Year 11 girls who were the backbone of the team left us.

What's worse, Zoe nominated *me* to be the new captain. Even though I was the top goal-scorer, I wasn't expecting it because I was only in Year 9. Besides, there were other girls who scored a lot too.

I was FUMING when she nominated me. I thought she was setting me up for an EPIC FAIL and wanted things to fall apart so that everyone would wish she was still around. But, to my shock, Miss Simpson actually agreed with her. So, near the end of last season, I became team captain.

Zoe and the other Year 11 girls came to watch us whenever they could. Having them cheer us on from the sidelines made us fight even harder to keep up our unbeaten streak. We almost slipped up a few times, but we managed it. We won a further seven games with me as captain – and guess what? Out of the blue, I became a *person*. Not popular by any stretch of the imagination, but suddenly people at school knew that I existed.

Usually, I'm just one of the many invisible losers who make it possible for popular people to stand out. However, thanks to my success as team captain, I started getting nods in the hallways! The day after the match against Morston High where we won 5–2 (!!) I even got some smiles.

But I don't play football for nods and smiles. I play because I love it. There's nothing like the thrill you get when you score a goal or win a match.

We only have four more games to go to hit one hundred games unbeaten, and I'm CONVINCED something is going to go wrong.

8.40 p.m.

Dear Diary, I figured there might still be more you need to know about me before we continue on our adventures together, so guess what? I'm going to give you a ROOM TOUR!! 🐵 🐵

I wish you could tell me what it's like to be an app, living in my phone, but I guess I'll just have to imagine. Is it anything like the movie *Emoji*? That would actually be pretty cool!

Well, I live with my mum, dad and the most annoying big brother in the world in a tiny terraced house that is nothing like the huge ones a few streets away that were built centuries ago. Ours is kind of modern, and it's REALLY small. You can hear the neighbours through the walls, which I don't really mind, because my room shares a wall with Jay's house (I've known Jay since I was, like, a baby) and the only thing I ever hear is his mum's old-school music.

We used to live in the high rise on the next street until two years ago when Jay's mum told us this house was for sale. His mum and my mum are best friends and have been following each other around since they were teens.

Sorry, this room tour is turning into a house tour with random info about my neighbours.

So, back to my room. Mine is the smallest room in the whole house, but it's also the best room, since I have much better taste than anyone else in my family. My room's colour scheme is black and white with pops of hot pink everywhere: my bean bag, my bedframe, my feathery lightshade, my lamp. I chose everything myself, and I'm really proud of how it all turned out.

I have a poster of the Lionesses on the back of my door. They're England's women's football team, and they're EPIC. I sometimes high-five it before big matches. I swear it gives me good luck.

The only other hint of my love of football is the two golden boot trophies I keep on the wall shelf by my bed. At the end of every season, they're awarded to the top goal-scorer. I would like to have more football stuff in my room, but since it's so small, anything else will make it look cluttered. I always keep my room tidy for the same reason.

Okay, okay, that's a total lie. The *real* reason I keep my room tidy is because it once got so messy and stinky (the stench was from Nala's litter tray, not me) that Mum threatened to put Nala up for ADOPTION! My room has never been messy since.

I really don't know why Mum is so obsessed with having an 'immaculate house', as she calls it. Me and Danny have to do so many chores because, according to Mum and Dad, we make most of the mess. That's the only time I'm glad our house is small. If it was any bigger, I'd be doing chores CONSTANTLY!

9.08 p.m.

Anaya just posted the Summer Selfie in our group chat. I scrolled back to find our selfies from the past two years and my friends all look so different now, while I just look the same, except a bit taller in each picture. My hair is exactly the same in every picture too – just stuffed into a bun. The bun has gotten a bit sleeker though. In the first picture it was really puffy with loose tufts EVERYWHERE. I looked like a TOTAL DISASTER.

I'm better at flattening my hair now, but having the same hairstyle for three years does show a complete lack of imagination, doesn't it?!

Oh, well. I have more important things to worry about than hair. Things like football and Marvel movies.

I re-posted the past pictures in our group chat and my friends started responding right away.

Anaya: OMG we looked like BABIES two years ago! 😄
Becky: Look at the state of my clothes! Why didn't you guys tell me that bow was hideous??
Kayleigh: It was your favourite accessory . . .
Becky: Did you guys think it was hideous?
Anaya: No, we thought it was cute.
Becky: DON'T LIE TO ME 😩
Me: You and your bow are FINE, Becky. Look at the state of ME. At least you guys have changed and look better these days. I'm still the same, and I'm still so flat-chested it's unbelievable!

Honestly, I don't mind my lack of imagination about my hair that much. That can change whenever I decide I'm ready to face my 'fro. But, seriously, why don't I have boobs? Everyone else is getting them!

My phone immediately began to buzz. Kayleigh was calling me. She's planning her glow up, and she's got something special in mind for tomorrow evening.

'Think of it as a taster session,' she said brightly.

I wasn't about to let her sway me, but before I could say no she said something that got me interested: 'It might help with . . . y'know, the flat-chestedness.'

She didn't say much after that.

9.24 p.m.

Okay, she did. She said a few things, but I don't know if I'm brave enough to type them in case someone reads it. I know I'm using an app and everything, but I've learned that you can never be too careful.

One minute you think your secrets are safe. The next, you're picking up MOULDY PIZZA in your brother's SMELLY room. (Can you tell I'm still traumatised?)

Anyway, Kayleigh said to come to her house tomorrow after 'moonrise' as she called it.

OMG, it's pathetic how excited I am.

I CAN'T WAIT!!

2

My Cyclops Chest

Friday 31 August, 9.43 p.m.
Tonight has been the most EMBARRASSING night of my life. Honestly, on a scale of 1 to 10 it's 100!

I'm never letting Kayleigh Lawson talk me into anything EVER AGAIN. I've finally managed to stop my teeth chattering, but I still can't get over the muddy boobs.

How, you may be wondering, does a fourteen-year-old girl (fifteen in two months – yay!) get her boobs muddy?

Before I tell you, let me clarify two things:

1. When I say boobs, dear Diary, I'm being waaayyy generous. I'm so flat-chested I pretty much have two backs. One of them is my front.

Actually, it's not really fair to say that, because I'm

not completely flat. I do have a little bit of something going on, but what's weird is that my left boob is bigger than the right one. Leftie is a solid A cup while rightie is still a double A. I'm like a Cyclops, but a boob version. I'm the one-boobed girl. Maybe my body is doing this for Hallowe'en, to save me the cost of a costume . . . 🎃

Anyway, I digress.

2. THIS WAS NOT MY IDEA. It was Kayleigh's.

Back to what happened: I took myself off to Kayleigh's house after nightfall. Her only instruction was 'bring a jacket', which I did. Becky, the other innocent victim who Kayleigh had talked into her little glow-up activity, was there too. Anaya didn't come.

In my defence, Kayleigh didn't tell me exactly what we were going to be doing. She did mumble something about chanting as she led us into her vast front garden, but that was all.

'The back garden would have been better,' she told us, 'if it had some trees. Out front, we have the perfect tree, and we'll be hidden by all the bushes.'

Why would we need trees? Why would we need to be hidden by bushes?

Well, dear Diary, I didn't ask. I was just eager for a solution to my BOOBLESSNESS!

I was already imagining myself with a pair of 34Cs. My

cousin Sadé is eighteen and has 34Cs. Since we're a similar physique, 34Cs would look perfect on me too.

Then I noticed that Kayleigh had a shovel.

Ten minutes later, Kayleigh, Becky and I were lying in the mud.

Other people go to parties on Friday nights. Or the cinema. But I was lying in the mud with two of my best friends, burying our breasts in the soil under a magnificent oak tree.

Kayleigh said the soil must be particularly rich in nutrients since the oak tree had grown so big.

Why, I hear you ask, *were you and your friends burying your breasts in the soil???*

Big sigh

Well, we did it because Kayleigh swore it would make them grow.

#EMBARRASSING.

'How do you make something grow?' she asked me when I asked why on earth she thought digging holes in the mud and putting our boobs in them would work. 'You plant it.'

I understood that for SEEDS, not for boobs.

Then Kayleigh added, 'But it's not really about growing our boobs. It's about being one with nature and drawing from Mother Earth's calming feminine energy.'

The only thing that made it slightly less embarrassing was that we kept our bras on. If I'm being completely honest, I knew it was stupid, but after watching my friends sprout boobs at the age of, like, eleven, while my chest adamantly refused to grow, and then became a Cyclops chest, I wondered, what if?

What if it worked?!

I opened my eyes after about thirty seconds of being 'one with Mother Nature' (so far they'd been closed, as I needed to concentrate hard on 34Cs).

'How long do we have to do it for?' I asked Kayleigh.

She was lying next to me. Becky was on her other side.

Kayleigh didn't reply. She was busy muttering something. I'm not entirely sure, but I think she was chanting a spell from *Charmed* (she's obsessed with that show). If I hadn't already been feeling FABULOUSLY SILLY, that would have been my wake-up call!

'How long, Kayleigh?' I snapped. 'We look like right oddpots, burying our boobs in the mud!'

'Lara,' Kayleigh said in a tone you might use when talking to a toddler. 'We're not *burying* them, we're *planting* them. There's a difference. Burying has very negative connotations. Never use that word in association with your breasts, unless you want them to shrivel up, die and *need* burying. Planting is all about new life, evolution, expansion.'

She grabbed a watering can that she'd handily positioned within reach and watered the soil.

Great, I thought. *Now all the worms are going to come to the surface, thinking it's raining.*

I squeezed my eyes shut and tried to focus on the evolution and expansion of my non-existent boobs, but just then, I felt something tickly on my chest. Visions of worms, ants and God knows what else crawling through the soil and finding a new type of food – MY NIPPLES! – filled my mind. I pictured a very hungry caterpillar nibbling its way through the thin material of my bra, and I completely lost it. I jumped up so fast I got my feet tangled and almost fell over. I let out a yelp – and that was the WORST mistake ever.

Kayleigh had been careful to make sure we were hidden from view, even draping a blanket over the bushes in front of us, but when I yelped, people came running over.

'Is everything okay?' came a woman's voice.

Somehow, Kayleigh and Becky managed to get their tops on lightning fast while mine got all twisted because I couldn't see properly in the dark.

Kayleigh rushed out onto the garden path.

'Everything is fine,' I heard her say.

'Are you sure?' came a different woman's voice. 'What are you doing? Are you trespassing?' She paused. 'I can hear someone else still in there. Who is it?'

'Uh, just a friend,' Kayleigh said.

Becky quickly ran out of our hiding place to join her. They were assuring the women that they were fine when a light suddenly shone on me, cutting through the darkness.

Whoa! Can't people mind their own business?? Luckily, I'd just managed to get my top on. I hurried onto the path too, squinting in the light of the woman's phone. Even more embarrassing than strangers catching us mid-boob-growing was the fact that a bunch of boys chose that moment to walk past. I kept my gaze firmly away from them.

I was about to assure the women that we were not trespassers and that this was Kayleigh's home when one of the boys stopped.

'Lara?' he said.

I whirled towards him. It was Jay, my next-door neighbour.

'What've you been up to?' Jay asked, his gaze lowering to my chest. 'Why are you all muddy?'

'I . . . fell,' I lied.

Then I noticed that everyone was staring at my chest, so I looked down too.

The light of the woman's phone perfectly illuminated the two splotches of mud oozing through my T-shirt around my chest area.

I looked at Kayleigh and Becky to see if it was happening to them too, but they were both wearing jackets over their clothes now. Neither of them had told me to bring my jacket out. I'd left mine inside!

I turned and ran off.

Laughter rang out behind me from one of Jay's friends.

I just hope none of Kayleigh's sisters sees the holes

we dug under the oak tree and figures out what we were doing. We'll never live it down.

11 p.m.

To distract myself from everything that's happened tonight, I'm watching *Twilight*. Random, I know, but it's one of my favourite movies of all time. What better way to make myself forget the fact that I let Kayleigh talk me into BURYING MY BOOBS IN SOIL than by watching Bella Swan hyperventilate over a cute vampire for two hours?

It's also distracting me from the fact that I have only two more days of freedom. On Monday I'll be back to waking up early, boring lessons and piles of homework.

Nobody at school knows I like *Twilight* (except Anaya, Kayleigh and Becky, of course). I'm open about my love of Marvel, because that's kind of cool right now, but every couple of months I get into bed with my laptop and indulge in all things Bella, Edward and Jacob.

(I was never 'Team Jacob', because I already knew the whole plot before ever watching the movies, and knew it wasn't worth investing in that relationship.)

Anyway, I'm almost at the part where Edward sparkles in the sun, so bye.

(P.S. Anaya finds the sparkling hilarious. She has a conspiracy theory: Edward Cullen is secretly a fairy princess masquerading as a vampire.)

3
The Friendly Neighbourhood Vampire

Kayleigh: Hey Lara, are you awake?

Me: Yeah, now that my phone has buzzed from you texting me 😠

Kayleigh: Oh, sorry 🙈. Just wanted to say we should meet and plan our glow up properly.

Me: You know what? I've changed my mind about it. Sorry.

Kayleigh: Why??? Didn't you enjoy the taster session last night? That was so fun!

Me: Um, no it wasn't. It was embarrassing.

Kayleigh: 😥

Me: Sorry, Kayleigh. Maybe Becky will glow up with you though? xoxo

Saturday 1 September, 9.12 a.m.

I'm so tired after staying up late watching *Twilight* 😴.
I wouldn't even be awake right now if Kayleigh hadn't
messaged me at eight, saying we need to continue our
glow up 😠

I just tried to do something different with my hair,
and I was reminded of all the reasons why I started just
sticking with a bun in the first place. My hair is so thick,
so puffy and so BIG! I almost broke my comb trying to do
a side parting. It brought back many memories of broken
combs from when I used to try to style my hair. My hair is
a comb's GRAVEYARD.

After a few attempts, I gave up. Switching things up
with my hair just isn't worth the stress. I'd rather spend my
energy on something more 'productive', as Kayleigh would
say. (But no, not glowing up. Football and movies.)

9.28 a.m.

Kayleigh should have her own reality show. People would
watch just to witness her latest antics.

11.25 a.m.

I now know where I get my clumsiness from!!

Dad told me to go and meet Mum at the bus stop
because she was returning from a night shift at the

senior citizens' home where she works and had done some shopping on her way. She needed help with the bags.

'Why can't you go help her?' I asked, pouring a can of cat food into Nala's bowl.

Nala purred happily as I set it on the floor for her. Then she began to gorge herself. It was her favourite this morning: ocean fish.

Dad turned around and gave me his best 'who do you think you are?' look. 'Because, as you can see, I'm making her breakfast.'

At the weekend, Dad only makes breakfast for Mum, not for me or Danny. Before I was able to make my own breakfast, it meant Danny had to fix breakfast for me. It's one of the reasons why he hates me. He's had to do stuff for me his whole life.

'Why can't Danny go?' I demanded.

I could see the back of Danny's big head through the door to the living room. He was already hogging the TV, playing video games.

'Danny, Mum needs your help!' I shouted so that he'd hear me through his headphones. 'Duty calls, so please take a break from *Call of Duty*.'

'Can you stop shouting?' Dad snapped. 'I asked you, not Danny. Now can you get going?'

As I stomped out of the kitchen, Dad muttered something about how he would never have lived to have children of his own if he'd ever talked back to my great-aunt when he was growing up.

My great-aunt (Dad's aunt) lives in Nigeria, and the woman is a BOSS. She's small and plump, but I've seen her chase hooded lads who thought she was a vulnerable old lady they could mug. She's really strict too. She lived with Dad and his parents until Dad was fifteen, and I don't know how they survived.

'Your mother will be there now,' Dad called from the kitchen. 'Stop loitering!'

I grabbed my trainers from the shoe rack by the front door, dug my feet into them and headed out. I was half-way down the street when a blood-curdling shriek echoed through the air. Usually, if I heard a scream, my reaction would be: Mind. My. Business. Unlike the women outside Kayleigh's house last night, I'm not nosey. And I'm not looking to witness anything. Witnesses get hunted down and killed simply for being a witness. Um, no thanks.

However, this kind of sounded like Mum, so I broke into a run. Sure enough, when I got to the end of the street, I saw her lying on the ground a short distance from the bus stop.

Honestly, my mum is the most embarrassing mum in the world. Why on earth was she just lying there like some kind of damsel in distress? Her skirt had ridden up her thighs and her curls were a MESS.

Yup, I got the clumsy gene from her.

I hung back when a boy appeared down the street, ran over to her, and helped her up. I was too far away to see if it was anyone I knew, but I didn't think it was. He helped her onto a bench then ran off to get one of her shoes, which was lying in the middle of the road.

He and Mum exchanged a few words then he disappeared into Mo's, the newsagent's.

I hurried over and had almost reached Mum when the boy stepped out of the newsagent's again with her shoe – and a hammer. This time, I was close enough to see him clearly, and the sight of him literally STOPPED ME IN MY TRACKS. Dear Diary, I forgot how to breathe for a few seconds. He was tall, bronze-skinned and GORGEOUS. And no, I didn't know him.

His hair sat in cute deep-waves on his head and his voice was all deep and velvety when he spoke to my mum. 'They didn't have anything I could use to stick the heel back on. Mo, the man in the newsagent, said your best bet is to break off the heel of your other shoe so they're the same height, then you can walk home.' He waved the hammer. 'I can do it for you, if you want?'

He wasn't from around here. 'Here' being Liverpool. He had a distinctly London accent that was like music to my ears. Maybe he was here on holiday. But then he'd stay in a hotel, wouldn't he? Not out in Toxteth.

Suddenly I became aware that:

1. I hadn't had a shower yet.
2. I hadn't even brushed my teeth.
3. I was wearing my pyjamas. They're not cute
   either. They were once cream, but they turned
   pink after Danny threw in a pair of red football
   socks with my washing once.

So, I hid. I stepped into the alleyway between Mo's and a hair salon, and hoped the boy would leave soon.

'Don't worry about it,' Mum whimpered to him. She really did sound like she was in pain. 'I'll call my husband.' She rummaged through her bag and produced her phone, then let out a heavy sigh. 'My battery is dead.'

'Do you live far?' the boy asked, still holding Mum's shoe. 'Can I call you a taxi?'

'I just live on the next street,' Mum replied.

'I can walk you home if you like,' he offered gently.

I frowned. Why was he being so nice? Weren't good-looking boys supposed to be too cool for things like helping clumsy adults?

'That would be very kind,' Mum said.

He crouched to put the shoe on Mum's foot. I cringed. I bet her feet were crusty as heck. They're always crusty after a night shift. She hadn't had the chance to put any cocoa butter on them yet.

'I'll just return the hammer,' said Mr I'm-Nice-To-Middle-Aged-Women-With-Crusty-Feet, 'then I'll walk you home.'

Once he was gone, Mum glanced around and I quickly stepped out of my hiding place before she realised I'd been hiding.

'Lara!' she exclaimed.

'Mum, are you okay? What happened?'

She patted the scarf around her neck as she launched into a story about how her scarf blew away when she got off the bus. Instead of just letting it go, she'd decided to chase it down the street, leaving all her shopping bags at the bus stop. I would understand if it was Gucci or Chanel like the scarves Aunt Maggie wears, but it's just this tatty scarf that Dad bought her aeons ago. Of course, she fell while chasing it.

I rolled my eyes. 'So you got your scarf but you twisted your ankle and broke your shoe. Was it worth it?'

Mum glared at me as she stretched out an arm. 'Help me up.'

I helped her stand up from the bench, hoping to get her to our street before that boy returned.

No such luck. He emerged from Mo's just then.

'Caiden,' Mum called. 'Come and meet my daughter.'

The boy – Caiden – smiled, and I got a sloping feeling in my belly, like I was on a ROLLERCOASTER that had just descended down a big dip. Suddenly I felt breathless. And sweaty. And SCATTERBRAINED!

Looking into his eyes made it worse. They were the darkest brown, and they reminded me of everything magical and mysterious: onyx stones, obsidian, the night sky . . .

'Lara, this is Caiden,' Mum said. 'He's such a lovely young man.'

She started telling me about how he came to her rescue. Usually, I find it annoying when Mum gabs on and on at me. But for once I was grateful, because I didn't have a clue what to say. My brain didn't kick into gear until Caiden nodded at me and said, 'Hi, Lara.'

My name on his lips sounded like music. And his accent was so swoony.

'Hi, Caiden,' I managed. Suddenly I remembered I was in my PJs and my face got so hot I was sure it was going to BURST INTO FLAMES! Thankfully, I'm way too dark to blush, so nobody ever knows when heat is flooding my cheeks.

'Caiden and his mother have just moved up from London,' Mum informed me.

So he's not just visiting. He's here to stay?

Mum thanked him again for helping her out, then I grabbed her shopping bags from by the bus stop and the two of us began the slow trek to our house.

'What a lovely boy,' Mum said loudly.

I glanced back to see if Caiden was still there, but thankfully he'd gone.

1.05 p.m.

ARRRGGH!!!

What is wrong with me?

I'm such a big, whopping DISASTER.

Nothing ever goes right in my life!

A list of five things that are very wrong with me:

1. I'm the kind of person who leaves the house without even brushing my teeth.

2. I'm clumsy.

3. My hair is always a mess. Especially when it rains. Even just the slightest bit of humidity turns it into a PUFFY CLOUD OF CHAOS!

4. I stepped in a puddle of Nala's wee when I got home from rescuing Mum this morning. It had soaked into the carpet in my room and I couldn't get it all out. Nala is trained but she occasionally has little accidents. My room stinks, and now I stink too.

5. My right eye has been twitching since noon. This usually happens when I'm tired and/or have been staring at screens too much. One, or both, of my eyes just randomly begin to wobble in their sockets and it freaks out anyone who sees it happen. Today that unfortunate person was Jay, who stopped over to ask if he could borrow my calculator. He was only just getting around to doing his holiday homework, but

was *he* grounded for leaving it so late? Noooo. Thankfully, he didn't bring up last night, and the muddy patches he saw on my chest. And he didn't say anything about my twitching eye either. He just stared at my eyes for a moment, in a sort of perplexed way, then left.

In light of the above list, no, I'm not the kind of girl who cute boys from London are remotely interested in ☹

8 p.m.

I can't stop thinking about Caiden. I hate myself for leaving the house in my PJs and without even brushing my teeth. Who does that? Kayleigh would say I'm in dire need of her glow up if she found out.

I've only had one serious crush in my whole fourteen-going-on-fifteen years of existence. It was back in primary school when I was ten. His name was Jamal and he had a thick 'fro that was always perfectly round. He also had the nicest smile ever. I found it impossible to speak whenever he was around. The connection between my brain and tongue would simply CEASE TO WORK. He was only in my class for one term before he moved school again.

I've had crushes since Jamal, e.g. Alex. But none of them have been all that monumental. I only had a crush on Alex for, like, a month. I can't believe it's come back to bite me. I should never have journaled about it.

Anaya and Becky think it's weird that I don't like any of the boys in our school, but it's not my fault that the quality of boys at Prince's Park Academy is ABYSMAL. Caiden puts all the snickering, irritating, immature boys at school in the shade. He's so gorgeous he was practically glowing in the sun. Maybe he's a vampire – not the scary Dracula kind, but the mysterious Edward Cullen kind.

Yes! Caiden is so cute, he's *got* to be a vampire.

I still couldn't stop thinking about him when I went to the cinema with Anaya and Becky this evening. Becky was telling Anaya about the whole boob-growing thing and Anaya was laughing her head off, but I was in my own little world – until we were comfortably seated with our bags of popcorn and Anaya said, 'I saw Sienna this morning. She came into my mum's café with Matt.'

Sienna is this girl who has been the bane of my life since Year 7, and Matt is her boyfriend. Sienna is tall, blonde and really pretty, and she seems to think that gives her the right to be a total bully. Like being pretty liberates her from the need to be a decent human being.

She once posted a video on TikTok of me eating a burger in the lunch room. I looked ridiculous, trying to fit the burger into my mouth. Our school supposedly has a 'zero-tolerance policy on cyberbullying' (there are posters about it in all the hallways, and we have long, boring assemblies about it) but nothing happened when I reported her.

Another time, she 'accidentally' spilled glue in my hair during an art lesson. Luckily, Anaya helped me get it out before it dried and did any damage.

But the worst thing Sienna has done is spread a rumour about me only being good at football because I was doping. DOPING?!

SERIOUSLY!!

I don't even know where to buy performance-enhancing drugs, never mind have the money to actually purchase some. I get a fiver a week in pocket money, so how am I going to afford to dope???

But the weird thing is, some people believed her.

Anaya smirked. 'I put salt in her Diet Coke.'

Becky and I giggled.

'Did she notice?' Becky asked.

'No. It was just a little bit. But she did notice the fiery chilli peppers I added to her panini.' Anaya took out her phone and showed us a picture of a red-faced Sienna Willis with her tongue hanging out.

Becky and I collapsed into giggles.

'I'd post it on Instagram,' Anaya said, 'but knowing my luck, I'd probably get suspended for cyberbullying. Plus, I don't want to have to deal with her.'

I don't blame her. Sienna fights dirty.

'Hey, I heard we're getting a new boy from London,' Becky said. 'Heard he's super-cute too.'

'Are you sure?' I asked. 'Where did you hear that?'

I must have sounded totally intense, because Becky shot me a sideways look. 'Okay, calm down.'

'Is his name Caiden?' I asked.

'Dunno. I just heard from Lottie that a boy from London is starting on Monday, and she thinks lots of girls are going to have a crush on him.'

Lottie's mum works at our school, so she would know. Lottie goes into school during the holidays and everything.

Suddenly my heart started hammering so hard I was sure there was something wrong with it.

'Are you okay?' Anaya asked me.

'Uh, I met the London boy today.' My voice didn't sound much like my voice. It was a bit breathless, which is ridiculous.

'And . . . ?' Becky asked.

'And what?' I asked back.

'What's he like?'

I decided to be honest. 'Mind-numbingly gorgeous!'

Becky and Anaya squealed because, well, I NEVER like anyone.

'He must be something to have awakened *your* dead urges,' Becky said.

And that just sounded gross. It's the kind of thing adults say. *Teenage urges.*

But anyway, I told them all about him.

Sunday 2 September, 10.16 a.m.

This morning, I sneaked into Danny's room to raid his sock drawer. That's where he stashes all his pocket money in an old wallet. It's only fair that I get him back in some way after doing all his chores on Thursday. The only reason he didn't make me do them again yesterday was because Mum and Dad were home all day.

(By the way, I'm testing this dictation function on my journaling app. It's pretty cool. I'm talking to you out loud, dear Diary, like a real friend.)

Anyway, I know I should have asked Danny before helping myself to his cash, but he was downstairs playing *Call of Duty*, and I was gasping for some Flamin' Hot Monster Munch. Since I had a fiver I also got myself some jawbreakers, bubblegum-flavour Millions and a Capri Sun.

It was bad timing to pinch his cash though, because a few minutes after I got back from the shop, he must've decided to get himself some snacks too. I heard him come upstairs and I was praying he wouldn't check his money stash.

My prayer was not answered. Next thing, Danny was banging on my door, asking why five pounds had gone missing from his wallet. I pretended not to know anything about it. My plan was to ask Mum for the money when she gets back from work, and replace it. Dad is in, but I'm not asking him. Mum will lecture me, but give Danny the money. Dad will lecture me and take it out of my pocket money for this week, meaning I'll get NOTHING!

Mum is usually the stricter one, but she's less likely than Dad to follow through with punishments. (You've got to know which parent to approach in each situation 😉)

I must have been pretty convincing because Danny believed me and walked out, only to burst into my room a few minutes later, WITHOUT KNOCKING, and catch me eating all my goodies.

'You definitely pinched my money,' he growled. 'How else did you buy all that? I'm telling Dad.'

'Then I'll tell him it was me who did your chores on Thursday,' I replied.

He paused, and I could tell his mind was working overdrive. He didn't bother threatening to tell Alex about my old crush, because I think he realised that that would mean he wouldn't be able to blackmail me any more and he'd be back to doing his own chores.

(I've switched to typing now. I just realised that speaking my journal entries isn't safe. Someone – i.e. Danny – could overhear me.)

Danny promised not to tell on me if I continue to do his chores. I promised to continue doing his chores if I can have regular access to his cash. MWAH HA HA!!

I guess Danny enjoyed that extra hour of hanging out on Friday night because he said, 'Well, you have to ask me first.'

But he did look a bit depressed about it.

10.48 a.m.

Mum is home from work now. She and Dad are SO ANNOYING!! I just asked them to increase my pocket money from a fiver a week to ten and she said no. It's not fair. Why does Danny get ten pounds a week just because he's sixteen?

Dad is annoying because he always goes along with whatever Mum says.

I stormed back to my room after they refused to even give me an extra pound a week. The next thing, they burst into my room without knocking, just like Danny did. I have ZERO privacy in this house. I asked if they could knock next time and they looked at me, all blank, like the idea had never occurred to them. Then they sat on my bed and explained that they're trying to teach me the 'value of money'.

Money doesn't grow on trees, they said.

Learning to manage money well is an important life skill, they said.

Yada yada yada.

Then Mum COMPARED ME TO DANNY. She said, 'Take a leaf out of Danny's book. Even when he was on five pounds a week, he saved and often had plenty of money whenever he wanted to make a big purchase. Now that he's on ten pounds a week he's even smarter with it.'

Mum thinks the world of Danny, just because he gets

good grades, saves his pocket money and builds weird robots with Alex.

Unlike me, Danny had a *very* productive summer. He's such a nerd. He had no holiday homework because he's just done his GCSEs, but he actually looked for work to do by entering a competition with Alex. It was for teen roboticists, and the robot they built looked like a metal scarecrow!

I've never seen Mum happier than on GCSE results day. Danny and Alex were in the local papers because they got all 9s – the highest grades possible.

Anyway, when Mum finished monologuing about the value of money, she asked if I understood where she was coming from. I nodded, even though I don't. All I understand is that Danny is a two-faced goody-two-shoes who has our parents wrapped around his pinky!!!

11.13 a.m.

I think I should go for a run. I really need to start training in preparation for football season starting again. Plus it'll help me burn off some of my frustration at Mum and Dad.

Next door, Jay's mum is blasting her Sunday morning cleaning music, and it's thumping through the walls. She only ever listens to old music. Destiny's Child today.

I wish Beyoncé would adopt me. Or Naomi Campbell. Or Barack and Michelle Obama. Actually, the Obamas would make me work hard. They'd probably expect me to go to Yale or something. And Beyoncé might not work out either because I heard she's a quiet, introverted person. I might be too much for her.

I think Naomi Campbell is my best option. I reckon she would give me lots of freedom and let me do whatever I want.

Yup, I've narrowed it down to Naomi Campbell. Just imagine. I could live with her in her mansion. I would probably get a massive room all to myself with an en-suite bathroom, instead of this box that I live in. As much as I love my room and how I've decorated it, I NEED MORE SPACE. And I DEFINITELY need more privacy.

Please God, let Naomi Campbell adopt me before I get too old to be adopted. Amen.

I wonder if you can be adopted as an over-18.

NAOMI CAMPBELL, YOU HAVE FOUR YEARS TO FIND ME AND WANT ME!!

4.15 p.m.

Since my epiphany about my goal (one hundred matches unbeaten and all that), I've been worried that I haven't been doing enough to prepare, so around noon I went for a run through Prince's Park. Kayleigh came with me. She isn't on the team, but she likes running with me. Thankfully, she didn't say anything about glowing up.

I haven't been training as hard as I should have 😖. I've played no competitive football all summer. I've only had kickabouts in the park with any girls from the school team who were free, as well as other random people who happened to be around. It hasn't been enough to keep me at 'optimal performance level', as our coach, Miss Simpson, calls it.

I really wanted to go to a football camp this summer, but Dad said no. And he felt totally justified about his decision when he found out, halfway into the holidays, that I hadn't done any of my holiday homework. He and Mum say I don't take my schoolwork seriously enough and think football is a huge distraction to me. They don't really support me being on the school team. They pretend to, but I know they'd prefer me to be brainy, like Danny, and just focus on schoolwork.

Anyway, the school football season starts again next Saturday, and I don't feel prepared! I can't let the school down. Being captain of the girls' football team is the one responsibility I've ever been given in my life. I CANNOT mess up.

For some reason, Kayleigh was videoing our run for TikTok. She and Becky are obsessed with social media. I'm on all the socials too, but I don't get why people need to share their innermost thoughts in public. That's what journals are for, right? I sometimes post funny videos of Nala, but all the important stuff is reserved for you, my dear journal!

Anyway, we usually split up when we get to the boat-house in the park: I take a longer route through the park and around the lake, and Kayleigh takes a shortcut. Then we meet up back at the gates and run home.

We'd just parted ways, and I was running my usual route around the lake when I almost slammed into someone coming around a bend in the path.

I managed to get out of the way, but he tried to dodge me in the same direction so we still ended up colliding. I went flying to the ground AND HE LANDED ON TOP OF ME!!

I was about to slap him and wrestle him off when I realised who it was.

Caiden!

Suddenly, I couldn't breathe.

He rolled away and I tried to stand, only to slip on a muddy patch of the lakeside path. I went sliding towards the water and might have fallen in if Caiden hadn't grabbed the back of my top.

He steadied me, while I cringed inwardly.

'Sorry about that,' he said.

I could only manage a noise that sounded something like *Ngffft*.

'Oh – Lara, is it?' he asked, recognition sparking in his deep, dark eyes.

Somehow I managed to say, 'Yeah. Hi, again.'

This time I wasn't wearing PJs. I was wearing a cute pair

of dark purple leggings and a white hoodie. Also, I'd brushed my teeth, showered and had my hair in its usual neat bun.

I wasn't sure whether to turn and carry on running. To be honest, I was kind of in a trance, unable to move.

'How's your mum?' Caiden asked.

I blinked. 'Oh, she's fine. Her ankle's sprained so she had to put some ice on it, but she was okay to go to work last night. She said it only hurt a little bit. She made sure to wear flat shoes for her shift . . .'

I clamped my mouth shut. He didn't ask for all the boring details of my mum's life.

Caiden's lips curved into the dreamiest smile I've ever seen. 'I love how you all talk up here.'

I wasn't sure what to say. I'm NEVER not sure what to say, but both times I've been around Caiden I've been all confused and speechless.

'Mind if I jog with you?' he asked. 'I don't know the park that well. It'd be nice to have a local lead the way, so I don't get lost.'

He gave me this imploring look that seemed totally flirtatious. I know a flirtatious look when I see one because I've seen boys give them to other girls. But never to *me*.

'Yeah, of course,' I said quickly. I started jogging again. 'Follow me. Prince's Park is 110 acres, so it's very easy to get lost.'

Caiden fell into step with me, and I told myself I must have imagined the flirty look. He started running a bit faster, then seemed to realise he was outpacing me and slowed down. But that only meant I felt pressured to run harder. I picked up my pace and he matchedme easily. One stride of his was probably equivalent to three of mine. In fact, he found my pace so easy that he continued to chat. 'So, have you always lived in Liverpool?'

'Yeah,' I puffed.

'What's it like?'

I shrugged. 'Dunno. It's just home.'

'Oh.'

With each step, a delicious tangy smell wafted over from him. That meant he was getting a waft of my scent too. I hoped I'd managed to get the smell of cat wee off my skin.

'I'm starting at Prince's Park Academy tomorrow,' he told me. 'It's just around the corner.'

Ha! He had no idea how far the news of his arrival had already spread. I acted surprised anyway. 'Really?' I gushed, then figured I'd overdone it when he cast me a glance. 'I go there,' I said with a little less gusto.

'Oh, good. I'll at least have one friend.'

'Who . . . says . . . I'm your . . . friend?' I puffed.

Caiden grinned. I wished he wouldn't. I was already breathless. 'I've kind of claimed you,' he said. 'You're my first friend in Liverpool.'

I was too out of breath to respond.

'Uh, do you want to slow down?' he asked.

I nodded and slowed, giving up on trying to impress

him with my speed. 'So how come you've moved up here?'

For the first time, a shadow seemed to pass over Caiden's face, lending him a broody aura that was just as appealing as his smile. He was quiet for a moment, and I realised it must be something personal.

'Race you to that tree,' I said, pointing, so that he wouldn't feel like he had to give an answer. Then I took off, running my hardest.

Caiden easily beat me.

'Show-off,' I said, when he gave me a triumphant little smirk.

We continued around the lake, and he was quiet until we reached the halfway point of my running route. I stopped to catch my breath in my usual break spot by a little playground.

'Uh, me and my mum moved,' Caiden said quietly, finally answering my question. 'My parents have split up.'

'Oh.'

He didn't meet my gaze. 'She's from Liverpool, and she wanted to move back now that they're over.'

'Well, I think you'll like it here,' I told him. 'Everyone at school is really friendly.'

For ordinary mortals like myself, that was a lie. But for someone like Caiden, it would be true. He would have no problem making friends. He was easily the coolest person I'd ever laid eyes on in the flesh, with his trendy trainers and southern swagger.

I took out my phone and timed my break. Once my minute was up, I started to run again.

Caiden jogged lazily beside me. 'Anything I need to know about school?'

'Yeah, the teachers hate us all. Last year, I got detention for not sitting still in maths, but I needed a wee so I couldn't sit still. I was BURSTING for the loo!'

Caiden was quiet for a moment. That's when I realised that talking about urination with a boy – especially one as gorgeous as Caiden – was probably not the best idea!

He burst into laughter. He laughed so hard, he had to stop running and lean against a tree.

I felt oddly triumphant as I watched his shoulders shake and his eyes crinkle at the corners. I, Lara Bloom, had made the friendly neighbourhood vampire laugh. And not just a little chuckle either. He was practically clutching his sides.

'So, no different to my school in London then,' he said when he'd pulled himself together.

'Schools are all the same,' I replied as we continued to run.

My running route is four miles, and it usually feels like eternal torment. Every second drags and I curse myself for subjecting myself to such torture. But today it was over in a flash.

'Do you run every day?' Caiden asked as we neared the park gates.

'Most of the time. On school days I run in the evening though.'

'What time?'

'Five. I start at the park gates,' I told him, in case I could tempt him to join me.

I didn't mention Kayleigh. She won't mind if I want to run with Caiden instead.

He nodded. 'I'll be there.'

At the gates he gave me a wink and then headed off in the opposite direction from my house.

While I waited for Kayleigh, I watched him until he was a speck in the distance.

I really hope he's a vampire.

Note to self:
- Google what boys mean when they wink.

4

Sienna and her Flying Monkeys

Monday 3 September, 7.13 a.m.

Why are school uniforms so ugly? Honestly, I've never seen a nice one. They're always GROSS colours that make you look hideous. Prince's Park Academy makes us wear a navy-blue skirt or trousers, white shirt and maroon cardigan and blazer. MAROON!

And what's with the cardigan? What are we, grannies?

Luckily, I just managed to save my cardigan from Nala's clutches. She was about to tip her litter tray on it. If that had happened, I would've been not just a granny, but a smelly one too.

Anyway, when boys wink it can mean they're being friendly, being funny, being cheeky or they like you.

Why is nothing ever straightforward??

7.53 a.m.

ARRRGH!!!

My hair can't decide if it wants to be curly or frizzy today. It's trying to be BOTH. I LOOK LIKE A HEDGEHOG! I swear the strands of my hair have had a meeting with each other and agreed to do this.

Strand by my temple: *Listen up, fellow strands of hair. It's Lara's first day back at school so let's do something wild. I'll be curly.* *Nudges strand next to it.* *Why don't you be frizzy? And you, behind me, stick out sideways for maximum chaotic effect. We can do this! Together we can make Lara look like a SCARECROW. Hurray!!*

I tried to slick it all down in my usual bun, but it wouldn't co-operate. It's all puffy. Danny made sure to snicker about it – he never misses an opportunity to be irritating. I'm so glad I don't have to deal with him at school any more. He's in sixth form now, and after his amazing GCSE results (Yawn! Eye roll!!) he's now going to a 'good school' across the city.

Whoa! Dad is yelling that we're leaving in twenty minutes, whether I've had breakfast or not. He walks me to school, then continues to his workplace. I better hurry.

It's not even eight o'clock yet, and this is already turning out to be the WORST first day of Year 10 IMAGINABLE!

12.32 p.m.

It got worse.

I'd had fantasies about showing Caiden around the school and getting to know him better. But that is *not* how things went down.

First of all, I didn't even see Caiden at all until I went to stash my books in my locker at lunchtime, and guess what? He was surrounded by people and didn't notice me trying to talk to him. The crowd around him was so thick he couldn't see or hear me when I said, 'Hi, Caiden.'

Somehow, he managed to look good in our horrid uniform.

Citizens of Earth, I have now discovered a mortal who suits maroon.

Maybe he isn't a mortal at all. Maybe he's a VAMPIRE.

I tried again, a little louder this time. 'Hi, Caiden.'

He was still trying to listen to about a dozen people who were all trying to talk to him at the same time. He didn't hear me until I shouted, 'HI, CAIDEN!' and brought the whole hallway to a standstill.

Caiden craned his neck and finally saw me. I thought he might give me a funny look, like everyone else was, but he grinned and said, 'Lara! I've been wondering when I was going to see you.'

You should have seen the bewildered looks on everyone's faces. I could tell what they were thinking. *Caiden is friends with* her?

Question: How come being good at sports makes boys cool and popular, but nobody on the girls' football team is *really* popular, except for Steph Gonzales? And that's only because she manages to look all cute and Selena Gomez-ish, standing in goal barely doing anything.

I was about to say, 'How are you finding your first day at Prince's Park Academy?' when there was a slam at the end of the hallway. Everyone turned.

The red lips were the first thing I saw. So scarlet and glossy.

It was Sienna, of course. Who else? She and her minions, Paige and Molly, came sashaying up the corridor, like they were on some kind of catwalk. They were quite a sight: Sienna with her long blonde hair and long, long legs; Molly with her auburn hair and vivid green eyes; Paige with her voluminous brown hair and glowy tan. Their school skirts were so short we'd all see their knickers if they bent over even slightly.

Sienna's hair was even blonder than usual – almost white. And she looked as fresh as a daisy. Even beside Paige and Molly, who are absolutely gorgeous, she still stands out. This is why people like her. Because of her supermodel looks. She also manages to seem all innocent and harmless too, but I know better. There's a very ugly heart behind that pretty exterior.

I tore my eyes away from her and focused on Caiden, only to find him watching Sienna. The way he was smiling at her cut my heart in two.

'Hey, Caiden,' Sienna said breezily as she strutted by. She even gave him a wink.

A WINK!

And somehow she managed not to look ridiculous, or like she was trying too hard.

Why is she winking at Caiden when she already has a boyfriend? I wondered. *She should get lost!*

'Thanks for helping me find my form room this morning,' Caiden said.

Sienna stopped walking. 'No worries. I'm just heading to the lunch hall. I can show you the way.'

Caiden slammed his locker shut. 'Great. Thanks.'

He spared me another of his knee-weakening grins before stepping around me and following Sienna down the corridor.

I wanted to THROW SOMETHING!

I had to spend twenty minutes of my lunch break watching Caiden chat with Sienna at her usual table by the vending machines. Her friends left them after about five minutes and I knew it was on purpose. She must have told them to.

'Doesn't she have a boyfriend?' I asked Anaya, Becky and Kayleigh.

'She broke up with him this morning,' Kayleigh said.

'Apparently she took one look at Caiden and decided Matt needed to go,' Becky added.

Great!

'He really is gorgeous,' Becky said, putting on her glasses so that she could see Caiden better. 'But not as gorgeous as Richard.'

Anaya shook her head. 'I don't get why everyone's so obsessed. I've already seen his name scratched into the doors in the girls' toilets. He's just okay, nothing amazing.'

I stared at them in disbelief. They actually looked serious.

'His accent is nice,' Kayleigh said, taking a sip of her water – no juice drinks for her during her glow up. 'Apart from that, I don't see the big deal either.'

Then they changed the subject and started talking about Kayleigh's red highlights (apparently, her new hair colour is called 'strawberry blonde'), even though I wasn't done griping about Caiden and Sienna yet.

Between me and you, dear Diary, I might not like Sienna, but there are clearly things I could learn from her, e.g. confidence. *Ugh!* I feel so ICKY writing this!!

12.55 p.m.

I've just discovered that one of the perks of journaling in an app rather than an actual diary is that people assume you're texting. And they think you must be WILDLY POPULAR to be doing so much typing – so many friends to respond to.

Lots of people have made that assumption today. I didn't correct any of them ☺

2.43 p.m.

Why do teachers hate me???

It's all Dad's fault. Ever since Year 8 parents' evening, when he told Mr Griffiths, our rickety old headteacher, that he wanted the teachers to push me harder, they've been having a field day!

Today, we had a new teacher for last period maths, so I thought I was going to get a break from being pushed harder.

As soon as Anaya and I walked through the door, I spied Caiden lounging in a seat at the back of the room, looking all deliciously cool.

'This is your chance,' Anaya whispered to me. 'Go and sit with him.'

'But I want to sit with you,' I protested.

'Sienna is in this class,' Anaya hissed under her breath. 'Go now, before she gets here.'

That sealed it for me.

I was sauntering over to the desk beside Caiden – I might have been trying to copy Sienna's runway walk a bit – when a voice boomed, 'OMOLARA BLOOM, IDENTIFY YOURSELF THEN SIT AT THE FRONT OF THE ROOM WHERE I CAN SEE YOU!'

I turned in annoyance. 'Why do I have to sit at the front?'

The new teacher, a mountainous man with chubby cheeks and a massive nose, glared at me. 'Because Mr Griffiths told me to keep an eye on you,' he said.

How did 'push her harder' become 'keep an eye on her'? Talk about a message getting lost in translation!

'But, sir, none of the other teachers make me sit at the front –'

'I'm not going to repeat myself, young lady!' The teacher stabbed a finger towards a lone desk at the front of the room. He'd written his name on the whiteboard behind him in bold black letters: Mr Savage.

Ugh! Well, it suited him!

Of course, Sienna chose that moment to breeze in, hair sailing after her like a shampoo ad, lips especially red and shiny, as though they'd just been given a fresh coat of lip gloss. She brushed past me and slid into the seat next to Caiden.

I stared at the front desk in annoyance. It had been pushed way forward and was just a step from the teacher's desk.

'I don't have to sit at the front in lessons,' I told Mr Savage again. 'I'm not in trouble. I just have to do extra work because my dad –'

'Omolara Bloom, you are on VERY thin ice here,' Mr Savage bellowed.

There was a ripple of muted giggling around the room.

I hate it when people call me Omolara. It reminds me of my great-aunt and her epic tongue-lashings. 'Just Lara is fine, sir –'

'ONE MORE PEEP OUT OF YOU IN MY LESSON AND IT WILL BE A DETENTION! NOT A VERY

GOOD WAY TO START THE NEW SCHOOL YEAR, OMOLARA BLOOM!'

People weren't giggling quietly any more. They were outright laughing, like this was the funniest thing ever.

'Peep,' I muttered as I stomped towards the seat at the front.

'WHAT WAS THAT?' Mr Savage exploded.

'Nothing!' I said quickly.

Sienna raised her hand. 'Sir,' she said innocently, 'she said "peep".'

What a *snitch*.

'And what does that mean?' Mr Savage asked, already crimson in the face. He probably thought it was some new swear word.

'You told her not to make another peep, but she said "peep",' Sienna explained.

'OMOLARA BLOOM, GET OUT OF MY SIGHT!' Mr Savage roared.

'For saying PEEP?' I roared back.

'YOUNG LADY, YOU WILL NOT USE THAT TONE WITH ME.' Mr Savage stalked to his desk, where a red button sat beside his computer. If he pushed it, the assistant head, who is also the director of behaviour management, would come and cart me off to his office, where he might call my parents. Mum and Dad would kill me if the assistant head called them.

I dashed out of the room – making sure to 'accidentally'

knock Sienna's orderly pink pencil case off her desk on my way – and took myself off to the detention room early.

Skipping detention would guarantee a call to my parents.

3.55 p.m.

I was expecting my friends to have left by the time I finished detention (we usually walk home together since we all live near each other), but they'd hung around, waiting for me. You'd think that means they're good friends, right? IT DOESN'T. Anaya was falling all over herself, laughing about my exchange with Mr Savage. She could hardly get the words out as she told Kayleigh and Becky all about it. She even had tears in her eyes.

'It was almost as funny,' Anaya gasped, 'as the time Mrs Laurent went ballistic over Lottie hacking the interactive whiteboard in French.'

I had to crack a smile. That *was* funny. Mrs Laurent had been trying to play a YouTube video of 2D animated characters singing the days of the week: *lundi, mardi, mercredi* . . . But the whiteboard kept switching to 'Anaconda' by Nicki Minaj. And Nicki and her dancers kept shaking their bums at the camera.

When Mrs Laurent finally figured out what was going on, she totally lost it.

'Charlotte Ramsbottom-Reed!' Becky mimicked, giggling.

'No,' I said. 'It was: CHARRRLOTTE RRRAMS BOTTOM-RRREED!' I rolled all the Rs just like Mrs Laurent had. 'YOU *NAUGHTY* GIRL!!'

Then she'd switched to French, and I'll bet she was shouting all the worst French swear words. Words she couldn't say in English because she might be struck off from being a teacher 🤭

After we'd laughed so hard we were all breathless, I reminded my friends about my run with Caiden at five. Unlike them, I had a whole bunch of stuff to do before I could go for my run. I had to eat, do my homework, and then do Danny's chores. Danny texted me while I was in detention to say I should do his chores quick before Dad gets home. The CHEEK!!

The only reason I'm not as annoyed about it as I was on Thursday is because there's now something in it for me 🤑🤑🤑. I'm not going to do his chores quite so well though. Danny needs to stop being rewarded for MY hard work.

Why do we have to do so many chores, anyway? I'm pretty sure it's child labour!! None of my friends have to do the dishes, so I don't see why me and Danny have to. Anaya's family has a dishwasher. Becky's doesn't, but her mum works part-time and usually does all the housework before Becky gets home from school. Kayleigh is the youngest of four sisters so she gets away with murder. Her big sisters do everything.

'Maybe you'll have to skip eating to make it to the park on time,' Becky said after I explained my dilemma.

'Skip a meal just because of a boy?' Kayleigh asked, incredulous.

I agreed with her. Caiden is gorgeous, but a girl needs to eat. Especially if she's going to be running four miles with him. The last thing I want is to collapse halfway around the lake due to starvation.

To do:
- Spend no more than half an hour on my homework.
- Eat while doing my homework.
- Activate BEAST MODE and get dishes, hoovering and dusting done in twenty minutes max.
- Wear my pink leggings and matching hoodie for my run with Caiden.

7.40 p.m.

He didn't show up.

I waited at the park gates for twenty minutes in the cute pink sports wear I got for my birthday last year, but there was no sign of him.

I wondered if he'd forgotten. Or if he'd remembered but decided he wasn't interested in being friends any more. Maybe he'd only wanted to be my friend yesterday because he didn't have any other friends and didn't yet know that I'm far from 'cool' at school.

I decided to still go on my run, but truth be told, I was running really slow, just in case he was late, so he could catch up with me.

That didn't happen.

On my one-minute break at the halfway point, I texted Anaya.

Me: Caiden didn't come.
Anaya: Really? Why?
Me: How am I supposed to know?
Anaya: Did he text to say he couldn't make it?
Me: He doesn't have my number.
Anaya: Oh. Well, maybe he just forgot.

I hoped that was the case. That would be better than him remembering but deciding to blow me off. But forgetting wouldn't be a great sign either. Boys don't forget girls like Sienna. Or Paige and Molly.

Why am I so easily forgettable?

I continued to run, trying to put Caiden out of my mind and not admit how devastated I was.

It turns out, I had every right to be devastated, because after I finished my run, I decided I wasn't ready to go home yet (secretly, I was still hoping Caiden would show up). Anyway, I wandered deeper into the park, and guess who I saw? Caiden and Sienna!

Okay, it wasn't just Caiden and Sienna. Paige and Molly were there too, as well as a bunch of boys, including Jay.

I got kind of frozen and just stood there, taking in the pale grey tracksuit Caiden was wearing and how amazing he looked in it. Then Jay noticed me and shouted, 'Stop staring at me, Lara. You're practically drooling!'

His friends, Ollie and Chris, laughed.

Caiden hurried over, an apologetic look on his face. 'Hey,' he said. 'Are you okay?'

Um, why wouldn't I be? Sure, I was upset that he hadn't shown up for our run and had blown me off to hang out with Sienna.

Not just Sienna, the rational side of my brain pointed out.

But *he* didn't know I was upset. And if he was assuming that I was, that could be evidence of an inflated ego. To be honest, at this point I was just searching for a reason to get turned off him, and an inflated ego seemed like a good reason to forget all about him and return to my carefree, pre-Caiden equilibrium.

'I'm fine,' I said as lightly as I could manage. 'Great, actually. Never been better. I just had a lovely run around the lake.'

'Really?' Caiden's face fell. 'I was at the gates waiting for you. I was early too. But Paige said you wouldn't get out of detention until, like, four thirty and that your parents would definitely ground you so you wouldn't be allowed out tonight.'

I frowned. 'Why would they ground me over my first detention of the school year?'

'She said you got suspended twice last year and almost got expelled, so your mum and dad are really strict on you now.'

I frowned deeper. Paige made up a bunch of lies about me?

I was about to tell Caiden that none of it was true when Sienna appeared in a flash of ice-blonde hair, shrieking with laughter.

'You have to see this, Caiden,' she trilled, clamping a hand around his arm and dragging him over to some of the boys, who were all staring at something on their phones. It sounded like a prank video. Jay, Ollie and Chris are obsessed with them.

I decided I wasn't interested in hanging around, watching Sienna flirt with Caiden. As I walked away, I thought about this really old movie that my mum likes, called *Shallow Hal*. In it, this man gets hypnotised so that he can only see women based on their inner beauty, not their looks. If that movie was real life, Sienna, Paige and Molly would look like MONSTERS.

Anyway, I'd better go. I'm FaceTiming my friends in a minute. I need to tell them everything.

9.04 p.m.

'It's got Sienna written all over it,' Anaya said after I told her and Kayleigh what happened.

My phone's screen was split into three and she was in the top right. Kayleigh was top left, massaging essential oils into her scalp. I was at the bottom, looking strange on camera as usual. The screen always makes my head look kind of oblong. Becky had been in the call but had had to go after a few minutes. Her mum has a new rule: no screens after 8 p.m.

'I agree with Anaya,' Kayleigh said. 'Paige has no interest in Caiden. Even if she does, she wouldn't dare go after him when Sienna clearly wants him. Sienna made her tell Caiden those lies.'

'Why make someone else do it?' I asked, not completely convinced that Paige was innocent.

'So Sienna can maintain her innocent façade,' Kayleigh said, like it was a no-brainer. 'She knew Caiden was going to find out it was a lie, so she had someone else tell the lie rather than risk her own reputation with him. It's Narcissism 101. I was just reading about it as part of my spiritual glow up. It was this article about protecting your energy from toxic people, and narcissists are some of the most toxic people ever.

'Every narcissist has something called flying monkeys – people who do whatever they say, even at their own expense. It's like in *The Wizard of* Oz. All those flying monkeys came after Dorothy just because the Wicked Witch of the West told them to. They were doing her dirty work the same way that Paige and Molly always do Sienna's.'

Sometimes, after one of Kayleigh's monologues, nobody knows what to say. This was one of those times.

Eventually I steered the conversation back to the matter at hand. 'I wish I'd said something to defend myself instead of just walking away after Sienna dragged Caiden off.'

Okay, I was in shock over Paige telling such blatant lies about me, but WHY DIDN'T I SAY SOMETHING???

'Well, why did you call?' Kayleigh asked, still massaging her scalp. 'Just to moan about Sienna, or because you've now recognised the need to up your game?'

Kayleigh can read me like an open book!

I took a deep breath. 'I can't compete with Sienna. I need help, Kayleigh. I think I need your glow up.'

5

Bulletproof Bras

Tuesday 4 September, 12.50 p.m.

Kayleigh, the cheeky thing, said no then hung up on Anaya and me last night. I called her over and over for the next hour, but she wouldn't answer.

This morning I followed her around between classes, GROVELLING – which is exactly what I knew she wanted. But she still said no.

'Let me stop you right there, Lara,' she yelled over the sound of the hand dryers in the toilets this morning. 'You don't level up to compete with someone. You improve your life because it's what *you* want.' Then she flounced off.

At lunchtime I joined her and Becky at our usual table by the grimy window overlooking the football field. Caiden was out there, kicking a ball around with Jay and some other boys.

I looked meaningfully at Becky, who I'd brought up to date about last night's call during geography this morning.

'Have you spoken to Caiden today?' Becky asked me, as planned.

'No,' I replied.

'I think you need Kayleigh's glow up,' she said.

Kayleigh rolled her eyes at Becky. 'Did Lara tell you to say that? Are you now Lara's flying monkey?'

Becky frowned. I'd omitted the 'flying monkey' stuff when I was bringing her up to date, so she looked offended. 'Did you just call me a monkey?'

Anaya dropped into the seat beside Kayleigh, her eyes shining with excitement. 'This morning I saw that St Michael's boy at the bus stop again.'

I rolled my eyes. There's this boy that Anaya sees, like, every six months, and she has a huge crush on him, but she knows nothing about him apart from that he goes to St Michael's High. And she only knows that because of his uniform.

Personally, I'm beginning to think she's made him up.

'I overheard him telling this other lad that he's starting a job at Mo's newsagent's on Thursday evening,' Anaya said.

'Don't tell me you're gonna go,' Kayleigh said snootily, as if she never used to follow a boy called Gary Giles around in Year 8.

'Of course I'm going. You're all coming too. You need to

finally see him.' Anaya's eyes turned shy. 'And one of you needs to find out his name.'

'What d'you think we are?' Kayleigh asked. 'Your flying monkeys?'

I was about to tell her to quit with the whole flying monkeys thing when Anaya grabbed Kayleigh's hands and said, 'Tell me more about your glow up.'

'Oh, so now you're interested?' Kayleigh snapped. 'I've been talking about it since the beginning of summer and you all just turned your noses up.'

'Okay, I wasn't into it at first,' I acknowledged. 'But now I see that glowing up is a fantastic idea. I *really* want to do it now.'

Kayleigh just rolled her eyes.

'I was into your glow up from the beginning,' Becky said. 'Didn't I do the cod liver oil face mask with you? And I came to your house for the, uh, "planting" exercise without a word of protest.'

'Yeah, but you only did it because you want Richard to notice you!' Kayleigh said way too loudly.

Everyone at the tables around us came to a standstill. Two tables away, Richard Mortimer, a spotty-faced boy in the year below, went bright red.

'Not you,' Kayleigh called.

Luckily for Becky, Richard is one of the more common names in our school.

'Come on, Kayleigh,' I said. 'All three of your best

friends need your help. If you say no, what kind of friend would that make you?'

Blackmail has never worked on Kayleigh. 'A good friend,' she snapped, glaring around at us all. 'Glow up for you, not for a *boy*.'

I wanted to shake her.

Anaya nudged me. 'We can create our own glow-up plan.' She included Becky in her gaze. 'Us three can do it without her. It'll be better, actually, because I'm not putting cod liver oil on my face. We'll start our own little glow-up club and –'

'Oh, okay then,' Kayleigh huffed. 'I'll help you. Let's meet after school – we can head into town and get this glow up started.'

6.30 p.m.

I have sooo much to tell you, dear Diary. My friends and I have had a very busy afternoon. They're all here in my room, right now.

Kayleigh and Becky are on TikTok, and Anaya is watching music videos on my laptop, which means I can journal in peace 😈

So, after school, I raced home to swipe twenty quid from Danny's not-so-secret stash. I tried to get more, but he was having none of it. He said twenty was the maximum despite the fact that his wallet is practically bursting with cash. Honestly, he's always saving his money for no reason.

'We don't want to do anything ridiculous like the other night under the oak tree,' I warned Kayleigh ten minutes later when I met her, Anaya and Becky at the bus stop.

Kayleigh just rolled her eyes.

'How much did you get?' Anaya asked me.

I waved the twenty-pound note.

Becky and Kayleigh both had twenty pounds too. Anaya, however, had her dad's credit card. Her mum had given it to her and told her not to spend more than fifty pounds!

'What about your money from working in your mum's café all summer?' I asked.

'I told her I want to save it, and she was all impressed and gave me Dad's card instead.'

Ha! My mum would never have fallen for that. But Anaya's mum is pretty soft and hardly ever questions anything Anaya says.

'I told her about our plan to glow up,' Anaya added. 'She said it sounds like a great idea.'

'My mum said I'm fine as I am and I shouldn't give in to peer pressure,' Becky said.

'Ha!' Kayleigh exclaimed. 'Did you tell her it was you guys pressuring *me* to help you glow up?'

It's funny how Kayleigh has managed to turn the tables on us and act like we're begging her for her help.

'My mum would probably say the same,' I told Becky. 'My dad too. He wants me to be a feminist and "not need a boy to complete me".'

'Does he still say you're not allowed to kiss anyone until you're thirty?' Becky asked, chortling.

My dad only said that once, and it was just a joke. A semi-serious joke, but a joke nonetheless.

'Feminists don't kiss, eh?' Kayleigh asked.

She looked like she wanted an answer, so I paused, considering it. To be honest, I wasn't sure.

'Feminists do whatever the hell they like,' Kayleigh informed me.

'They certainly don't stifle their urges just because Daddy dearest wants them to never grow up,' Becky added.

What is it with Becky and the word 'urges'?

I felt the need to defend my dad. 'He was only joking –'

'Listen,' Kayleigh said seriously. 'Dads are part of the patriarchy. Ironic that he wants you to be a feminist but thinks your resistance should apply to every male except him.'

Becky chuckled.

'A lot of things need to change, Lara,' Kayleigh said.

'Things like what?' I asked hotly.

'Things like walking to school with your dad, hand in hand.'

Prickly heat flashed through me. I looked at Anaya and Becky, hoping one of them would come to my defence, but they just giggled.

I don't see what the big deal is. I like walking to school with Dad. We get to talk without Danny in our faces, upstaging me at every turn with his good grades and ability to build pathetic robots. I've also been able to negotiate some pretty important things on those fifteen-minute walks without Mum around to say no and make Dad agree with her.

I don't ask for things on *every* walk to school, or it'll stop working. We mostly just chat about random stuff, and I endure his occasional Dad joke, although he stopped telling me jokes after the look I gave him one time when he said: 'My wife asked me to buy six cans of Sprite from the shop. When I got home, I realised I had picked 7 up.'

Okaaayyy.

My point is, walking to school with Dad isn't that bad. But my friends were acting like it's some super-uncool thing to do!

(Okay, okay, maybe I *am* a bit too old to still be holding Dad's hand. Whatever 😳)

Thankfully, a double-decker appeared down the road.

'Uh, what's the patriarchy?' Anaya asked as it approached.

Kayleigh rolled her eyes. She seemed to be doing that a lot today. 'You all have a lot to learn.'

On the bus, a dozen boys were sitting towards the back. We hurried up the stairs, but it was even worse up there.

It was full of boys from St Michael's. Anaya said none of them was the one she liked though.

'So where do we start with this whole glow-up thing?' Becky asked as the bus lurched forward.

I couldn't understand her excitement. Her only motivation is Richard Skelley, and let's just say he's no Zayn Malik. Beauty truly is in the eye of the beholder.

Kayleigh opened her school bag and tugged out some printed sheets. 'We're going to do a self-assessment,' she said, 'because I want you to understand why, during this glow up, we're not going to rate ourselves on things like looks. Also, there's a point I would like to prove.'

'What is it?' Becky asked.

'I'll tell you after I've proved it,' Kayleigh replied. She handed each of us one of the papers. 'Read the instructions. It's self-explanatory.'

I gave the instructions a quick scan. Basically, I had to give myself a score out of five on looks, but it was broken down into skin, hair, style and development.

DEVELOPMENT???

I figured that meant 'womanly curves'. I took a deep breath and got to work:

Skin: 3

Luckily, I'm acne-free and always have been.

Hair: 1

Try as I might, I just don't know what to do with my PUFFY HAIR! And I'm not letting Mum near it because we can never agree on how to style it. Why can't my hair just lie in smooth ripples that don't puff up and stand on end all the time? 😫

Style: 1

Um, I'm the girl who's had the same look for three years now. Clearly, I don't know a thing about being stylish. I've been known to leave the house without brushing my teeth, so there's that too.

Development: 0!

Hello? Cyclops boob.

Everyone else has boobs. Why don't I? 😟

I once mentioned to Mum that I was worried about my boobs. She said not everyone has big ones, and that there's no specific way that boobs have to look. 'Everyone's boob size is perfectly fine, including yours,' she said. 'And you're still growing, so who knows what size you'll be in the end?'

I knew she was right, because I've seen a lot of people with big ones, and lots with smaller ones, and everything in between. But it's still so hard to stop worrying and comparing myself. (Especially when I'm on Instagram looking at pictures of perfect people with so-called perfect bodies 😫)

When I calculated my score, it was only 5 out of 20.

The next instruction was to turn over the paper and pass it to my friends to rate me. I flipped it over and handed it to Anaya, who was sitting beside me. She passed me hers.

'Be completely honest,' Kayleigh warned. 'There's no point in lying to each other. We all need the brutal truth.'

Anaya doesn't actually need a glow up. She's already pretty much perfect, with her flawless skin and big brown eyes, not to mention her long dark curls – which, unlike mine, lie in obedient ripples. She kind of looks like Leigh-Anne Pinnock. I gave her 5s for everything.

Kayleigh was next. She's pretty too. Her new strawberry blonde hair really suits her, and she's got long, thick eyelashes so she doesn't even need mascara. I gave her all 5s too.

Then I wondered if I needed to prove that I was being 'brutally honest'. I decided that I did, so I wouldn't get into trouble with Kayleigh. I tried to think of somewhere to deduct some marks. Then I decided I couldn't, because she's honestly pretty.

Finally, it was time to score Becky. I already knew she's prettier than me, just like Kayleigh and Anaya are. But in the 'womanly curves' department she's beating us all hands down. I might not feel so bad about my non-existent boobs if I didn't have to come face to face with Becky's heaving chest EVERY DAY!!

Anyway, I eagerly took my paper back from Becky as we got off the bus in town. My friends and I walked slowly through Queen's Square bus station, our eyes glued to our scores.

'Aww, all 5s,' Anaya said. 'Thanks, guys.'

I stopped walking. I had all 5s too, resulting in a score of 20 out of 20. I glared at my friends. 'You're LYING!'

'Why?' Kayleigh asked. 'Because we didn't tear you apart?'

'You even gave me 5s for development when I've got no boobs!'

'Does not having boobs make you any less amazing than anyone else?' Kayleigh demanded.

I supposed it didn't. But still, I wasn't sure.

'Does it mean you're not developing?' Kayleigh asked. 'You're developing in other ways – getting taller, stronger, older – so you do deserve a 5.' She gave us all a smug smile. 'I've proved my point perfectly. We're nicer to other people than we are to ourselves. As we glow up, we need to start being as kind to ourselves as we are to our friends. Plus, I was expecting one of you to point out that rating ourselves on stuff like this is ridiculous. How do you score hair or development? And if you don't like your hair or your body, what can you realistically do about it?'

'Uh, get a boob job,' I pointed out.

Anaya and Becky chortled.

Kayleigh shrugged. 'I suppose you could, but where does it end? If you don't work on loving who you are, you might still not like yourself after the boob job. You'll probably just analyse yourself all over again and come up with something else you want to change.'

'I want to lose weight,' Becky said quietly.

Kayleigh gave her an encouraging smile. 'Then lose it for you, not because you're trying to look like other people.'

Becky rolled her eyes. 'Easy for you to say, being stick thin and everything.'

'Well, I think that if you're going to lose weight you should focus on just being healthy instead of on how your body looks or trying to get it to look like an Instagram model or something. You can totally drive yourself to despair if you focus too much on your appearance rather than on feeling good and accepting yourself.'

Kayleigh took out her phone as we entered St Johns Shopping Centre. 'Look at this girl,' she said, tapping into Instagram. A picture appeared on her screen of a really pretty girl around our age with a halo of gorgeous curls. I checked her profile name: @TheMelaninKween.

'Some people just have it all,' I grumbled.

Kayleigh snorted. 'If only she was here to hear you say that. Read the caption.'

I took her phone from her and read it: I hate my face.

It's so round. I have no cheekbones. I can't stop thinking about it 😢😢😢

'What?' I exclaimed.

'Okay, her face is round,' Anaya said. 'But what's wrong with that?'

'Tell me people were kind in the comments,' Becky said.

I scrolled down to the comments. One from Kayleigh was right at the top: There is absolutely nothing wrong with your face, Melanin Kween. What's wrong is the media always telling us what is beautiful. We should all boycott it. You're gorgeous!

Kayleigh's comment had lots of likes and replies from people who agreed with her. She's probably going to start a revolution someday.

I scrolled further down and saw that most of the comments on the picture were nice. I handed Kayleigh's phone back to her as we entered St Johns food court.

'So, what should we be rating ourselves on, then?' I asked as we slid into seats at a table for four.

Kayleigh, who was sitting directly opposite me, leaned forward, her eyes brimming with excitement. 'Things like happiness, accepting yourself, self-care, and how much you're working on your mental health. That's what really matters. We can still work on our appearance, but the main thing about our glow up should be doing what makes us feel good.'

'I feel like we need some dramatic music right now,' Anaya said. Then, much to my horror, she began to serenade us with 'Diamonds' by Rihanna. At the top of her voice too. And Anaya can't sing to save her life. (Nobody's got it all, eh?)

Kayleigh and Becky joined in.

'Stop,' I groaned. 'People are looking at us.'

They sang louder.

'Good grief, girls!' an old man roared from the next table. 'You sound like a bunch of dying cats!'

At that, we all burst into laughter.

Then Kayleigh tugged a notebook out of her bag and opened it to a blank page. 'Right,' she said. 'We're going to be systematic about our glow up. It's time to plan it all out.'

'Step 1: Tackle flat chest,' I said, instantly morose. I'm all for 'accepting myself', but I do want boobs.

I expected Kayleigh to argue, but she wrote it down, even though I'm the only flat-chested one. Maybe she thought I was bothered about it 'for me' and not because of what 'other people think'.

'Not that there's anything I can do about it,' I griped. 'It's not my fault that I'm not developing.' I slumped down in my chair.

'Never you mind,' Kayleigh said with a wise air. 'You don't need to know what the solution is. It's your job to ask. It's the job of the universe to answer – even if that answer is to help you accept yourself.'

The universe?

She was totally serious. Anaya and Becky exchanged

looks. I covered my mouth with my hand so that I wouldn't laugh.

'Next?' Kayleigh asked.

'Step 2: Tackle hair,' I said. (Yes, I was making it all about me, as I'm the one who needs the most help!) 'Step 3: Tackle clumsiness.'

'Great,' Kayleigh said, writing it all down. 'Anything you want to add, Anaya? Becky?'

'We should have makeovers,' Becky said.

'Yeah,' Anaya agreed. 'And get our nails done and stuff. Not that I don't agree with everything you said, Kayleigh. Because I do.'

'It's fine,' Kayleigh replied. 'Our glow up can include beauty stuff. We just need to do it for the right reasons. We also need a spiritual glow up.'

'What's that?' I asked.

'Stuff that will increase our confidence. For example, embodying powerful archetypes.'

'What's that?' I asked again.

Kayleigh sighed, like it's my fault that I don't have four older sisters to learn these things from. 'Female archetypes are things like goddess, queen . . .' She paused, trying to think of more.

'Oh, I get it,' Anaya said. 'Yeah, we totally need to work on having goddess energy and carrying ourselves like queens.'

Kayleigh wrote down *Goddess energy. Queen energy.* 'We need two more,' she said.

'What are the other archetypes?' Becky asked.

'Mother is one,' Kayleigh said, 'which is why I did the Mother Earth exercise.' She gave Becky and me a sheepish look. 'Planting our boobs in the mud wasn't really about growing them. I only said that to make you come along.'

I narrowed my eyes. 'I kind of gathered that when you started talking about "being one with Mother Earth's calming feminine energy".'

Anaya snorted with laughter.

'Well, I can't remember the other archetypes right now,' Kayleigh said, 'so I say we just choose our own.'

We were all quiet for a moment while we thought about it. Then I suggested, 'Supermodel.'

Kayleigh wrote down *Supermodel energy*.

'Independent woman,' Becky suggested.

'Perfect,' Kayleigh said, adding it to the list. 'So that I don't have to do all the work, each of us will research one of these archetypes and lead the rest of us in a session on how to embody that kind of energy. You're doing supermodel, Lara, since you suggested it.'

'Supermodels have to walk, and Lara isn't very good at that,' Becky said, lips twitching.

I glared at her.

'They walk in heels too,' Anaya added. 'Lara and high heels must never meet.'

'Well, this is her opportunity to tackle her clumsiness,'

Kayleigh said. She gave me an encouraging smile. 'You can do it, Lara.'

At least ONE of my friends has faith in me!

'Becky, you're doing Independent woman,' Kayleigh said.

'I'll do Queen,' Anaya offered.

Kayleigh grinned. 'Great. I'll do Goddess.'

She set down her pen and we all stared at our plan for a few moments.

GLOW-UP PLAN
Step 1: Tackle flat chest
Step 2: Tackle hair
Step 3: Tackle clumsiness
Makeover (to include having nails done)

SPIRITUAL GLOW UP
Queen energy
Goddess energy
Supermodel energy
Independent woman energy

A new charge filled the air at the table right there in the noisy food court. An excited charge. The whole thing felt kind of . . . momentous. Sacred, almost.

'We should be able to get through all this in a month,' Kayleigh said, 'if we're serious about it and stay focused. Just think, by the end of this month we'll be brand-new versions of ourselves.'

I felt practically giddy with excitement. Finally, I'm getting my glow up, and I'm so glad I'll have my friends helping, because heaven knows I'd have no clue what to do on my own.

Caiden isn't going to know what's hit him. I know Kayleigh said we shouldn't glow up for a boy, but I had visions of Caiden running in slow motion towards a stylish version of me that was literally glowing, like I was made of pure gold. (Get it? I was *glowing* because I'd *glowed up* and become IRRESISTIBLE! 😊 😊 😊)

You don't understand how exciting this is for me, dear Diary. None of my crushes have ever liked me back! But with this glow up, the possibilities are endless!!!

After we'd spent a few long moments staring at the glow-up plan, Kayleigh said, 'Take pictures of it so that we each have a copy.'

After we left the food court, our first stop was a lingerie shop. I was expecting Superdrug first for make-up, but Kayleigh said we needed to all make sure we were wearing the correct bra size.

The thought of getting measured was a bit embarrassing. We made Kayleigh go first, so she could tell us what to expect, and when she said she had to remove her cardi but the lady let her leave her school shirt on because she didn't want to take it off, I relaxed a bit. But not enough to go second. I went last, so I could prepare myself.

In the end, there was really no need to worry. The lady didn't scream in horror and shout, 'CYCLOPS CHEST!' She said Anaya told her I'm a footballer, and started asking me lots of questions about it. I hardly even realised she was measuring my chest while I answered. (I think Anaya told her that on purpose so we would have something to talk about and I wouldn't have a spare moment to feel embarrassed ☺)

The whole thing was over before I knew it. And it confirmed what I already knew: all my friends are bigger than me ☹

'You might want to try a padded bra,' Anaya suggested after I pointed that out, 'if it bothers you that much. You can tackle Step 1 right away.'

I perked up at that. I've sometimes been tempted to stick some socks in my bra but my cousin, Sadé, told me about her friend, this girl called Simone, who tucked tissues into her bra one time, and when she did a handstand at school, the tissues fell out. Since then I've resisted the urge to fake having boobs. But with a padded bra, what could go wrong?

I found a rack of brightly coloured bras that were so padded, they looked like BULLETPROOF VESTS. I *loved* them, but they were SIXTEEN POUNDS! I couldn't spend almost all my money on a bra when I still needed to buy make-up.

Thankfully Anaya found some for twelve pounds. I added a pretty pink one to my basket. The label promised to make you look THREE CUP SIZES BIGGER!

'Won't people suspect something if I suddenly look three sizes bigger?' I whispered to my friends.

Kayleigh shook her head. 'No, they'll just think they never noticed how big you were before.'

Becky also added a three-sizes-bigger bra to her basket, even though she's already a respectable size and doesn't need the extra help.

Next, Kayleigh said we all needed thongs.

'Why?' Anaya asked. 'Nobody can see our knickers anyway.'

'It's not about what people see,' Kayleigh replied. 'It's about how we feel.' She wiggled her brows. 'We'll feel super-hot in thongs and start carrying ourselves in a whole new way.'

Becky smirked. 'Actually, people do see Lara's underwear quite frequently. The next time she falls flat on her face, we'll all be spared the sight of her holey granny knickers.'

Anaya laughed uproariously.

I couldn't believe that Becky had the audacity to bring up my fall at Anfield Stadium. 'I wouldn't want to be wearing a thong the next time I fall over,' I retorted.

'Everyone'll see my bum. At least my knickers covered it . . . except for the little part that showed through the hole.'

Becky sighed. 'Trust me, it would have been better to see your whole bum than those granny knickers with the massive hole.'

Whatever! I thought.

After the lingerie shop, we went to Superdrug, where Anaya helped me choose foundation. 'Not that you need it,' she said. 'It's just for any time you might want your skin to look extra-smooth.'

I liked the sound of that.

Next, I got mascara, eyeliner and a clear lip gloss. I didn't bother with a coloured gloss because I knew there was no way Mum would let me wear it. She lets me use some of hers on special occasions, but that's it. It's so not fair. All my friends are allowed as much make-up as they want. Kayleigh is even allowed to dye her hair!

When we finished shopping we debated about whose house we should go to to continue our glow-up talk.

'Come to mine,' I suggested. I needed to get home before Dad so he wouldn't get on my case about me not doing my homework or chores before gallivanting around the city.

Dad is always keeping tabs on whether I've done my homework. It's so aggravating. I feel like he would be totally happy with my grades if it wasn't for Danny always getting results that make mine look bad in comparison.

'It depends on what's for tea in your houses,' Anaya said.

'Spaghetti Bolognese at mine,' Kayleigh told her.

'Jollof rice at mine,' I said. 'My dad made it last night so that it's ready for when we all get home today.'

That sealed the deal. My friends all love Dad's jollof rice.

Luckily, we got home at four thirty and I had time to rush my chores then do my homework. With my friends' help, I got all my homework done before we heard Dad's key in the lock.

Note to self:
- Follow @TheMelaninKween and leave her a nice comment.
- Padded bras are God's gift to flat-chested womankind.

By the way, how am I supposed to teach my friends about supermodel energy? I didn't even know that female archetypes existed until today. Supermodel isn't even one of the archetypes. Neither are goddess or independent woman. I just googled them, and they're queen, mother, maiden, huntress, lover, sage and mystic.

I prefer ours.

My mum and dad are such fakes! They act all super-nice whenever my friends come over. They even gave us money for ice cream after dinner when the ice-cream van came.

When do I ever get ice cream? The answer is NEVER! Not unless my friends come round and Mum and Dad want to act like cool parents.

Mum and Dad found out I went to town because my friends were talking about it, but they assumed I must have done my homework first because Dad checked my books and everything was all done. He didn't notice that my English homework was all in Anaya's handwriting.

Mum's ankle is still swollen and a bit sore, and she told my friends all about how kind Caiden was on Saturday while I just wished she would stop talking.

Since they were preoccupied with playing host to my friends, I secretly fed Nala bits of jerk chicken under the table. Dad hates it when I give Nala our food, but he didn't notice. He was too busy lapping up my friends' praise over how nice the jollof rice and fried plantain was.

His jerk chicken has come a long way. Even Nala loves it. Whenever we visit Grandad, he always says in his thick Jamaican accent, 'Is my son still playing chef, serving my grandkids his BLAND, UNSEASONED CONCOCTIONS?' He thinks his jerk chicken is better than Dad's and I play along to make him happy (he always gives me a tenner, after all). But really, Dad has surpassed him.

After dinner, I was glad to get back to my room and back to glow-up talk. We decided to do 'Step 2: Tackle hair' and the makeover right away. Anaya helped me choose a hairstyle in one of Mum's Black hair magazines: a straightened fringe, cornrow braids running from the front of my head (except the fringe) to halfway up my head, then the hair at the back straightened too. We used Mum's straighteners and had to put them on maximum heat for them to actually work.

I trust Anaya with my hair. She's good at braiding (she learned from YouTube tutorials) and sometimes does her mum's hair. She even does her own, usually with coloured hair extensions. She's had red, blonde, and even black with curly blue tips. But she only tends to wear braids in the winter.

I've never asked her to do my hair before because I've been content with my bun. But now that I'm glowing up, Anaya's hair skills might come in handy.

'You have gorgeous hair,' she told me as she did my braids. 'You just need to learn how to work with it instead of against it.'

That made me feel less hopeless about my hair, and like maybe cute, stylish hair was possible for me.

'You should ask your mum for tips, since her hair is the same,' she suggested.

I thought of Mum's carefree 'fro and snorted. Her hairstyle's nice for a woman her age, but I don't want to wear mine like that. Mum used to braid my hair when

I was younger, but she always did it really tight, which hurt, and it would take forever. We often ended up falling out too. Once I turned twelve I decided I wasn't letting her touch my hair any more.

'So when are we doing our archetype sessions?' Kayleigh asked as Anaya worked on my hair.

I was only half listening, because suddenly I was worrying about whether my hair would turn out well. The style looked good on the girl in the magazine, but she's really pretty, and I'm . . . me. Anaya's best efforts might not be enough to transform my look.

Then I started stressing even more, because if it didn't turn out nice and I took it out before school tomorrow, Anaya might think I didn't think she did a good job, and she might get all offended.

'Weekends are probably best,' Becky said. 'Maybe two this weekend and two the next?'

'Okay.' Kayleigh gave us all a stern look. 'But don't think that means we won't be glowing up on weekdays too. I will continue my research and share anything useful with you on weekdays at school.'

'We can do the queen session tomorrow after school,' Anaya said. 'I already have ideas.' Then she tugged me to my feet and steered me towards the mirror on my closet door. 'All done.'

I was shocked when I looked at my reflection. The hairstyle actually turned out pretty well. In fact, it looked

NICE! I was so relieved. I threw my arms around Anaya and jumped up and down while Kayleigh and Becky giggled. I can't wait to show up at school tomorrow with my new straightened hair.

'Wow, a fringe really suits you,' Becky said. 'You look like a young Naomi Campbell.'

That was a total stretch, since Naomi Campbell is a supermodel and everything. Becky probably only said it because she knows I follow Naomi Campbell online, but I accepted the compliment anyway.

'The final piece of our glow-up puzzle,' Kayleigh said as we all settled down to do each other's nails, 'is that we also have to work on inner beauty and self-love. Glow ups are more than just makeovers. There's no point in changing the outside but staying the same on the inside.'

'How do we work on self-love?' I asked.

'Well, you can't love what you don't know,' Kayleigh said, 'so first you have to get to know yourself. How do you even know what kind of boy would be right for you if you don't know who you are?'

After Becky finished painting Kayleigh's nails pink, Kayleigh grabbed her phone and sent us all a link to an ebook called *101 Self-knowledge Questions*.

'Journal on these questions every day,' she instructed.

And now, I shall proceed to do just that. I don't know why I just said 'shall', but it feels like kind of a big deal. Y'know, self-knowledge. I wonder if I'll find out something

I don't already know about myself. That doesn't seem likely since I've known myself since, uh, birth.

I'd better just do it though, so Kayleigh doesn't get on my case. At least it isn't something crazy like the boob-burying thing. It's just more journaling, which is something I already do anyway.

Self-knowledge Questions
Favourite singer: Ariana Grande
Celebrity crush: Zayn Malik & Anthony Joshua
Girl crush: Zendaya
Book boyfriend: Selwyn from Legendborn
Secret wish: To be adopted by Naomi Campbell. Becky said I look like her. Maybe that was a sign that it's going to happen!

10.05 p.m.
Anaya just posted in our group chat saying we're going to need milk and honey, as well as some old underwear or a swimming costume, for her queen session after school tomorrow. What on earth has she got planned?

6
Milk and Honey Mayhem

Wednesday 5 September, 8.13 a.m.

Good morning, dear Diary,

Are you ready for some new knowledge?

Well, 'patriarchy' means 'a system of society or government in which men hold the power'.

I asked Dad about it over breakfast and he said I can and will thrive and succeed, patriarchy or not. Danny said maybe I should move to Bribri, Costa Rica, where it's matriarchal, which means women hold the power.

Dad was impressed that Danny knew something he didn't know, and that's how Danny hijacked the whole conversation!

10 a.m.

I'm in French, but the lesson hasn't started yet. Mrs Laurent only just walked in and is sorting out her worksheets.

We're not allowed to have our phones on us at school. We're meant to leave them in our lockers, but you can get away with it if you're careful.

Anyway, this morning

11.04 a.m.

Sorry I had to stop the last post so suddenly. Mrs Laurent called my name. I thought she must have seen my phone, but she just wanted me to give the worksheets out. Phew!

It's break time now and I'm with my friends in the school library. Anaya and Becky are quickly doing last night's homework before their next class. Clearly their parents don't moan at them to do their homework every night. Kayleigh is on TikTok watching dance videos – mostly people twerking. I will *not* be impressed if she starts trying to twerk now.

Anyway, what I wanted to tell you in my last post was that I think Dad was a bit offended when I told him I didn't want him to walk me to school today, never mind hold my hand.

He works at a warehouse a few streets from my school so we've always walked together. He just nodded when I told him I would be walking on my own, then he watched me cross to the other side of the road. I glanced back and found him still standing there with a funny look on his face. I felt a bit sorry for him, so I gave him a little wave.

He waved back and called, 'Your hair looks nice, love.'

I cringed. The street was full of people hurrying to school or work, and he was shouting like that? I quickly turned around and hurried off.

Danny came to my room this morning while I was giving my fringe a bit of a curve so that it didn't just lie flat against my forehead. He said my hair looks like I'm trying too hard. He tried to mess it up. I set Nala on him, and as soon as she bared her teeth and hissed, Danny ran out of my room, shouting, 'That cat is evil. It must belong to a WITCH!'

I owned the title and cackled loudly.

Anyway, when I walked through the school gates people STARED. It was really strange. I knew it was because of my hair. I was wearing a bit of make-up too. Since I couldn't tell what they thought of my new look, I didn't know whether or not to be flattered, as my own family's feedback had been so mixed. Dad liked it; Danny didn't. Mum didn't notice since she was in such a rush to get to work. For day shifts she has to be there by eight, so she leaves home around seven.

Just when all the gawking was beginning to make me feel like a ZOO ANIMAL, I spotted Kayleigh by the school entrance and ran over to her. Unfortunately, that made my fringe blow up. I felt the wind lift it, but when I stopped running, I didn't feel my hair flop down again.

That's my hair for you.

'Your hair's sticking up,' Kayleigh said.

'I know. Got a mirror?'

She slipped one out of her bag and held it up so I could look into it and fix my hair. Yes, my fringe was STANDING ON END. After I smoothed it back down, we went inside. We ran into Jay in the hallway.

'Good morning, James,' Kayleigh sang, putting on a posh accent. 'You look dashing as always. What a pleasure. How are you today?'

Jay turned, grinning. 'I'm fine, dearest Kayleigh,' he said in his best *Pride and Prejudice* voice. 'And how are you?'

'Oh, dear James, I'm marvellous!'

Jay's nose wrinkled at the sight of me. 'You smell like you had a fight with a perfume counter.'

Jay can say things like that to me and get away with it – but only because we've known each other forever. I see him almost like a brother – just slightly less annoying than Danny.

He looked at my hair next, and his eyes widened. 'What happened to your hair?' he asked.

I took another quick glance in Kayleigh's mirror to make sure it wasn't sticking up again. It wasn't. 'I straightened it,' I told Jay.

He looked bewildered. 'Why?'

'Because she wanted to,' Kayleigh told him. She linked her arm through mine. "Come on, Lara. See you later, Jay."

Next, we ran into Lottie coming out of the girls' toilets as we were about to go in and check our reflections in the bigger mirrors. (Pocket mirrors can only show you so much.)

'You look different,' Lottie said. 'What have you done to yourself?' Her eyes raked me over from head to toe, trying to figure it out.

'My hair's straight,' I told her. 'I had a makeover.'

Lottie's eyes snapped to my hair. 'Ah, a makeover,' she said. 'Is that what they call it when you give in to the pressure of societal beauty standards?'

Lottie has big hair. Apparently, her great-grandad was from Barbados. She wears her hair out in a gravity-defying mass. It suits her. She kind of looks like Tori Kelly. She's also too deep for me. She and Kayleigh have endless conversations about 'society' and 'the plight of humanity', and I can never keep up.

She told me last year that she's never had a crush on a boy, only on girls. And I told her that my cousin, Kemi, has a girlfriend. I didn't tell a soul about what she said, but then Lottie told everyone herself after a while.

'Not everyone will applaud your glow up,' Kayleigh whispered to me as we shoved past Lottie and entered the toilets. 'Such people are either just resistant to change or have crab mentality.'

I didn't know what crab mentality was so I had to google it. Basically, if you put a bunch of crabs in a bucket and one tries to escape, the others will pull it back down. A good way to sum it up is: 'if I can't have xyz, neither can you'.

Anyway, it's almost the end of break, but I have time to squeeze in a self-knowledge question.

Self-knowledge Question
Write a letter to your biggest physical flaw.
This one is a no-brainer. I'm going to write to my HAIR!!

Dear Afro hair,
    Why do you like to EMBARRASS ME??
    Why do you stand on end instead of lying nice and
    flat like other hair types?
    Why do you frizz up and like to be PUFFY rather
    than just sitting in nice orderly curls?
    Why do you need so much time and attention???
    I GENUINELY want to know!
Sincerely,
Lara Bloom

12.45 p.m.
This must be what it feels like to be popular, admired and NOT AN INVISIBLE LOSER! All morning people stared

at me, and lots of them complimented my hair. Kayleigh was right. Jay and Lottie were just being killjoys.

So that you understand how momentous this new development is, no one EVER compliments my hair!!! Not since Year 7, when I used to have braids and people would compliment me whenever I got a new braid pattern done. Once I stopped wearing braids and started just stuffing my hair into a bun every day, the compliments stopped.

At lunchtime, I couldn't wait to see Caiden. He's not in any of my classes except maths with Mr Savage, so I hadn't seen him all morning.

I made sure to walk by his locker on my way to the lunch hall, and there he was. And all alone too. He was putting on his trainers, probably planning to go play football again.

I was just about to go over when my left eye began to wobble.

WOBBLE WOBBLE.

TWITCH TWITCH.

Arrrgh!

My eyes hadn't twitched since the weekend. Why was my left eye doing it again now???

I changed my mind about going to talk to him, but he spotted me and waved for me to come over, so I had no choice.

DO NOT TWITCH, I yelled at my eye internally. *AND NO WOBBLING EITHER*!!

Surely my brain should be able to control my eye, the

way it can control my legs to walk and my mouth to speak or not speak.

I felt another spasm in my eye. I wanted to scream.

During the summer holidays I asked Mum to take me to the doctor about my twitching eyes, convinced it meant I had some terrible medical condition, but after a couple of tests the doctor said it was just fatigue – and could also be too much screen time. Mum gave me a new bedtime of nine o'clock, but after a few days she – thankfully – started leaving me to my own devices again. (Ha! She knew she wasn't getting my phone off me so she didn't even try.)

'Why didn't you tell me?' Caiden asked as I approached him.

'Tell you what?'

SPASM SPASM, went my eye.

I rubbed it. Then I remembered I was wearing mascara. The back of my hand came away black. Did that mean I'd smeared it all over the place?

If I had, Caiden didn't seem to notice. 'That you're the captain of the girls' football team, and that you guys have won the Liverpool Schoolgirls' Football League six times and are almost at one hundred games unbeaten?'

'Oh.' I shrugged. 'I suppose I just didn't think to mention it. I've only won the league with them twice though.'

To be honest, I was surprised by how impressed Caiden looked.

'I heard the Year 10 boys' team is rubbish,' he said.

Unlike the girls, who only have one team for the whole school, there are LOTS of boys' teams. Most of them are separated by Year group. It's annoying, but the girls wouldn't even have a team at all if not for teachers across the city coming together like a decade ago to create a special league for girls. It was meant for schools that didn't have enough girls interested in football to make one team per year group, and they allowed teams to include girls from Year 7 to Year 11.

Our school needs to change things up, though, because more girls want to play now. Lots of other schools now have multiple girls' teams and play in lots of different leagues. Why can't we?

'Yup,' I said to Caiden. 'Most of the boys' teams are pretty bad, but our year is an absolute joke. They always finish the season in the bottom three. If it was the Premier League, they'd be relegated.'

Caiden pinched the bridge of his nose and groaned.

'I saw you playing yesterday lunchtime,' I told him. 'You're good.'

Caiden's brows lifted slightly and I wondered if I'd sounded like a stalker.

'You should join the team,' I added. 'With your help they might escape the bottom three this year.'

'Yeah, I might join,' Caiden said. 'But I'm not really used to defeat.'

'Did you play back in London?'

'Yeah. We won our league in Year 7 and came second last year. I was the top goal-scorer for the whole league last year.'

I snorted. 'Anyone can make big claims when there's no way people can check if they're true or not.'

Caiden looked insulted, and it was the cutest insulted look I've ever seen.

'You think I'm lying?' he asked. He stepped forward, locking eyes with me.

I giggled and backed away, only to hit my back against a locker.

'Seriously?' Caiden raised an eyebrow. 'Are you calling me a liar, Lara Bloom?'

I was trying to think of something cool, funny or witty to say when my eye wobbled FEROCIOUSLY, reminding me that I wasn't a girl with shampoo-ad hair who knew how to flirt.

Before I could figure out what to do next, Sienna trilled, 'Caiden, *there* you are. I've been looking everywhere for you!'

There she was, flicking her shampoo-ad hair as if conjured up by my thoughts.

Ugh! Her syrupy voice annoys me so much.

The next thing I knew, she was dragging Caiden off down the corridor.

I was feeling decidedly morose when I joined my friends in the lunch room. Caiden had been nice enough just now, but he hadn't seemed to notice my glow up. I told my friends about it when they asked what was wrong, and Becky said, 'Well, he's new so maybe he thinks this must just be one of the ways you usually wear your hair.'

My eye had stopped twitching by then, and that told me one thing loud and clear: it's not just my HAIR trying to sabotage my life. MY EYES ARE IN ON IT TOO!

'I don't stand a chance with Caiden,' I muttered into my bowl of tomato soup.

Kayleigh had the nerve to roll her eyes.

3.09 p.m.

The STRANGEST thing happened after lunch!!

Sienna is in my chemistry class and she kept staring at me. Once Mr Adeola finished droning on about safety precautions and let us loose in the lab, Sienna came over and said, 'Your hair looks nice. A fringe really suits you.'

WHAT???

There and then I almost forgave her for – well, everything. Maybe even the doping allegation.

'Thanks,' I said, a tad shy.

Sienna tucked a silky straight handful of hair behind her ear. 'Molly said she heard Anaya and Becky talking about you guys doing a glow up.'

I nodded and told her all about it. Her gaze sharpened when I mentioned the journaling component, reminding me of our first ever conversation back in Year 7.

Believe it or not, Sienna and I were once BFFs. We latched on to each other on our first day at Prince's Park Academy. We were both nervous because we didn't know anyone. I spotted a cute, glittery red journal poking out of her school bag and my eleven-year-old self thought I'd found a kindred spirit.

'I journal too,' I told Sienna.

'Really?' she asked. In those days, her voice was so quiet, I had to strain to hear her. It was nothing like the loud sugary voice she puts on these days.

'Yeah,' I said. 'I LOVE journaling.'

'ME TOO!' she cried in a voice that was loud for her but still quieter than most people. 'I've been journaling since I was, like, seven.'

'Same!'

Then we grinned at each other and our friendship was born.

Anyway, back to today. I asked, 'Do you still journal?'

She nodded. I couldn't believe it. Back in Year 7, after she ditched me for Paige and Molly, she got them to make fun of me for journaling all the time. They said only two types of people journal:

1. People with no life.
2. Weird people with massive issues.

I pointed out that Sienna journaled too, but she denied it.

All this flashed through my mind as she smiled innocently at me and said, 'I never stopped.'

I wanted to SHAKE HER. Instead I said, 'I use an app now for better security.'

Sienna lifted her perfectly arched brows. 'Me too!'

It turned out we both use the journalpixie app.

'My sister read my journal once,' Sienna said, rolling her eyes. 'That's why I decided to go digital.'

'Same here! Danny read my journal, so I wanted something more secure.'

I can't believe it. We're practically living parallel lives, trying to survive the trauma inflicted on us by evil siblings.

'It's so good, because if you're short on time you can just do a voice note or shoot a quick video,' she said.

'I've used the voice note function a few times,' I told her. 'But I haven't done any videos yet.'

'I do mostly videos now,' Sienna said. 'The app transcribes them so that you can skim-read what you said if you don't want to watch the whole video.'

At that point Mr Adeola noticed us gabbing and said, 'Girls, would you like to share your riveting conversation with the rest of the class?'

'No, sir,' Sienna and I said in unison.

'Then I suggest you switch on your Bunsen burners and get to work!'

I wonder if, now that I'm kind of 'pretty', Sienna wants

to be friends. If she does, should I say yes?

What will Anaya, Becky and Kayleigh think if I start hanging out with her?

Self-knowledge Question
Do you have a best friend? If so, who is it and why?
Anaya, Becky and Kayleigh are my best friends.

Why? Because they're funny, silly and nice. And even though we tease each other sometimes, we're all very supportive of each other.

I might have the most annoying family EVER, but in the friendship department I can't complain!

Being friends with Sienna first makes me appreciate Anaya, Becky and Kayleigh even more. Sienna had *no* sense of humour when we were friends. I don't know if she's different now.

P.S. Don't tell Kayleigh, but I'm actually enjoying these self-knowledge questions. They're a great way to think about what I think about things – if that makes sense ☺

8 p.m.
After school, I had training with the football team. Saturday's match is fast approaching. It'll be Match 97 in our unbeaten streak and it's against Sefton College. WE HAVE TO WIN!!!

My friends hung around, waiting for me to finish training, then we all rushed to Anaya's house because we had a lot to get through (Dad gave his permission yesterday over jollof rice). (I didn't tell my friends about my chat with Sienna, in case they thought I was about to ditch them.)

I love Anaya's house. It's in a brand-new street of brand-new houses and inside it's all white marble, fluffy cream carpets and mirrors. Neither of Anaya's parents ever gets home before six, so we had plenty of time. And, lucky her, she doesn't have any siblings.

She led us outside to the back garden, which is half paved and half grass. Kayleigh helped her carry the coffee table from the living room out onto the paved section.

'You can put your milk and honey on it,' Anaya said.

I removed from my bag the two-pint carton of milk I'd bought on my way to school that morning. Another perk of not walking with Dad is privacy. If we'd walked together, he would have wanted to know why I was buying milk and honey. He'd have found it ridiculous if I'd said that Anaya had told me to but I didn't know why.

'You can sit down,' Anaya said after we'd all placed our milk and honey on the table.

We sat. She remained standing.

'Well, go on then,' Kayleigh said eagerly.

'Welcome to the queen energy session,' Anaya

announced. 'Cleopatra, one of the most famous queens of all time, bathed in milk and honey.'

Becky and I groaned, but Kayleigh clasped her hands together in glee. 'I knew it! I've always wanted to bathe in milk and honey!'

'It sounds kind of . . . sticky,' Becky said.

'And weird,' I added.

'Ignore them,' Kayleigh told Anaya encouragingly.

'I'm surprised at you, Anaya,' I said. 'Since when are you open to stuff like this?'

Anaya went a bit pink. 'Kayleigh has convinced me about this whole spiritual glow up, okay?'

'How is having a bath in milk and honey going to help us?' I asked.

'Clearly, there'll be skin benefits,' Kayleigh said. 'There'll also be spiritual benefits because we're channelling CLEOPATRA. Think of the confidence benefits too. Tomorrow when you walk into school and see everyone else strutting around, just think to yourself: *Have they ever bathed in milk and honey like Cleopatra? No! Have I? YES!*'

I lifted a brow.

Kayleigh threw up her hands. 'If that doesn't give you queen energy, I don't know what will.'

Becky looked at the bottles of milk and tubs of honey on the table. 'Well, it's hardly enough to have a bath in. I'm going first though. I'm not bathing in anyone's dirty milk.'

'We don't have enough to fill a bath,' Anaya said. 'So we're having a shower in it instead. A milk and honey shower.'

Kayleigh sighed. 'So creative.'

Anaya grinned. 'Thanks. Let's do it.'

'Out here?' Becky asked.

'Yeah,' Anaya said. 'We can't have milk going everywhere in the house.'

'But the neighbours'll see us,' Becky protested.

Anaya gestured to the tall wall beyond her garden fence. She doesn't have neighbours opposite, or on the right, as hers is a corner house.

'Nobody's in next door,' she said, nodding towards the house on the left.

So we stepped inside to get changed, then returned to the garden in our knickers and bras. It's a good thing it was still warm for September. What wasn't good was that, this morning, I was so focused on remembering my football kit that I forgot to pack a change of underwear like Anaya told us to 😬

Anaya and Kayleigh were wearing old, faded underwear, and Becky was wearing a yellow swimming costume, while I was in my new padded bra.

I usually wear a sports bra under my football shirt, which would have been perfect. But I didn't pack one today as I thought it might be a bit weird going from a three-sizes-bigger bra to a sports bra. People would be suspicious, wouldn't they?

(In case you're wondering, no it was NOT fun or at all comfortable wearing a three-sizes-bigger bra for training!)

'Rub your honey onto your skin like shower gel,' Anaya instructed.

It was easy for the others, since they'd all bought honey in squeezy bottles. I, however, had bought honey in a glass jar 😊. But I managed it.

'Now, we'll take turns having milk poured on us,' Anaya said. 'Becky first. We'll be your attendants and pour it over you so that you get the full queen experience.'

Becky struck a regal pose. We all laughed as we poured her two pints over her. 'It's COLD!' she squealed.

Next was me. I couldn't believe I was going to get milk on my gorgeous new padded bra, but I supposed getting queen energy was worth it. I did what I imagined was a powerful dance, rubbing the honey into my skin as the cold milk poured down me.

'What are you doing?' Becky asked.

'Being a fierce, powerful queen,' I replied.

Kayleigh snorted. 'I thought it was an exorcism.'

Becky giggled.

Next we did Kayleigh, who revelled in the flowing milk like it was liquid diamonds.

Finally, it was Anaya's turn. She sang 'God Save the Queen' – very loudly and very badly – while we poured her milk over her.

When we finished, we stared at each other, all sticky with honey and dripping with milk. Then we burst into laughter.

Anaya opened a drawer in the coffee table and took out some face towels and shower gel. Then she switched on the garden hose so we could clean ourselves up. She was very organised.

Once we were all back in our uniforms, our wet, milky underwear now in our schoolbags (and me underwear-less since I forgot to pack spares!), Anaya read us a poem about queens that she said she'd found online:

She walks down the street
With her head held high.
She smiles at strangers,
Catching many an eye.

She's secure in who she is,
She won't be manipulated.
She cares little for popular opinion,
Whether she's loved or hated.

Her smile lights up a room,
She exudes regal grace,
She shatters social norms,
Unafraid to take up space.

She loves the skin she's in,
And from within she glows.
She's a queen in her own kingdom
Everywhere she goes.

'That was kind of depressing,' I said when she finished.

'Why?' Anaya asked.

'Because I just realised why Sienna is so popular. She totally has queen energy.'

Anaya shook her head. 'No. During my research I read that queens lift others up; they don't put them down. They're kind, not cruel. I'd say Sienna has princess energy.'

'Princesses are nice,' Becky disagreed.

'Not really. They're all 'somebody save me', 'rescue me', 'I'm so fragile', 'I'm so naive I would eat a poisoned apple from someone who looks totally suspect and isn't even trying to hide the fact that she's a WICKED WITCH'.'

Anaya had clearly done a lot of research, so we shut up and listened.

'Queens don't sit in locked towers waiting for someone to climb up their hair,' she told us. 'They would blow that tower up and be out of there. Queens don't lie asleep for decades waiting for someone to kiss them; they wake up and kiss themselves – as in, self-love. Queen energy is "I'm in charge, I'm in control, I rule, I don't need permission from anyone to do anything". And they're positive and kind.'

I sighed. 'I still need permission for everything. I needed permission from my parents to come here today.'

'Yes, but you can still have "I don't need permission" energy.'

'Anna and Elsa are princesses but they're badass,' Becky said, still trying to disprove what Anaya had said about princesses.

'Technically, Elsa was a queen all along because her dad died when she was little,' Anaya replied.

'Oh yeah,' Becky said.

'Anna's a queen too, because of the second movie,' Anaya added.

'Queens aren't *all* nice,' I said. 'What about that evil queen with the mirror in *Snow White?*'

'She was rogue,' Anaya replied. 'But she still wasn't a fragile pushover. We can learn from that.'

'So Sienna has evil queen energy then.'

'Maybe,' Anaya conceded.

Even though Sienna was nice to me today, I wouldn't be surprised to find out she has a magic mirror that she uses to make sure she's the fairest of all the girls at school. Well, she'd better get prepared to see me in that magic mirror soon, because I'm glowing up and her days of being the queen of Prince's Park Academy are numbered. *Everyone* at school had better get ready for a new queen – *moi* – to emerge. Sienna's reign of terror is OVER!

I couldn't help floating off into a daydream. I imagined

myself walking regally into school tomorrow and Caiden totally sensing my queen energy. I, on the other hand, hardly even notice him as I strut around school, queening and generally being cool and awesome.

At lunchtime he's waiting for me by my locker, and all the thoughts in my head *don't* instantly evaporate at the sight of him. No, I'm a queen, and I'm totally calm and casual. 'Hi, Caiden,' I say with a measured smile that isn't too wide and doesn't make me look like I'm desperately happy to see him.

Caiden is all nervous and doesn't say anything, and I'm like, 'What's up? Did you want to tell me something?'

He nods quickly. 'I was wondering if you're free on Saturday afternoon. I was thinking we could go to the cinema or something.'

I twirl a lock of my hair (which is smooth and sleek) around my finger. 'That sounds like fun. Sure. What time?'

And the rest is history . . .

'Earth to Lara,' Anaya said, and I snapped back to attention.

I'm not sure what I missed while I was daydreaming. Nothing too important, I hope.

'This has been a great session,' Kayleigh said. She pushed back her strawberry blonde hair with a satisfied grin and looked at Becky and me. 'Anaya has set the bar high. I hope you two will put the same effort into your sessions.'

All I could do was nod.

7

Game of Phones

Thursday 6 September, 9.25 a.m.

Dear Delightful Diary,

You must be wondering what might have changed since yesterday's glow-up session. Do I feel Glowed Up? Am I having any queenly thoughts and feelings?

Well, I've been walking a bit taller today as I traverse the hallowed (not) hallways of the wonderful (not) Prince's Park Academy. Becky said it isn't necessarily because of the milk and honey shower. She said we just feel more confident because we're taking better care of ourselves in general.

I'm in English language right now, and I managed to sneak my phone in. Miss Robbins hasn't noticed. She's busy marking at her desk while we're all supposed to be getting on with the work on the whiteboard.

I've finished, so I might as well do some self-knowledge questions.

Self-knowledge Questions
Favourite subject at school: English lit is okay. I might even actually like it if we got to read good books about whirlwind romances with vampires, or warrior girls slaying evil, magical beasts. But no, we get books from centuries ago about star-crossed lovers who speak in *thees* and *thous* then die!
Favourite colour: Orange
Favourite food: Dad's jollof rice and Becky's mum's king prawn vermicelli
Favourite Song: '7 Rings' by Ariana Grande
Favourite movie: Most Marvel movies and *Twilight*

Oops, Miss just stood up.
   Ciao!

3.05 p.m.
I'm so ANNOYED!!

I just got out of ICT, my last lesson for today. Before class, I was minding my business, playing Candy Crush on my phone outside the computer room while we waited for Mr Collins to arrive, when, suddenly, Paige snatched my phone and ran off.

'GIVE IT BACK!' I yelled, chasing her.

I don't know if queens yell, but then I figured they must do! I can't imagine bygone queens using a quiet simpering voice whenever they said, 'Off with their heads!'

Paige disappeared through a set of double doors that lead to the maths department. I didn't notice Molly standing there, or the foot she put out to trip me, until it was too late and I was sprawled on the floor, having bashed my head against the door frame. Laughter broke out behind me.

Molly ran off as I dragged myself to my feet. At that point, there was only one thought on my mind: I'M GOING TO MAKE MOLLY AND PAIGE REGRET THIS!!!

I didn't get my phone back until Paige showed up late for ICT. As soon as she walked through the door, I stalked over to her. 'WHERE'S MY PHONE?!'

'LARA BLOOM, YOU WILL NOT CREATE ANY DISTURBANCES IN MY CLASS –'

'Sir, she took my phone!' I told Mr Collins.

Thankfully, Mr Collins is one of those rare teachers who actually listens. Any other teacher would have started lecturing me about why my phone wasn't in my locker, but he didn't. He looked at Paige. 'Did you?'

Paige gave him a wide-eyed, innocent look. 'No, sir. I don't know what she's talking about.'

'Your phone is on your table,' Molly piped up from across the computer lab.

I spun around. Sure enough, it was lying by my computer keyboard. Paige must have passed it to Molly when she walked in.

I stomped back to my table and grabbed my phone. I checked all my apps to see what she'd done, but nothing looked amiss.

'What did you snatch my phone for?' I called to Paige. 'What did you do?'

'Lara,' Mr Collins snapped. 'If you would like to talk about the data protection exercise on page 103 of your textbook, we would be happy to oblige. For all other matters, please wait until after class.'

4.15 p.m.

Paige and Molly legged it after ICT so I couldn't make them tell me what they did to my phone. Maybe they've rigged it with a bomb and it's going to explode or something. Just in case, I've told everyone who'll listen so that they'll know who to tell the police to arrest.

After school, me and my friends saw Caiden with Jay and some of Jay's annoying football-fanatic-but-rubbish-at-playing-it buddies. Jay is a decent footballer though.

I waved at Caiden. My eyes have stopped spasming today, so I thought it would be a good time to actually talk to him, but he just turned abruptly and acted like he didn't see me.

I was mortified, dear Diary. MORTIFIED!

Anaya and Kayleigh noticed the snub, but Becky didn't because she was too busy watching Richard Skelley run past, playing air guitar and singing 'Stairway to Heaven' at the top of his voice.

I wanted to talk about it, but Anaya started going on and on about Mr St Michael's, who we're all finally going to see today.

'Here's the plan,' she said. 'We'll walk in and buy something, then one of you will ask him what his name is and if he has a girlfriend –'

'He'll think we like him,' Becky protested. 'You ask.'

'You have nothing to lose if he thinks you like him because you don't actually like him,' Anaya said. 'I, on the other hand, have plenty to lose if he thinks I like him, because I do. That's why I can't ask.'

It made sense, in an odd kind of way.

Kayleigh volunteered to do the asking.

Mr St Michael's wasn't in Mo's when we arrived, and we figured he would still be on his way over from school. He might also stop at home first to get changed out of his uniform. Since my house was the closest, we went there to wait until five.

We're at my house now. When we got here, Jay was emerging from his house next door in shorts and a T-shirt, probably off to play football. 'Why did you send Caiden that text?' he called.

'What text?' I asked.

'I was defending you,' Jay said, 'saying you would never say stuff like that, and that it didn't even sound like you. But then he showed me the number it came from, and when I checked on my phone it was your number.'

'What are you talking about?' I asked. 'I don't even have Caiden's number.'

Kayleigh frowned. 'Didn't you say Paige snatched your phone?'

'Crap!' I groaned. I looked at Jay warily. 'What did the text say? Do I even want to know?'

Jay approached the low fence that separates his little front yard from mine and held out his phone. 'He forwarded the text to me.'

I took his phone and read:

You think everyone likes you, Caiden. But I don't. You think you're so cool, but what are you actually good for, except swanning around looking pretty? You should get an 'L' tattooed to your forehead because you're a total LOSER!!!

Lots of hate from your not-so-secret HATER, Lara

'WHAT?!' I exploded. 'I didn't write that! I would NEVER send anyone a message like that!'

'What did Caiden say?' Anaya asked.

'He wasn't that offended,' Jay replied. Then he looked at me again. 'He just thought it was odd, and asked me if you have a weird sense of humour.'

'And what did you say?' I asked.

'I said I didn't know.'

'You don't know?'

'Yeah. How am I supposed to know? You've been acting all weird and different this week.'

'YOU DON'T KNOW?'

Jay looked at my friends. 'Is she overreacting, or what?'

The last thing I wanted was for Jay to figure out I have a crush on Caiden, so I quickly wiped the frown off my face. 'Uh, well, thanks for letting me know.'

But Jay still gave me a weird look. 'I'm just the messenger, okay? I didn't know it was my job to be your PR team with Caiden.'

With that, he walked off.

'Jay really is getting kind of cute,' Kayleigh mused.

I almost gagged. 'Please don't.'

I see Jay the way I see Danny. In other words, I *don't* see him. Not in *that* way.

Nala greeted me enthusiastically when I unlocked the door to my house, but I was too preoccupied with what Jay had just told me to pay her any attention. Anaya picked her up and tickled under her chin just how she likes, and she let out a purr.

I checked my messages, but there were no strange ones that I hadn't sent. 'Paige texted him then deleted it from my phone so I wouldn't know. What a WITCH!'

'This is a whole new level of low life-ness,' Anaya agreed. 'Sienna probably told her to do it.'

I think she's right.

I really hope Caiden doesn't think I actually sent that horrible message 😩

4.45 p.m.

Anaya is practically hyperventilating right now, since we're leaving for Mo's again in a few minutes. I can't work up the will to be excited though, because my phone just buzzed as I was browsing through pictures on a Black hair website (I've been wondering what hairstyle to do next. I might also have been trying to distract myself from stressing about that text, and whether Caiden will believe that I didn't send it).

It was a text from Paige. We NEVER text each other. We only have each other's number because we had to work together on a group essay in English last year. She hardly did any of the work, but she always had plenty to say about how the essay wasn't good enough.

I thought she might want to apologise for what she did. Then I got real. Who was I kidding? She probably just wanted to gloat.

I opened the message . . . then froze.

It was a picture of Sienna and Caiden. He had his arms around her, holding her close.

Nala must have sensed the instant shift in my mood because she crawled into my lap, meowing.

I threw my phone at the wall.

'LARA!' Danny yelled from the next room. 'WHAT WAS THAT?'

'I . . . fell,' I called back.

'Oh, so nothing new then,' was his only response.

Unlike our parents, Danny doesn't make any effort to be nice when my friends are around.

Becky picked up my phone and looked at the screen. Then she showed it to Kayleigh and Anaya.

I have to say, my crush on Alex was so much easier than this crush on Caiden, because I knew Alex and I would never get together so I didn't even dare to hope. Letting myself hope that Caiden would like me – just because he's nice to me sometimes – has been the BIGGEST MISTAKE EVER.

'I have two questions,' Kayleigh said. 'One: why are they trying so hard to make Caiden hate you? And two: why are they making such an effort to rub him and Sienna in your face?'

I don't know the answer to either question. But I do know one thing: *Sienna* didn't have to bathe in milk and honey, but she still managed to get Caiden.

Mr St Michael's was CUUUUUUUTTTTTTEEEEE!

I didn't get that tingly feeling in my chest that I always get around Caiden, but there was no denying that the boy was the definition of GORGEOUS. No wonder Anaya has been raving about him for TWO YEARS!

He was tall with skin the colour of autumn leaves, and close-cropped hair that would curl if it was any longer. And his eyes . . . They were perfectly dark and almond-shaped.

'Look at his lips,' Kayleigh whispered as we hid behind a rack of birthday cards, staring at Mr St Michael's through a crack between the shelves. 'Why would a *boy* have such perfect, full lips like that?'

'He's got a bit of a beard going on though,' Becky whispered. 'He might be too old for you, Anaya. Kayleigh, that's one of the questions you should ask him.'

'I can't ask too many questions or he'll think I'm a stalker,' Kayleigh replied.

'No, he won't,' Anaya whispered. 'Stalkers don't ask direct questions. They just hide and watch you from the shadows.'

'And from in between card racks?' I asked.

Mr St Michael's glanced up at a screen to his right. No doubt a CCTV monitor.

'Move!' I hissed. 'He'll see us on the camera, staring at him.'

In our haste to turn around and act normal, Becky elbowed me in the neck and Anaya stamped on my foot.

I let out a yelp and slammed against the card rack. To my horror, it moved. No, not just moved; it completely gave way to my weight and fell over. I grabbed the rack of magazines next to it to steady myself, and that toppled too. I went crashing to the floor, cards and envelopes flying around me. Then a thick magazine landed on my head and almost knocked me out.

As my friends helped me up, Mo, the shop owner, came running over, yelling in horror and saying we couldn't sue him since his shelves weren't designed to be leaned against.

He eyed a piece of shelf that had broken off. 'Liam!' he hollered. 'Come and pick all this up while I fix the shelf.'

Mr St Michael's came over and started to pick up cards and magazines.

'We're so sorry to have caused you more work,' Kayleigh said, dropping to her knees. 'Here, let me help.'

I was so mortified, I just said, 'I'm really sorry, Mo', then walked off. Anaya and Becky hurried after me.

A few minutes later, Kayleigh met us down the road at the bus stop and said, 'His name is Liam Brown, he's sixteen and his TikTok is @LBrownTheClown. He said he has a girlfriend but is open to a new adventure.'

'Good work!' Anaya gushed.

'Yeah,' I said stiffly. 'I'm glad some good could come from my embarrassment.'

'But he said he's "open to a new adventure",' Kayleigh said. 'Don't you think that's weird?'

'What does he mean?' Becky asked.

'Obviously that he's had enough of his girlfriend,' Anaya said happily.

'He shouldn't really be open to new adventures when he has a girlfriend,' Kayleigh told her.

Anaya rolled her eyes. 'I expected him to have a girlfriend. A boy like that isn't going to be floating around available.'

'Well, a new adventure could mean he wants you both,' Becky said.

Anaya frowned. 'Oh.'

'I can go and clarify,' Kayleigh said, turning to walk back to Mo's.

Anaya grabbed her hand. 'No. Let's just go.'

Just then, Liam stepped out of Mo's. 'Which one?' he called.

Kayleigh pointed at Anaya.

Anaya looked like she wanted to die.

But Liam actually looked chuffed. 'I don't really have a girlfriend,' he called. 'I just said that in case I needed an excuse to turn you down.'

Anaya grabbed my arm. 'Why is he shouting across the street? Make it stop!'

Anyway, what happened next is Liam came over, told Anaya she's gorgeous and that he's noticed her a few times on his way to school but thought she must have a boyfriend. Then, just like that, they exchanged numbers and he asked if she'd like to go to this crazy golf place in town this weekend.

Anaya lives a CHARMED LIFE. She likes someone. He likes her back. And they just SAIL OFF INTO THE SUNSET!

I wanted to puke as they grinned at each other and made plans to meet up.

The most interesting thing about Liam, though, was that after hugging Anaya and promising to call her, he looked at me and said, 'You're Lara Bloom, aren't you? Caiden's friend. He's my cousin.'

Ugh! I have to go now. I'm downstairs watching crappy evening TV game shows with Mum while we wait for dinner, and she just said, 'You're always on your phone, Lara. It's far too much.'

Then Dad called from the kitchen, 'If only she had as much interest in maths as she does in texting!'

9.18 p.m.

Of course Caiden has cousins in Liverpool. He said his mum is from here, duh!

11.47 p.m.

Should I read anything into the fact that Caiden has clearly talked about me to his cousin, and must even have pointed me out? I'm trying to imagine them spying on me through a crack in the shelves at Mo's, but somehow I just can't picture it. I'm no goddess in the looks department.

Friday 7 September, 12.15 a.m.

Okay, I really need to stop wondering what Caiden said to Liam about me and try to sleep!! It's practically Friday now, which means Match 97 is, technically, TOMORROW!

Miss Simpson always says sleep is very important for athletes.

1.44 a.m.

I wonder what Caiden said about me to Liam . . .

8

Match-Day Disaster

Friday 7 September, 10.40 a.m.

I haven't seen Caiden ALL MORNING. I need to tell him that I didn't send that text, but he's NOWHERE to be found. I just texted Jay to ask if Caiden is in and he said

12.50 p.m.

Sorry, I had to stop the last entry because I was in history and Miss Lord said, 'If I find, Lara Bloom, that you are on your phone in my lesson, that phone will be CONFISCATED and you won't see it again until MONDAY.'

I quickly slipped it under my books and said, 'Phone? What phone?'

Luckily, Miss just said, 'Go and put it in your locker and never bring it to class again, Lara.'

I felt kind of empty, having to be without my phone for the rest of the lesson.

Anyway, it's almost the end of lunchtime now and I *still* haven't managed to talk to Caiden. He was in maths just before lunch, sitting with Sienna as usual. She grabbed his hand as soon as I entered the classroom and began to whisper something in his ear.

I wanted to tell him I didn't send that message, but I didn't want to have that conversation in front of Sienna. So I just made my way to my special desk at the front of the room – right under Mr Savage's nose – and slumped into my chair.

3.02 p.m.

I'm just squeezing in a quick update before football starts at quarter past three. (No, I'm *not* wearing my three-sizes-bigger bra for training today!)

Anyway, I'm sighing right now. Sighing *heavily*. Because I don't know what else to do. Here's what happened just before last period today:

Caiden was standing at my locker when I went to switch books between classes. It made me think of my silly daydream during Anaya's queen energy session. But no, nothing that I daydreamed about happened. My insides twisted into a knot at the sight of him. I forced a smile, but he didn't smile back. He just took out his phone and held it up. It had the text that Jay told me about on the screen.

'I didn't send that,' I said.

'What's your number?' he asked.

'That *is* my number, but I swear I didn't send it.'

Then I explained that Molly and Paige snatched my phone yesterday, and *they* had sent it.

I don't know if he believed me. Sienna showed up before he could respond. She's always showing up as soon as Caiden and me start talking.

'We're late for geography,' she told him, then dragged him off down the hallway.

Seriously, why would I send a message like that? It's basically BULLYING. I wouldn't do that. If Caiden thinks I did it, then he must also think I'm a bully.

5.24 p.m.

Caiden and Sienna must have *a lot* of classes together.

How ANNOYING!!

10.23 p.m.

Becky knows how to throw a PAR-TAY!

Tonight was her independent woman session, and it was so good. I was late because I had to stay behind at school for training. When I got to her house, Becky popped a party cannon that sprayed me with confetti, then my friends dragged me to the living room, where there was a punch bowl, a tray of spring rolls and samosas, another tray of chicken satay and cocktail sausages, and another tray of cakes.

Becky dimmed the lights then made an announcement: 'We are independent women. We have independent energy.'

I couldn't help laughing at the forceful politician voice she was using.

'Why are we independent?' she asked. 'Because when you act like you don't need boys, they get all intrigued and want you to need them.'

'Preach!' Anaya shouted.

'Actually, we're not being independent to make boys like us,' Kayleigh said. 'We're independent because we want to be!'

'That too,' Becky said. 'What are we, girls?' She looked around at us expectantly.

'Independent women!' I shouted.

'What are we?' Becky hollered.

This time, Anaya and Kayleigh joined me in yelling, 'Independent women!'

The living-room door opened and Becky's mum popped her head in. 'If you're so independent, go rent your own place.'

'NO!' Becky shouted. 'Being independent means I get to say no to that!'

The rest of us burst into laughter 😂😂😂. Becky's mum rolled her eyes and retreated.

'Alexa,' Becky said, addressing the smart speaker across the room, 'play my Independent Women playlist.'

'Independent Women' by Destiny's Child began to pump from the speaker and we danced our hearts out.

'Feel the energy,' Kayleigh shouted. 'Feel the independent vibe!'

Next it was 'Power' by Little Mix, then 'Run the World' by Beyoncé, then 'I'm Every Woman' by Chaka Khan. We went wilder and wilder with each song.

'She Wolf' by Shakira was playing when Becky's stepdad got home and came to tell us to keep it down.

'NO!' we all shouted. Becky's mum dragged him away, saying something to him in Mandarin.

'I heard that!' Becky yelled. 'She said we've gone berserk.'

We all roared with laughter.

It was a great evening. So good that I forgot to think about Caiden and the fact that Sienna seems to be sinking her claws deeper and deeper into him.

My friends and I hung out at Becky's until pretty late. And when our parents called to ask when we'd be home we said, 'I'll come home when I like!' then hung up.

At least, Anaya and Kayleigh hung up on their parents. Before I got to hang up on Mum, she said, 'It's almost ten and you have a match tomorrow, remember?'

I hadn't forgotten. I'd just pushed it to the back of my mind.

I groaned and hung up. A few minutes later, I said bye to my friends, then left.

Self-knowledge Questions
Favourite sport to play: Football
Favourite sport to watch: Football
Favourite sportsperson: Should there be an 's' on the end of that to make it sportspersons? Because, seriously, how do you expect me to pick just one? I'll try to limit it to five:

1. Lucy Bronze – I mean, she's won Women's Player of the Year and everything. At this point she might as well just be crowned QUEEN OF FOOTBALL.
2. Marcus Rashford – I support him only when he plays against any team that isn't Liverpool, and when he plays for England.
3. Anthony Joshua – I never understood why boxing is considered a sport until Dad explained that it's the ultimate test of strength and physicality. Literally FIGHTING for your title.
4. Lewis Hamilton – Car-racing, record-breaking CHAMPION!
5. Serena Williams – I don't think I need to explain this one.

Saturday 8 September, 2.03 p.m.

The one time I'm not clumsy is when I play football. Somehow, when I'm on the pitch with a ball between my feet, I have balance and co-ordination.

I marched onto the field at Sefton College today at noon for Match 97 with the rest of the team, all in our garish yellow kit. It's a mustardy shade of yellow that makes you want to puke if you stare at it for too long. The Sefton College girls had an equally horrifying vomit-green kit.

I expected to see a bunch of parents and people from school there to watch. What I did *not* expect to see was Caiden! He looked AMAZING, dressed all in black – and kind of like a rebel 😎. A stress headache immediately started behind my temples. Why oh why did he have to come and watch me run, jump and scrap with twenty-one other girls for ninety minutes? Not to mention all the yelling I have to do as the captain. There are some Year 11 girls on the team who don't like having to answer to someone in Year 10, so I have to shout louder at them. Also, I'm always a sweaty mess ten minutes into a match.

Then I noticed Sienna pushing through the little crowd, ponytail bobbing, lips cherry-red, obviously heading for Caiden. Sienna hardly ever comes to watch our matches, since she won't be the centre of attention. I bet she only came today because she knew Caiden would be there. And she looked all great and girly in jeans and a cute pink top. I couldn't help comparing myself. I was wearing a puke-inspired football kit.

I decided not to look in Caiden's and Sienna's direction. I told myself to just focus on the match and on getting one step closer to ONE HUNDRED MATCHES UNBEATEN.

Seven minutes in, I scored, and I went pretty wild. First goal of the season scored by MEEEEEE!!!

My teammates jumped on me and we went crashing to the ground. When I got up again, I was covered in mud. I felt a bit embarrassed until I heard Jay yell, 'Go, Lara!'

I didn't look at him because he was standing not far from Caiden.

Everything was going pretty well until I noticed how grey the clouds had gone. The braids at the front of my head had got a bit messy so I took them out this morning and straightened that portion of my hair. Then I'd gathered it all into my usual high bun. It was nice and flat since I'd straightened it, and I didn't want rain ruining it.

But soon after, the heavens opened and sheets of rain began to pelt us. I don't care too much about getting cold or wet . . . but MY HAIR!!!

I've played through rain before and had my hair transform into a puffy, shrunken DISASTER. Usually, I just laugh it off when people stare or giggle.

Today? I. Wanted. To. DIE! 😩😩

I prayed that my bun was tight enough to keep my hair together. I prayed that the fact that I'd straightened it would count for something.

But I knew better.

At half-time, I dashed into the girls' locker room and ran to a mirror. It was worse than I'd expected. My reflection was TRULY HORRIFYING. My hair had freed itself from the bobble I'd used to put it in a bun, except for a little handful in the middle. And it was all puffy. AND it had shrunk to a quarter of its length. It was also all sticking up like I'd been ELECTROCUTED.

WHY???????????

I texted Anaya, but Miss Simpson said no non-team members were allowed into the room. Then she yelled at us for the rest of half-time, saying we should be 3–0 up but we were only 1–0 up because we were playing like little girls instead of SIX-TIME CHAMPIONS. By the time she was done, I hardly had time to change into a dry kit, never mind work on my hair.

I looked desperately around at the other Black girls on the team. There are six, but only two have the same hair texture as me. Tasha had hers in long braids that she'd twisted into a bun. Bisi had straight hair that was STILL SOMEHOW STRAIGHT!

Bisi and I needed to talk.

In the meantime, I needed bobbles. I managed to get four from my teammates, then Tasha helped me section my hair into quarters and gave me four tight Afro puffs – the type of style your mum does for you when you're six years old. I felt so ridiculous as we ran back onto the pitch. So much for glowing up and becoming a better version of myself!

I made the mistake of looking at Sienna. She had a bright pink umbrella and was nice and dry.

I didn't look at Caiden.

Lottie scored halfway through the second half. By then it had stopped raining, but the pitch was a muddy mess so we were skidding all over the place as we celebrated.

Then near the end of the match I was about to score again when one of the Sefton College girls swiped my legs out from under me in a BLATANT FOUL!!

All the Prince's Park Academy supporters erupted with anger. I could hear Jay's voice the loudest. 'That was a full-blown attempted murder!' he shouted.

People laughed.

'Lara's too good for them, so they've always got to try and assassinate her,' called Darren, Jay's friend. Everyone calls him Daz. He doesn't even go to our school, but he always follows Jay to our matches. Probably to ogle girls in shorts – pretty ones like Steph Gonzales, who still didn't have a speck of mud on her.

'Penalty!' the spectators began to chant. 'Penalty! Penalty! Penalty!'

I rolled around in the mud a bit, just to make sure the ref had definitely seen. Sure enough, she blew her whistle and pointed to the penalty spot.

'Go on, Lara!' someone shouted. 'Bang it in!'

Lottie tossed me the ball. I caught it and put it on the penalty spot. More people began to shout their encouragement, but I barely heard them. I was in the zone. That place where it's just me, the ball, and the net – my target.

The Sefton College goalkeeper already looked defeated. I was going to score *easily*.

'Love the hair, Lara,' sang a sweetly smug voice that cut right through my focus.

Sienna!

The referee blew and I kicked. The moment my foot struck the ball, I knew it was going wide.

There was a collective groan from the supporters as the ball blasted outside the right goal post.

The rage that filled me was so strong, I literally couldn't see straight for a good ten seconds!

How does Sienna always know exactly what to do to get under my skin? Actually, I know how. Back when we were friends, I told her all about my hair struggles. I can't believe she'd use that against me. So much for thinking she might want to be friends again after our little chat about our journaling apps!

My teammates slapped my back to comfort me. Tasha

muttered, 'Chin up.' But I *couldn't* lift my chin. I felt worse than the time I scored an own goal back in Year 7 when I tried to pass the ball to Steph for a goal kick and she couldn't catch it.

I sank to my knees, despair making my head swim.

It's just a game, I told myself. But football ceased to be just a game for me the moment I started playing competitively in Year 7. It's serious. Important. And right now, making it to Match 100 without losing has become my reason for EXISTING.

I should have scored that penalty!

Apart from the fact that balls move faster than goalkeepers so every penalty *ought* to go in, it was a perfect opportunity to show Sienna that I don't care about anything she says. That she can't hurt me. But I failed.

I began to raise my hand self-consciously towards my hair, but I stopped myself quickly. Touching my hair would just confirm to her that I was insecure about it.

When the whistle blew at the end of the match, I was glad to get off the pitch. We'd won, but I couldn't shake my disappointment over missing that penalty.

I'm on the school bus now. It takes us to matches and drops us off at home after. It's also MAROON and like a HUNDRED YEARS OLD! Honestly, it's a DEATH TRAP! All its rattling and clattering isn't helping my mood right now.

2.40 p.m.

I'm back home and I still can't stop thinking about that penalty I missed.

Why is Sienna so mean? She should know better. Here's why: back in Year 7, Sienna was really quiet. She told me she started journaling because she was bullied at her old school. I asked why she was bullied, and she said she didn't know. Then another time she told me her bullies used to say she was ugly. I couldn't believe it! Sienna is really pretty. She's like a Barbie doll come to life. I told her that whoever said that must have just been jealous, but I could tell she didn't believe me.

Another time, she told me her mum said she has low self-esteem and was trying to get her to read a book about confidence, but she wasn't interested in reading it.

She was on the football team back then. She tried out with me and we both got through, but she didn't last long.

I know some of her secrets:

- Her hair is blondey-brown. She gets highlights to be an ice-blonde.
- She only dated Adam Knox in Year 7 because he was popular and she wanted to be popular too.
- She's TERRIFIED of being bullied again.
- Even though she's pretty, she doesn't see it. I mean, I think she knows *other* people think she's pretty, but *she* doesn't feel pretty. Low self-esteem is a thing. SHEESH!

I don't know why we stopped being friends. I suppose we just drifted apart after she dropped out of the football team. Then she started hanging out with Paige and Molly. I figured it was because she was getting more into make-up and stuff, and I didn't have a clue about make-up and wasn't even allowed to wear it.

Anyway, I now have three amazing friends so I'm not complaining. But here's a secret of mine: I would actually like to be friends with Sienna again DESPITE EVERYTHING SHE'S DONE TO ME!!

I like my friends, and I would never ditch them. But I don't need haters or enemies. Kayleigh, Anaya and Becky would still be my BEST friends. And Sienna would be someone I hang out with occasionally.

3.43 p.m.

After having a nice hot shower to get the chill out of my bones, I asked Mum if I could have my hair relaxed. I spoke to Bisi after the match and she said her hair survived the rain because it's relaxed. It's the ONLY SOLUTION.

Hair relaxer is this creamy stuff you put on your hair and leave in for a few minutes, then when you wash it out, your hair's magically straight.

Mum was hardly listening to a word I was saying. She was more bothered about whether my muddy kit was in the washing machine yet and if I'd cleaned my football boots 😊

Once I told her that the answer to both her questions was yes, she started lecturing me about how damaging the chemicals in hair relaxer are, and how I shouldn't be putting my hair through all that at such a young age.

'It's my hair!!' I said in annoyance. 'And I'm nearly fifteen!'

I'm so sick of my parents always deciding everything for me. Why don't I have a say over what I do to the hair growing out of my OWN HEAD??

I ran out of the house, almost tripping over Nala, who chose that moment to dart from side to side in the hallway like a furry, grey ping-pong ball. I headed towards Mo's for some coconut and vanilla flavour popcorn. A girl needs some comfort food after missing a penalty.

The way Miss Simpson yelled at us after the match, you'd think we lost. She singled me out for a talking-to, which I guess was to be expected.

I knew Liam wouldn't be at Mo's. His date with Anaya was at three. Good thing too. I wasn't in the mood for seeing anyone.

I flounced out of the shop with my popcorn, only to see Jay, Caiden, Daz and a whole host of boys coming up the street. I hurried away.

'Lara!' Caiden called. 'Wait!'

I groaned. Hadn't I just put it out to the universe that I didn't want to see anyone? And why were Jay and Caiden constantly hanging out together, acting like BBFs (best bros forever)?

I adjusted the hat I was using to hide my shrunken hair as I turned to face Caiden. The other boys crossed the road and continued to wherever they were going without him.

'Girl, you've got *skills!*' Caiden said as he closed the distance between us. 'You were so good out there.'

'Thanks,' I mumbled.

'We're going to this arcade that just opened near the park,' he told me. 'Wanna come?'

'I'll have to pass. I'm meeting my friends in a bit.'

(I'm not meeting them until six, and when I say 'meeting' I mean on FaceTime, but that's beside the point. I didn't want to go to the arcade. I knew Sienna would probably be there, and I would probably try to kill her!)

'Well, walk with me,' Caiden said. 'Please.'

I shrugged. 'Okay.'

But I didn't know why he wanted me to walk with him after he'd been blanking me since Thursday and didn't seem to believe me when I said I didn't send him that nasty message.

He took out his phone and tapped the screen a few times then handed it to me. It was a school website. The article talked about the school's football team and highlighted last year's top goal-scorer: Caiden Hayes. There was a picture of him in a red and white kit, smiling for the camera.

'Cool,' I said, handing the phone back to him. 'So you were telling the truth.'

'Of course. I've been training with the boys' team, by the way. Our first match is a week on Wednesday.'

'You're going to lose.'

Caiden slitted his eyes. 'Thanks for the vote of confidence.'

'I'm not being mean, but you're playing Aldersfield High. They're a posh little private school where everyone is a maths genius. They have no business being so geeky and yet so good at football, but they are. They're like robots. Annoyingly precise robots that don't get tired and score every time they get into the eighteen-yard box. They're going to maul you like lions against poor wildebeest. Five-nil would be a good score. But it'll probably be worse.'

'Wildebeest can defeat lions sometimes,' Caiden deadpanned. 'Like that stampede in *The Lion King*.'

'The stampede that killed Mufasa?' I scowled. '*Why* would you remind me about that on a perfectly good day when the sun is shining and all seems right in the world?'

'The sun isn't shining,' Caiden replied. 'It's pretty grey and rainy today, actually.'

I know, I thought miserably. *My hair certainly knows.*

We fell into an awkward silence for a few moments, then Caiden started talking about football. Good topic. I can talk about football endlessly. He told me he supports Chelsea. I couldn't believe it, but then I suppose he is from London . . .

'Just don't tell anyone you support Chelsea,' I told him with a snooty sideways look. 'Pretend you support Liverpool and you'll be safe here.'

'Yeah, I've gathered that.' He shrugged. 'I do have a lot of respect for Liverpool. Decent team.'

'Decent? You mean *champions*.'

He rolled his eyes and it was cute.

Even cuter was the fact that it started raining again, and he took off his jacket and held it over both our heads as we walked!! It meant I had to step closer to him, which also meant I could smell that tangy signature scent of his. Today, it was mixed with the smell of damp clothes and was even more amazing.

I sighed.

'Still feeling bad about the penalty?' Caiden asked.

'I wasn't, but now that you've mentioned it I am.'

'Oh. Sorry. You played really well though. You should come train with the boys' team sometime. It would be fun.'

I used to play football with boys at break times in primary school, mostly because only boys were playing. Since getting to Prince's Park Academy I haven't played with boys.

'We've decided we're not just going to do the required training sessions at school,' Caiden said. 'We're going to train on our own too. You can come to some of those sessions if you think you're hard enough.'

I snorted. 'The question is, are you guys hard enough for *me?*'

'Probably not,' Caiden said, grinning, 'but you should still come.'

We were almost at the park now and I could see the arcade in the distance. I was willing to bet that Sienna was waiting inside.

'By the way,' Caiden said, 'I know that weird text wasn't from you. Jay got to the bottom of it. Like you said, it was Paige.' It had stopped raining so Caiden lowered his jacket, tying it around his waist. 'He also said the stuff she told me about you almost getting expelled last year wasn't true.'

'Yeah, it was all lies. I've never been suspended either.'

Caiden looked puzzled. 'Why doesn't she like you?'

I shrugged. 'I don't know. I think it's Sienna who's behind it all though. It's her who doesn't like me.'

'Sienna?' Caiden shook his head. 'She only ever says nice things about you.'

Really now? Ugh! Sienna is one clever minx!

'She's nice to everybody,' Caiden said.

I decided not to argue with him. It would just look like I was jealous of her or something.

We passed a bus stop with a poster for a new Marvel movie on it. 'I can't wait till that comes out,' I said to change the subject.

Caiden glanced at the poster, then at me. 'Me too. We should go see it together.'

I kind of froze.

Did Caiden just ask me out on a date?! To the CINEMA?? Just like I imagined in my daydream???

I started to feel all flustered. This was the whole reason for the glow up, and I've only had two sessions. It was working already!

But before my heart could do a happy dance, Caiden quickly added, 'With your friends too. And Jay, Ollie and Chris.'

My heart plummeted. No. He didn't just ask me on a date. *As if!*

Suddenly I felt incredibly silly. I couldn't even look at him any more, in case my thoughts were written all over my face.

Sienna, Paige and Molly arrived just as we reached the arcade, dropped off by Sienna's dad, who drives a silver Mercedes. The three of them looked like perfect little Barbies in their various shades of denim and pink.

'Or we can, like, go, uh, alone,' Caiden said, stumbling all over his words. 'To the cinema, I mean. It's up to you.'

I wasn't sure what to say. Was he just saying that because he could tell I was disappointed that he wanted to go in a big group?

I noticed he hadn't once looked at Sienna yet. He was watching me. Closely. I wasn't sure why. Maybe a tuft of puffy hair was poking out of my hat.

'Caiden!' Sienna sang, sashaying over. 'Oh, hi, Lara. Great match! What a shame about your penalty. Please don't be too hard on yourself about it.'

I wished I could do something to wipe the smug smile off her face 😠

'Are you sure you don't want to come in?' Caiden asked me.

I glanced through the door. I could see lots of flashing lights from the arcade machines. It looked like fun, plus I'd get to chat with Caiden even more.

'You do!' Caiden said. 'Come on.'

We all approached the entrance and Caiden held one half of the double doors open for Sienna. I went to walk through the other side, which was already open . . . and smacked hard into a pane of SOLID GLASS.

Okaaay. So it *wasn't* open. In my defence, the door was completely transparent. Practically INVISIBLE!

Sienna, Paige and Molly snickered.

'Are you okay?' Caiden asked me.

'Yes,' I said airily, like my nose wasn't throbbing from almost getting smashed into smithereens against the door.

I tried to pull the door open.

'Uh, Lara,' Sienna said sweetly. 'It says "Push".'

Paige and Molly howled with laughter.

I pushed it open with way more force than necessary, only to find that the door was pretty lightweight. I went flying forward, but thankfully didn't fall.

Cue more laughter at my expense!

I'm now in the arcade toilets, locked in a stall and trying not to die of embarrassment. Everyone is probably wondering where I disappeared to.

Self-knowledge Question
What do you want to learn more about?
1. How to stop being clumsy and AWKWARD. How to stop falling down stands at stadiums and walking into doors at arcades. Basically, how to navigate the world WITHOUT EMBARRASSING MYSELF EVERY TEN SECONDS! This glow up isn't helping. I've seen ZERO improvements so far!
2. Boys. But I don't think there's really any point. They're impossible to understand. It would confuse me. Yeah. It would be a COLOSSAL waste of my time!!

9

Party Pressure

Saturday 8 September, 4.45 p.m.

It's all well and good having fun conversations with Caiden about football, but it wasn't ME who he followed around the arcade for the brief time I was there. It was SIENNA. Caiden and Sienna might not be able to connect over a common love for football, but maybe that's working for her – the fact that she isn't sporty and instead is all girly and ANNOYING.

I left after about twenty minutes of watching them huddle together over one machine after another. I just couldn't take it any more! It's good to be back in the comfort of my own room with Nala. It's Saturday; I shouldn't have to deal with Sienna on my weekend. Monday to Friday is more than enough!

4.57 p.m.

So, this is kind of embarrassing, but I just posted a question on this website called *Q&A* where you can ask anything and people will post answers.

Mum and Dad used to block it using parental controls, but now that I'm fourteen, it's allowed. They did lecture me about being careful. Nothing new there; they're always lecturing me. I even got lectured before being allowed to post comments on YouTube and book reviews on Amazon.

'Stranger danger' applies to the internet too, they said. *There are weird people out there.*

Anyway, I just hope I get some good answers.

There's this boy I like, and we get along really well. But he also gets along well with this other girl at my school. She's snobby but pretty so ... yeah. Anyway, we both like football (me and this boy), but I'm starting to wonder if being good at football isn't helping matters. He came to watch me play and he said I've 'got skills', but do boys like girls who are good at football? Do they consider them girlfriend material? Or do they prefer girls who aren't sporty?

Thanks in advance for your advice!

I posted it anonymously, of course. The username I chose was GlowedUpGal.

Now I just have to wait and see if anyone bothers to reply.

5.13 p.m.
I have replies!!!
   Three, to be precise. Woohoo!!
   BRB!

5.21 p.m.
The first reply was from someone called I_BE_ALWAYS_
YELLING:

It depends. Are you obsessive about football? Do you
have a STRICT DIET and refuse to eat anything but
CLEAN CUISINE? Do you SACRIFICE FUN ON THE
ALTAR OF FITNESS AND WINNING GAMES?

Then he ranted IN CAPITALS about his ex-girlfriend,
who was a total knockout but was no fun to be around
because all she ever did was count calories, obsess about
meal prep and go to the gym. It was a really long post, but
it wasn't very helpful. Mum and Dad are right. There *are*
strange people out there.
   The second response was from someone called
AlienOnEarth:

Dear GlowedUpGal,
If he prefers a horrible snob just because she's pretty,
why are you still interested in him? Forget him! Over four

billion of this planet's population is male. It's safe to say that at least some of them will be into sporty girls. But how would I really know? I'm a Martian, after all.

WHY ARE PEOPLE SO WEIRD???

Anyway, the final response was from someone called ArianaGrandesPonytail:

Who cares, sweetie? Focus on school and start trading on the stock market. Boys will still be there after you've got your qualifications and built some wealth. All the best. *Swish*

I'm guessing the *swish* was supposed to be the sound of the ponytail as it walked away?

Not. Very. Helpful.

I read all these replies to Nala and even she purred in disapproval (I swear she can understand me).

See? I knew trying to understand boys would be a WASTE OF TIME!

5.38 p.m.

I just got another response. It was from someone called TooKool4Skool: Maybe he doesn't see you as a girl.

I replied: But I am a girl.

TooKool4Skool replied right away: Maybe he doesn't see you as a GIRL girl.

I still didn't really get it. But then they sent another response: Maybe he sees you as 'one of the guys'. Sports are a one-way ticket to the dreaded friend zone.

FRIEND ZONE??

Nooooooo!

I think TooKool4Skool might be right. Caiden is definitely nice and he's friendly enough, but maybe liking football and being good at it *is* turning me into 'one of the guys'. Maybe he sees me the way he sees Jay, or his other guy friends.

I don't want to be friend-zoned! 😩😩

I definitely don't want Caiden thinking I'm his GUY friend 😟😟

7.05 p.m.

This evening, on FaceTime, I told my friends that I might stop playing football.

'Why?' they chorused, all instantly looking concerned.

Everyone knows how much I love football.

It was hard to explain why, but I tried. I'd been thinking about it all afternoon and basically it's because of today at the arcade. I only stayed for a bit, but it was long enough to see how Sienna's girly helplessness made Caiden cater to her every whim. She is both Powerless Princess *and* Evil Queen. Boys get the princess mode, but with girls, she slips into her full Evil Queen persona. She pretended not to know how to play any of the arcade games – I say 'pretended', because they were so simple a four-year-old could figure them out – and she asked Caiden to help her so he learned how to play a few of them then began to teach her.

'Maybe that's what boys like,' I told my friends. 'Ditzy girls who need help with every little thing.'

'But you enjoy football,' Kayleigh said. 'How much of yourself are you going to change just for a boy? Remember, a glow up isn't about becoming someone else to impress other people. It's about becoming more of who you are. The best version of *you*.'

'Yeah, I probably won't quit,' I said with a sigh. 'But I think it's better to not be sporty.'

'Are you kidding?' Anaya asked.

'I wish I was sporty,' Becky said.

Anaya leaned close to her phone's camera, making her face look huge. 'If I was as good at *anything* as you are at football, NOBODY would be able to talk to me without an APPOINTMENT!'

Becky and Kayleigh chuckled, but I wasn't convinced. To be honest, I've never thought about these things before. I've always just done whatever makes me happy, and since playing football makes me happy I go ahead and play it.

But today, I've been rethinking my whole life.

I told my friends about my conversation with Caiden. The one we had as we walked to the arcade.

'Hmm,' Becky said when I finished.

'Hmm what?' I asked.

'Well, Caiden might've opened the door for Sienna and helped her with the arcade games, but he sheltered you from the rain with his jacket. Now, that's something.'

'He was sheltering himself too,' I pointed out.

'Yeah, well, when he opened the arcade door for Sienna, he was opening it for himself too,' Becky replied.

I sighed. I didn't know what to think. Why are boys so hard to understand??

I decided I didn't want to talk about it any more, so I asked Anaya about her date with Liam. That was all the permission she needed to gush about it for eight minutes straight (I timed her). In a nutshell, she beat him at mini golf, he asked if she wants to go ice-skating tomorrow, and she said yes. So she has another date tomorrow. Two dates in one weekend.

'He must really like you,' Kayleigh said.

'Then why didn't he ask me to be his girlfriend?' Anaya asked.

'You only just met him on Thursday!' Becky said. 'He probably thinks you need to get to know each other a bit more – hence why he asked you on another date.'

'Oh,' Anaya said, like she hadn't thought of that.

Of course, it wasn't because Liam saw her as not a *girl* girl or thought she was 'one of the guys'.

There's this question I always ponder: do perfect little pretty girls know that they're perfect little pretty girls? Like, does Anaya know that she's stunning?

I asked her and she shrugged. 'Sometimes I feel hideous,' she said. 'But sometimes I'm, like, who cares?'

'So what do you give yourself out of ten on looks?' I asked. I couldn't remember what score she gave herself when we did that self-assessment on Tuesday.

Anaya shrugged. 'Uh, maybe a six.'

Ha! So not a five. That means she knows she's above average.

'You're a nine,' I said morosely.

'I'd say she's a ten,' Becky said.

'Nobody is a ten,' I replied. 'You can't give anyone a ten.'

'Well, what's Caiden?' Kayleigh asked.

And that's when I had to give in. 'Okay. There are tens.'

'Anyway, can we get to the purpose of this call?' Anaya asked. 'Guess what!!'

Her eyes were shining like she had amazing news, but what she said made me BREAK OUT IN HIVES.

'I have a new goal for this year,' she sang. 'After today's match, I spoke to Miss Simpson. We're going to throw a party if you get to one hundred matches unbeaten.'

I just stared at her in shock for a few seconds, unable to believe my ears. Okay, I know a party should be exciting, but it isn't! It's actually VERY STRESSFUL. Because what if we slip up and lose a match?

'That's amazing!' Kayleigh cried. 'When's the party going to be?'

'Match 100 is on the 19th of September, which is a Wednesday,' Anaya said, 'so the party will be on the Friday. The 21st.'

Kayleigh squealed. 'I can't wait! We need to be all glowed up by then. I say we shift the end date of our glow up so that we finish before the party and show up as our new glowed-up selves!'

Her excitement filled me with even more anxiety. We still have three matches to go. Anything could happen. Plus, Match 100 is against WESTLAKE HIGH!!! They're GOOD.

Under normal circumstances, nobody would blame us for losing against them, but with a party at stake, we'll become public enemies if we lose. And as team captain, all the blame will be placed squarely on my shoulders!! I don't want to be responsible for ruining our chance of having a party!

'Uh, Lara doesn't look very happy,' Becky said.

Anaya paused what she was saying about getting a party committee together to help with the planning, and her bright smile dimmed a bit. 'What's wrong?' she asked.

'What if we lose a match?' I asked.

'You won't.'

'We don't know that!'

'We do know that. You guys are now ninety-seven matches unbeaten. If you can do ninety-seven, you can do a hundred. I had this idea ages ago, but I didn't suggest it to any teachers until now because you guys are so close. It's definitely going to happen.'

Her certainty about it only made me feel worse. Anxiety gripped me so hard, I felt sick. I had to hang up.

Thankfully, they didn't try to add me back to the call.

Anaya should NEVER have suggested this!

7.38 p.m.
   Anaya: The whole school believes in you. Maybe you should try believing in yourself too.

Anaya just texted me. I didn't reply. I've decided to put the party out of my mind.

Self-knowledge Questions
What is something you regret doing?
Posting that silly question on Q&A. None of the answers helped.
What is something you regret not doing?
I really regret not scoring in spite of Sienna's taunt about my hair. Scoring would have been the perfect response.

Sunday 9 September, 9.12 a.m.
You know what would be awesome?
   Arriving to the party as Caiden's date!!!

Just imagine: captain of the girls' football team. Just won Match 100. HOT DATE.

Hearing about the party made me feel *very* anxious, but you know what? It's also made me realise just how far the team has come. I mean, I know we're doing well, but having a party on the horizon as a reward for all our hard work kind of made it dawn on me all over again. There is nothing else in my life that I'm this good at. Football really is *so* important to me. There's no way I could give it up! Who am I kidding?

I now have two goals:

1. Score goals and remain unbeaten.
2. Be so glowed up and amazing that Caiden can't help asking me to be his date for the party.

So exciting. (But still nerve-racking!!!)

Me: I agree with Kayleigh that we should change the end date for our glow up. We need to finish before the party.

Kayleigh: Yes! We'll launch our new selves at the party.

Becky: But this gives us less than TWO WEEKS!

Kayleigh: We can do it. We just have to stay focused.

7.43 p.m.

Today, Nala and I binged the Spiderman movies. (Well, she mostly lay on my lap snoozing and growling in annoyance whenever an on-screen explosion disturbed her.)

It's been a day well spent. (I was mostly just trying to distract myself from thinking about the party.)

I went for a run with Kayleigh this morning, before I started my Spiderman binge, and she asked me if I'm still quitting football. I assured her that I'm not. I didn't *seriously* want to quit. It's just kind of depressing that playing football could get a girl friend-zoned. But that won't happen to me because I'm glowing up, aren't I? Glowing up has got to count for *something*.

Can you tell I'm trying to stay positive about this glow up? (If I'm really honest about it, though, I sometimes think I'm a lost cause. I'm always embarrassing myself ☹)

Mum and Dad would probably be happy if I quit football. When I got back from my run this morning, Mum asked if I'd done my homework. (Danny, the total nerd, did his weekend homework as soon as he got back from school on Friday.) I said I was going to do it right away, and she gave me this unimpressed look. So what if homework isn't the first thing I do in the evenings and on a weekend? It still gets done, doesn't it? 😐

Mum and Dad need to accept that I'm not Danny – and I never will be!

Anyway, I did a bit of my homework, then decided

to watch *Spiderman*. I'm doing the rest of it now, but I can't focus, because I can't stop thinking about how my issues are much bigger than getting friend-zoned for playing football.

I walked into a DOOR right in front of Caiden. I talked about URINE in our first proper conversation. Stopping football isn't going to change the fact that I'm a walking disaster! It won't stop my eyes from wobbling or make the rain stop doing diabolical things to my hair. I'll still be the same old klutz, pulling doors I'm supposed to push, falling over and flashing my knickers, and just generally being a danger to myself and others.

Okay, positive thoughts, Lara.

Deep breaths.

Think about rolling meadows and peaceful streams.

Exhaaaale.

Right . . . I'm calming down a bit.

I think.

8.57 p.m.

Self-knowledge Question
Free-write about something you desire.
The thing I desire is Caiden asking me to be his date for the party.

Here's how it might happen:

Wednesday 19 September, the day of Match 100, dawns bright and sunny, not a grey cloud or a hint of rain in the sky. My hair co-operates when I straighten it and ISN'T PUFFY. It obediently lets me slick it into a neat bun. I put on some light make-up then leave for school.

Everyone is nice and kind all day. Even Sienna, when I see her in chemistry after lunch, says, 'Good luck for tonight, Lara. I'll be rooting for you and the girls.'

And I graciously say, 'Thank you, Sienna. Much appreciated.'

After school, we head to Westlake High on the rickety school bus, but the bus is less rickety today. It knows that spluttering and clanging won't help our winning vibe.

When we arrive at Westlake, they already look defeated. They watch us walk onto the pitch, their eyes filled with dread. And they're right to be afraid. Because as soon as the match starts, I SCORE.

In fact, I score a hat-trick. Lottie also scores. And Bisi and Tasha. Even Steph, the goalkeeper, does a goal kick and the ball ends up in the net at the other end of the pitch.

The final score is 10–0 TO PRINCE'S PARK ACADEMY ⚽ ⚽ ⚽

I go BALLISTIC with joy.

The whole team goes WILD.

The spectators are MIND-BLOWN.

And Caiden . . . Caiden falls in LOVE!!!

He is UTTERLY OVERWHELMED by my hat-trick, my skill and my amazing leadership as team captain. He is GOBSMACKED by us going one hundred matches unbeaten. His eyes turn into hearts as he gazes at me (like this 😍) and he runs onto the pitch and asks me, right there and then, to be his girlfriend!!!

I say 'YES!' Then we melt into a kiss 🏉🏉🏉

🐺 Wait a minute! That would be my *first* kiss!

I don't know *anything* about kissing. The thought of it is actually pretty terrifying. But since this is just a self-knowledge question-turned-daydream, I can make the kiss whatever I want it to be, right? I'm writing about a glowed-up version of me, and glowed-up Lara doesn't mess up the kiss. She doesn't collapse from panic or do anything embarrassing like accidentally head-butt Caiden in her eagerness to kiss him. She just goes with the flow and fireworks explode in her heart. Caiden's too.

The next morning, we make our school debut as a couple. Then the day after that, which is the PARTY, we show up in matching outfits that were totally not planned but that demonstrate how in tune we are with each other, and we DANCE THE NIGHT AWAY!!!

9.32 p.m.

Dear Diary,

I shouldn't have written that last entry. I know you're a non-judgemental piece of software, made up of code that looks like gibberish, but still . . . I shouldn't have written it, because now I'm even more nervous about the upcoming matches. And I'm sweating with dread at the thought of trying to kiss Caiden and accidentally head-butting him when HE ISN'T EVEN MY BOYFRIEND YET!

Look at me saying 'yet' as if it's definitely going to happen. Honestly, I'm rolling my eyes at myself.

Right, that's it. I'm not thinking about this party or Caiden ANY MORE.

Monday 10 September, 7.57 a.m.

Another Monday 😊. Another week of school ☹

I just finished washing cat wee off my hands because Nala did a wee in one of Mum's shoes 🐾. I don't know why she keeps RANDOMLY WEEING IN RANDOM PLACES these days. My only explanation is that she's picking up on my stress. The last time she did a random wee on my bedroom carpet it was the morning after boob-burying with Kayleigh and Becky, and I was feeling pretty stressed then too.

Mum only found out that Nala had done a wee in her shoe when she put her foot in it and felt the warm wetness 😖

The way she yelled at me, anyone would think I'd *told* Nala to do it.

Then she reminded me of all the rules I agreed to before they let me have a cat:

1. I will be fully responsible for her.
2. I will empty her litter tray every day.
3. I will clean up after her.

Well, guess what? I just googled pet ownership and, by law, adults are responsible for their children's pets. I can't legally be held accountable for anything to do with Nala until I'm sixteen.

So Mum is responsible for Nala weeing in her shoe.

But did I say any of that? Nope. I just poured the wee into the toilet and cleaned Mum's shoe.

IT WAS SO GROSS.

This is the last thing I need just before school, and with two matches coming up this week!

11.15 a.m.

You know how I said I wasn't going to think about the party any more? Well, this morning I walked into school and there was a HUGE banner in the hallway saying *CELEBRATING OUR GIRLS' FOOTBALL TEAM*. It had the date of the party on it and wavy writing that said

You are all cordially invited to a party for our girls' football team. Then in small print at the bottom it said *providing the team remains unbeaten for 100 matches*.

CAN YOU FEEL MY ANXIETY, DEAR DIARY?

My heart is rattling around in my chest like a MARACA! And my lungs are kind of frozen. They won't let me breathe properly.

Throughout history and English lit this morning, I could think about nothing else but the party. During morning break, I felt sick with worry, but I still went to sit with my friends outside.

On my way, I saw Caiden with Jay and some other boys, and I instantly remembered the head-butt-kiss I wrote about. My face got REALLY hot and I felt like the fact that I'd journaled about kissing him might be written on my forehead.

He and Jay waved, but I was so embarrassed, I pretended not to see and just hurried away. I'm waaay too stressed out right now to talk to Caiden.

I found my friends sitting at the picnic tables, and they quickly stopped talking when I slid into the empty space beside Anaya.

'We weren't talking behind your back,' Anaya said quickly, tucking behind her ear a handful of curls that were blowing in the wind.

'Yeah,' Kayleigh confirmed. 'We were just talking about the party we might be having for the girls' football team. Planning has begun, and we can't say much about it in front of you.'

'I'll excuse you then,' I muttered, beginning to stand.

Anaya tugged me back into my seat. 'I know you're worried about it, but you guys are going to do it.'

Becky gave me a sympathetic look. I could tell she felt sorry for me – unlike Anaya and Kayleigh, who just want to party.

'There's something we're going to order for the party that I just *know* you'll LOVE,' Anaya said. 'I can't wait for you to see it.'

I didn't know what to say. I know Anaya is just excited, and she likes to make a fuss of people. She's sweet like that. But all the fuss is *STRESSING ME OUT!!!*

This party is a very bad idea. If we do make it to one hundred matches unbeaten, it won't be my – or the rest of the team's – doing. Other girls did most of the work. Sure, I've scored lots of goals over the years, but it's been a team effort, and many girls who were part of that have now left the school.

The team and I don't deserve to party without them.

12.53 p.m.

At lunchtime, I called a meeting with the girls' football team. I texted them all and asked them to meet me in the school gym. By then, the party was on all the hallway screens, periodically flashing up in between memos about saying no to cyberbullying and the healthy school lunches initiative.

'I'm sure you've all heard about the party,' I said, and they nodded. 'This is serious now,' I told them, like it wasn't already serious before. 'We're going to have to train more. Lunchtimes, after school.'

I expected some eye-rolling. Especially from Jamila, Kirsty and Heather, who are in Year 11 and always roll their eyes when I say stuff, but they didn't. They must be feeling the pressure too.

'Three more matches, girls,' Lottie piped up. 'We can do this!'

After our meeting, I hurried to the lunch room. By then, more than half of lunchtime was over and there was hardly any food left, but my friends were still at their table and Kayleigh was telling them about her goddess session.

'It's going to be on Saturday,' she said, 'but that doesn't mean we'll be doing nothing all week. We need to up our game with this glow up, especially with a party on the horizon.'

'I have two matches this week,' I reminded her. I know I agreed to finishing our glow up before the party, but now I'm wondering if it might all be too much for me.

'That's fine,' she replied. 'It won't affect your football. We'll do our glow-up stuff during lunchtimes rather than after school because of your training.'

I didn't bother telling her we might be training at lunchtimes too.

I feel a bit sad that I'm probably going to miss some glow-up stuff. Okay, I haven't seen much improvement since we started, but it's not like I have any other ideas for getting Caiden to like me. This glow up is my best chance.

Anyway, I just hope we manage not to lose any of the next three matches.

The next ten days are either going to make or break me. #FREAKING OUT!

Tuesday 11 September, 6.45 p.m.

Today has been soooo busy, I didn't even see my friends at all, and this is the first time I've come on my journaling app all day! I missed you so much, dear Diary, but I had training during lunchtime *and* after school. Then when I got home I had piles of homework. By the time I was done I was completely exhausted so Mum and Dad said I didn't have to do my chores (yay!!).

I'm going downstairs for dinner now. I'd better keep acting all tired and exhausted. The more sympathy, the better.

P.S. In case you were wondering, I only saw Caiden once today, by the vending machines. And he was with Sienna. While I'm busy with football, Sienna is moving in for the kill!!!

8.30 p.m.

Guess who came to our house for dinner. ALEX!

I honestly can't see why I EVER had a crush on him. He's as snooty and nerdy as Danny. He's also obsessed with *Call of Duty* and building robots, just like Danny. Plus, he's nowhere near as gorgeous as Caiden. He hardly even looked at me the whole time he was here. I think I'm actually invisible to him!

Danny said, right in front of him, 'You don't write in your journal much any more, Lara.'

I gave him a flat stare, knowing he was only bringing up my journal for two reasons:

1. As a taunt because of what he'd discovered about Alex when reading said journal.
2. To remind me of his power to TRASH MY LIFE.

'That's true,' Dad said, totally oblivious to the sneaky, underhand games Danny was playing.

'All she does these days is text constantly,' Mum said.

I almost snorted. Let them *think* that all I do is text.

Danny probably wishes I would go back to writing in my journal so that he'll have fresh information to use to continue blackmailing me. He, Mum and Dad know nothing about my journaling app – and it's going to stay that way. Seriously, I'm so glad I have this safe space to vent my frustrations in PRIVATE.

Anyway, Alex was at our house because Danny received a letter today containing the results of the robotics competition that the two of them entered over the summer holidays, and they wanted to open it together.

They won, of course. Danny ALWAYS wins things. He and Alex will be attending an awards ceremony next month to collect their trophy.

I don't know why Mum and Dad were so thrilled about it. It's not like they're getting a million pounds or anything 😐

8.55 p.m.

I'm absolutely fuming. Something just happened that is a perfect example of how much better Danny is treated than me in this house: HE'S GETTING A NEW PHONE!

If it was just because of winning that stupid competition, I might not mind, but it isn't. It's because he's 'becoming an all-round, well-adjusted, responsible young man', as Mum put it.

Basically, he's getting a new phone for his good grades, winning a competition AND cleaning the house really well (apparently!!).

It's not fair!!! He already has a bigger room and gets more pocket money, and now he's getting a new phone, while I'm stuck with this old iPhone that used to be Dad's. And all because of MY good cleaning.

Danny is clearly Mum's favourite. She went to watch him and Alex present their ridiculous robot at that competition last month, but does she ever come to watch me play football? NO.

Does she care that I've been the top goal-scorer in the Liverpool Schoolgirls' Football League for two seasons? NO.

Does she know we have three games left until one hundred matches unbeaten? NO!!

I told her all this, then walked out of the living room.

I just texted Anaya about it, and she pointed out that Mum always comes to watch pro women's football with me. Okay, so she doesn't mind watching pros, but does she bother to watch her own daughter?

NO!!!

Anaya also said I should have just reminded Mum and Dad that we're close to Match 100 instead of only telling her now because I'm annoyed. Being an only child and having the luxury of her parents' attention all to herself, she just doesn't get it. Why should I have reminded them? Why did they need reminding?

They don't care about my football. And since my grades are never as high as Danny's, they're never satisfied. I'm so sick of the pressure to be like Danny. I don't even understand how he gets such good grades and is so clever. I have to sweat for every high grade, but Danny spends obscene amounts of time playing *Call of Duty* and still manages to do well at school.

He says he wants to be a billionaire businessman like Sir Richard Branson, although he hasn't decided what business to start yet. He's mainly just thinking about the billions. And Mum loves it when he talks about how he's going to buy her and Dad a mansion.

Whatever!!!

9.22 p.m.

Nooooooo!!!!!

Mum just came to my room and said that she, Dad and Danny are coming to watch me play tomorrow 😩😩😩

That's the last thing I need!

I know I was all annoyed about them not being interested in my football, but of all times for them to decide to start coming to my matches, this is the worst! They haven't been to watch me since Year 7, but now that I'm stressed out and have so much at stake, they hit me with the added pressure of their presence. I need to focus on the match. It's Match 98, and them being there will throw me off.

I told Mum they can't come and she got all hurt, which made *me* look like the bad guy, when she and Dad have neglected my matches for two and a half years!!

While we were arguing about it, Dad came in and said, 'Why didn't you remind us that you're almost at one hundred matches unbeaten? This is *huge!*' Then he gave me a big hug, like I'm a little girl, and said, 'No pressure though. You'll still be my Lara even if you don't achieve it.'

Well, I know *that*. But I still want to achieve it – without them in the crowd making me feel nervous.

Anyway, in the end I gave in and said they could come, so long as they stand near the back of the crowd where I can't see them. Mum whooped, all excited.

So . . . my family is going to be there tomorrow.

And probably on Saturday for Match 99, and the following Wednesday for Match 100.

OMG, this is so stressful.

Well, I suppose if I can play in front of Caiden with an UNLEASHED AFRO, I can play in front of anyone!

Self-knowledge Question
You've just won a million pounds. How would you spend it?
Okay, so I've had a good think and I would do this:
- £100,000 for Mum and Dad (they can share it with Danny if they want. If not, too bad, Danny).
- £100,000 for Anaya, Becky and Kayleigh.
- £500,000 for charity (I haven't figured out which ones yet).
- £300,000 for me and Nala.

10

Bloodshed

Wednesday 12 September, 11.02 a.m.

Kayleigh clearly isn't impressed that I wasn't at the glow-up session she ran yesterday at lunchtime. In order to keep me included, she's resorted to texting. This morning, she posted in the group chat.

> **Kayleigh:** Confidence isn't 'they will like me'. Confidence is 'I'll be fine if they don't' – Christina Grimmie

Becky replied while I was walking to school. She was probably walking to school too, from all the typos:

> **Becky:** I dusgree. 'I'll be fine if they dpn't' is kind of pessimistic, like an insecure person alresdy thinking that ppl r gna not like them.

All morning my phone buzzed as they argued back and forth about it during lessons.

Just before the end of second period, Becky said:

Becky: Well, what do the others think? Anaya? Lara?

I considered it as I doodled in the margin of my French exercise book. I couldn't really tell which of them I thought was right until I applied it to Caiden.

Caiden Update

On Monday, he sat with Sienna again during maths. They're cosy little maths table buddies now.

Yesterday, I saw them eating together in the lunch room. Paige, Molly and Jay were there too, but Sienna was all over Caiden like a RASH, leaning against him, whispering in his ear, TWIRLING HER HAIR AROUND HER FINGER.

I don't know why I thought Caiden would ever like me. Anyway, I have independent woman energy and I'm not going to compete for a boy's attention. (Kayleigh would be so proud.)

So, confidence feels more like being fine whether or not Caiden likes me and asks me out.

Me: I agree with Kayleigh.

Mrs Laurent didn't notice me texting, even though she was at the next table helping Jay with translating the French poem she'd projected on the whiteboard. (It didn't rhyme in English.)

Kayleigh: Thank you, Lara!

Anaya: I think you're both right. Confidence is 'they will like me' and if you're proven wrong, confidence becomes 'Okay, they don't like me, but I like me, so I'll be fine.'

Becky: Thank you, Anaya!

Me: Actually, I agree with Anaya.

Kayleigh: Actually, I agree with Anaya too.

3.27 p.m.

'I think Caiden likes you.'

It was Anaya who said that.

After school.

In the middle of the hallway where ANYONE COULD HAVE HEARD HER!!!

I shushed her and she tugged me into the girls' toilets.

'Honestly, I think he does,' she said.

'And why would you think that?'

'I just spoke to him about you –'

'WHAT?!?' I practically yelled.

'I just spoke to Caiden about you,' Anaya repeated.

'Yeah, I understood the first time. When I said "what", I was just expressing my shock, horror and ANNOYANCE.'

'Don't worry,' Anaya said quickly. 'I didn't say anything about your crush on him.'

'What did you say?'

'Well,' Anaya said, 'I've been thinking about what you said about your conversation with him on the way to the arcade, so I wanted to see if I could get some answers and find out if he likes you.'

I covered my face with my hands.

'I asked how he's finding living in Liverpool, and if he likes school, and all that stuff. Then I looked at the hallway screen when it flashed up the party memo and casually said, "The girl's football team are amazing, aren't they? Lara's doing such a good job as captain." You should have seen the way his eyes lit up at the mention of you.'

I lowered my hands from my face. 'I don't believe you.'

Caiden hasn't talked to me all week. I haven't really seen much of him, except in maths, but still.

'Well, it's true,' Anaya said. 'He agreed with me, by the way. He thinks you're amazing at football. Then he said Paige told him she never snatched your phone and that she didn't text him using your phone. He doesn't know what to believe. I told him you would never do something like that.'

Ugh! I thought that was all sorted out now!

'Did he believe you?' I asked.

'I don't know, but he did say he wants to help with planning the party.' Anaya wiggled her brows like that's some secret code that means *I, Caiden Hayes, am irresistibly in love with Lara Bloom.*

'That doesn't mean anything,' I told her. 'The party is for the whole team, not just for me.'

'I know, but I think it *does* mean something.' She grinned wickedly.

I just walked out and hurried to join the rest of the team. I have a match to play.

9 p.m.

I'm absolutely exhausted, dear Diary. But I have to tell you all about today's match before I go to bed.

Hardly anyone ever shows up for midweek matches, but the place was packed. What's worse, Mum, Dad and Danny didn't stay at the back of the crowd, like I requested. They were right there at the very front, and Mum waved enthusiastically when I ran onto the pitch with the rest of the team.

'Your mum is waving at you,' Lottie told me.

She was busy trying to ignore her own mum, who was holding a banner with a photo of Lottie's face on it.

I gave Mum a small wave back then tuned her, Dad and Danny out.

My nerves were completely shot because we were playing Mossley Hill High, and their girls are big and stocky like RUGBY PLAYERS. And their captain, Angelica Locke, is notorious for getting into fights. She's a hefty, scowling BULLY who you wouldn't want to cross paths with in a dark alley! (At least, I wouldn't.)

She ran at me as soon as the match started, but I managed to dodge and run for goal. I was on the edge of the penalty area before three defenders barrelled over and tackled me. I didn't score on that attempt, but I did twenty minutes later (WOOP WOOP!).

Mum screamed and high-fived Dad. Dad whistled through his fingers. Danny, however, couldn't look more bored if he was watching the obligatory few seconds of a YouTube ad.

Just like in the last match, I got fouled in the second half. Seriously, this time. It seems people really want to stop us from getting to Match 100 unbeaten.

I didn't know how badly injured I was until after the match. In the heat of the moment, the adrenaline was running high and I felt okay so I told Miss Simpson I was fine to keep playing.

My leg was a bit sore though, and I couldn't run as fast as usual. On top of that, my football boots decided to choose that moment to start falling apart from all the rough tackles. I must not have been playing to my usual standard, because Miss Simpson ended up making me and

Lottie swap positions. BAD IDEA. Lottie plays midfield and feeds me the ball so I can score. Until now, I didn't realise how much work that is. It was down to me to chase the ball around and get it to Lottie, and it was soooo EXHAUSTING!

Then, like ten minutes later, I got WHACKED IN THE FACE!!! Angelica Locke just bashed her MEATY ELBOW right between my eyes. I think my spirit left my body for a few seconds and floated through outer space. When I came back to planet Earth, everyone was in UPROAR, chanting 'RED CARD! RED CARD! RED CARD!' and BLOOD WAS GUSHING FROM MY NOSE!

Mum, Dad, Kayleigh, Jay and Caiden were shouting the loudest.

Angelica got sent off, which was good riddance, but then Miss Simpson said I couldn't play any more. She meant it too. Tears welled up in my eyes and she realised how much it meant to me to be on that pitch, so she said she would have to call my parents. I told her they were right there, and she ran over to ask Mum. Luckily, Mum said I could still play if I wanted to.

The nosebleed stopped after a few minutes, but could I get anywhere near the ball? Noooooooooooooo!!!

ARGH!!

I felt like I still had goals left in me, but half the players from the other team surrounded me for the rest of the match, and I couldn't run, couldn't get the ball. I could hardly even MOVE.

Unfortunately, Mossley Hill High scored and I figured the match would be a draw since it was almost over.

Then, with like two minutes to go, Mossley Hill SCORED AGAIN.

I actually screamed. We were LOSING!

'We're not having this!' Miss Simpson yelled at us while the Mossley Hill girls celebrated. 'DO SOMETHING ABOUT IT!'

Some of my teammates ran over to me.

'What does Miss expect us to do about it?' Tasha growled. 'We only have two minutes left.' She doubled over, hands on knees, panting. 'It's over.'

I agreed with her, but Miss Simpson always tells me I'm 'the manager on the pitch' and that I can talk to the girls when she can't. So I made myself say, 'Two minutes is plenty of time.'

They all stared at me in outrage.

I felt a bit silly, to be honest, but I carried on. 'We just need to get the ball in their net, and we know how to do that. We've worked together to get balls into nets a million times before.'

Some of the girls nodded, as though realising that it really was that simple. Others didn't look convinced.

'As soon as the whistle blows,' I said, 'just get the ball to Lottie – or whoever is in position.'

And they did just that. As soon as the whistle blew, Bisi blasted the ball in an amazing cross-pitch strike that landed perfectly for Tasha to kick it to Lottie.

I ran as hard as I could to support her if needed. Three Mossley Hill girls trailed me.

Lottie ran towards the goal until she was one-on-one with the goalkeeper. Then she hesitated.

'SHOOT!' I screamed.

It was now or never.

But she didn't shoot. She turned and kicked the ball to ME. Even though I was still a good distance away, and SURROUNDED by Mossley Hill defenders.

The referee began to lift the whistle to her lips.

I ignored the throbbing pain in my right leg and dribbled the three defenders around me. I managed to break free.

A herd of Mossley Hill girls stampeded over as I ran towards the eighteen-yard box, and I knew I was going to get fouled again if I didn't act quickly. So even though I wasn't in a great position yet, I blasted the ball towards the goal.

One of the defenders kicked my feet out from under me and I fell, but she was two seconds too late.

The goalkeeper lunged for the ball. My heart was in my mouth as I watched it sweep past her and into the back of the net. Then the whistle blew for the end of the match.

For a moment, I just stood there in a daze, unable to believe that we'd managed to score in time.

The final score was 2–2.

Our schoolmates and parents flooded the pitch, yelling and screaming with joy. I felt tears stinging in my eyes. Not just because of this game, but because of the ninety-seven that had come before it.

We'd made it to NINETY-EIGHT games UNBEATEN!!

I got squashed among a zillion people who were congratulating us and I couldn't breathe, but I'd never been so happy in my life.

Jay gave me a piggyback ride around the pitch, which was hilarious. I screamed the whole way, sure he was going to fall over and kill us both. When we got back, Caiden was watching us with a funny look on his face. He must have thought we were being really immature. In fact, he kept watching as I chatted to all my friends and Jay and his friends, but he didn't come over. I was surprised to find him waiting to give me a high-five when I finally walked off the pitch with my teammates.

That's when I realised I was COVERED IN BLOOD 😲. It was *so* EMBARRASSING!!

Even worse, my leg started throbbing with EXCRUCIATING PAIN and I keeled over like a bag of spuds! Miss Simpson and a bunch of other people hurried over to pick me up. I guess the adrenaline had worn off, and the full impact of all the fouls had finally caught up with me.

Mum immediately rushed me to a walk-in centre, just

to make sure nothing was broken. Nothing is, but I'm still in so much pain, I'm limping.

Just when I thought things couldn't possibly get any worse for me (wild hair, wobbly eyes, graceful as a rhino on roller skates), I'm going to have to hold on to my friends as I walk around school tomorrow.

Self-knowledge Question
What is your proudest moment?
My proudest moment is still in the future. It's Wednesday 19th September, when me and the rest of the team are unbeaten in our hundredth match 😺 😺 😺

I think I might cry 🔈

Of course, Caiden asking me out and being my date for the party will be the cherry on top 🍒

He looked so cute at the match today: black hoodie, blue jeans . . . GORGEOUS FACE. And that high-five . . . it gave me tingles in my hand that shot straight to my heart.

A high-five is almost like holding hands, right? 🖐

Thursday 13 September, 11.04 a.m.
OMG! This morning, when I got to school, a whole bunch of boys led by Richard Skelley came running at me and picked me up.

I was so shocked, I squealed. And I NEVER squeal. That's for girls like Sienna, Paige and Molly.

They CARRIED ME THROUGH THE HALLWAYS all the way to my locker, and people cheered all the way. It was like CROWD-SURFING, and it was just as well, because my leg is still sore.

Best of all, Sienna was right there in the hallway looking as pretty as ever in her cherry-red lip gloss and heavy mascara. But I guess my goal yesterday, leading the team to ninety-eight games unbeaten, must be better than any amount of make-up. After all, no one ever carried someone around school just for looking pretty.

Can you tell I'm CACKLING?

My friends were waiting for me at my locker. At the sight of Richard, Becky's cheeks reddened, then she hurried away.

When the boys all put me down, Richard, whose eyeliner was especially heavy today (and even winged at the corners), turned me towards the screen at the end of the hallway. On it was a picture of me from yesterday's match, covered in blood. I looked like I'd just gone ten rounds with Anthony Joshua.

'Who put that on the reel?' I demanded.

'Me,' Richard said beaming. 'I'm now on the communications committee. Isn't it magnificent?'

'No! Take it down!'

Richard looked perplexed. 'What? Why? That picture is EPIC. We're calling yesterday's match the BLOODBATH.' He flung an arm around my shoulders.

'You survived the bloodshed and emerged victorious, Lara. You should be proud.'

I shook my head adamantly. 'It was a team effort. Put a picture of the whole team up, please.'

'I agree,' said Lottie, who happened to be passing. 'And now it's my turn to get carried through the hallways.'

(I spoke to her on the phone last night, and she said she'd passed to me because she was nervous. She didn't want to be the one responsible for us losing!)

Anyway, the boys immediately flocked over to her and picked her up. They all disappeared through the double doors at the end of the corridor, leaving just a handful of people left at the lockers.

Jay was one of them. 'Hey,' he said to me. 'How's your leg?'

'Not great,' I said honestly.

He gave me a once-over then cocked a brow. 'You forgot my birthday again.'

My brain went into overdrive as I tried to figure out what the date was. 'No, I didn't,' I said. 'It's today. I knew that.'

'Well, where's my pressie?'

Now he had me.

Jay always remembers my birthday and gives me a card and a gift voucher, but I think it's really his mum who reminds him. Unfortunately for me, my mum never remembers Jay's *or* his mum's birthday, so I get no reminders.

'Here's your pressie,' Kayleigh said, and gave him a loud wet kiss on the cheek.

I kissed his other cheek, and he actually looked embarrassed. It was HILARIOUS.

Anaya just rolled her eyes. 'Are you having a party?' she asked Jay.

He nodded. 'Bowling on Saturday. You're all invited, but only because my friends said I should bring some girls.'

'Well, it depends who else'll be there,' Kayleigh said.

'Yeah,' Anaya agreed. 'Y'know, we do have our street cred to think about before accepting random invitations. We can't have low-vibe people messing up our chi.'

'Chi?' Jay snorted. 'Well, it'll be me, Ollie, Chris, Daz –'

'So the usual suspects then,' Kayleigh cut in.

'I guess. Two of my cousins are coming as well.'

'What about Caiden?' Anaya asked, and I knew she'd asked so that I wouldn't have to.

'Yeah, he'll be there.'

'What other girls did you invite?' I asked, hoping he wouldn't say 'Sienna'.

Jay held his hands up in a defensive gesture. 'What's with the drilling?'

'That was the final question,' Kayleigh said. 'Who are the other girls?'

'It'll be only you guys,' Jay said, eyeing us warily. 'Becky too.'

I smiled inwardly. No Sienna 😬

12.53 p.m.

I've just finished a glow-up session with my friends. Kayleigh texted us all during third period to say she's leading a session at lunchtime about beauty tips. I was excited to learn some new beauty tips, especially with bowling coming up, but Kayleigh's tips were all boring things like 'drink more water' and 'get enough sleep'.

Well guess what, dear Diary: I'VE BEEN SLEEPING AND DRINKING WATER SINCE I WAS BORN AND IT DIDN'T AMOUNT TO A GLOW UP!

Other tips were:

- Smile more (is she for real?)
- Eat healthy food (I would eat more healthy food if healthy food wasn't so BLAND. Seriously, though, why is everything healthy disgusting?)
- Take time for yourself (to do what? Just sit and stare at the walls like there's nothing more interesting to do??)
- Move your body (I guess I'm covered on this one since I play football).

Basically, there were no REAL beauty tips.

4.02 p.m.

My friends walked me all the way home after school because of my sore leg. On the way, Anaya said, 'I had another chat with Caiden today.'

Ugh! She needs to STOP. If she keeps talking to him about me, he's going to figure out that I have a crush on him!!

It wasn't too bad this time though. She said he told her he's joining Mr Savage's Friday lunchtime maths club and he wanted to know who else is in it apart from Sienna.

'Sienna is doing extra maths?' Kayleigh asked. 'Since when?'

'Since Caiden decided he's doing extra maths,' Anaya replied. 'I asked him why he's joining maths club and he said his grades were terrible at his last school and his mum wants him to turn things around. Apparently, he used to hang out with lads who don't care about grades and stuff back in London. Moving to Liverpool is kind of like a fresh start for him. He said he promised his mum to stay out of trouble and try harder at school.'

'He's clever too,' Becky said. 'He's in my chemistry class and he's really good at it. Mr Adeola loves him.'

'His mum promised him driving lessons as soon as he turns sixteen if he gets his grades up,' Anaya said.

Becky frowned. 'I thought you have to be seventeen.'

'You have to be seventeen to be fully licensed,' Kayleigh informed her, 'but you can drive on private land before then. There are young driver centres that let you do that.'

'Wow, I wish my mum would negotiate with me like that,' I said. 'I just get orders.'

'Are you going to join extra maths?' Becky asked me.

'Uh, it's with Mr Savage. Do I look like a glutton for punishment? I wouldn't do extra maths with him if he was handing out free cash.'

My friends all started laughing about the 'peep' incident, then they got talking about other things, but all the way home, I thought about what Anaya said about Caiden and his quest to improve his grades. I wondered if that might be one of the reasons why he's nice to me but is kind of staying away from me.

He's trying to glow up his grades. Maybe he thinks I'll be a bad influence, or something. I told him on Saturday that I've never been suspended and that none of the stuff Paige said is true, but what if Paige is telling him more and MORE lies about me?

He probably doesn't know what to believe ☹️☹️!!

4.23 p.m.

There's no need to worry, because everything I'm thinking might not even be true. But what if it *is* true? What if Caiden thinks being friends with me would amount to 'getting in with the wrong crowd'?!?!

Anyway, Mum is home. She finished work early to take me SHOPPING. Woohoo!

As you know, my football boots fell apart yesterday so we're going to get some new ones before the shops close. We're leaving now.

6.14 p.m.

CAN I BE ADOPTED ALREADY????

I want to get on with Mum. I really do. But she's just so AGGRAVATING sometimes. Dad is usually okay, but he has his aggravating moments too. Why can't parents just not be annoying? Is that too much to ask?

Shopping was SO STRESSFUL! Instead of letting me choose the football boots I like, Mum kept trying to make me get this pink pair with glittery yellow stars on them. They were HIDEOUS. They looked like something a child would wear.

HELLO! I left primary school over THREE YEARS AGO!

I wasn't having it.

Mum wasn't impressed that I refused the 'pretty' football boots, but I told her there was no way I'd wear them. In the end, she got me the orange and silver ones I wanted, but kept saying how much nicer the pink ones were 😣

7.22 p.m.

Danny did my chores today because I'm injured. And he made sure to let Mum and Dad know. They were really impressed and started saying he's so responsible, kind, mature, a good big brother, blah blah blah. I almost cracked and told them EVERYTHING, but Danny waved his phone slightly and I knew that Alex would get an immediate text if I said anything. So I just walked out.

NALA IS THE ONLY LIVING THING IN THIS HOUSE THAT ISN'T ANNOYING!

Self-knowledge Question
What do you worry about the most?
Right now, it's three things:

1. Danny telling Alex about my crush on him. (Why did God create big brothers? They're horrible!)
2. My hair.
3. MATCH 100.

Friday 14 September, 11.11 a.m.
My leg is feeling much better today 🐝 😊 🐜. It's still a bit sore, but I should be able to play tomorrow. I told Miss Simpson this morning in PE, but she said no. She didn't even let me play hockey with everyone else during the lesson. I was only allowed to do a few gentle stretches, then I had to sit and watch everyone else having fun.

She said she wants me fully recovered for Match 100 next Wednesday, and she's not willing to take any chances. That means I'll be on the bench for tomorrow's match ☹

In happier news, she said that a local journalist might be at the match. The school has had some media interest because we've reached ninety-eight matches unbeaten, and Miss Simpson said that if they want to interview us, she's nominating me to be the main spokesperson since I'm the captain.

The whole team has been given consent forms for our parents to sign, just in case the journalist wants to take any pictures during the match.

Miss said not to get my hopes up because journalists sometime say they'll come, but then don't show up. But imagine if they do! I could be in the papers, just like Danny 🐺 🐺 🐺. His reign as the most promising Bloom child could be coming to an end.

MWAH HA HA HA HA!!!!

12.23 p.m.

I just had maths with Mr Savage (😳) and I couldn't stop thinking about the journalist who's coming tomorrow. Mr Savage yelled, 'WAKE UP, OMOLARA BLOOM,' like every five minutes, and each time everyone laughed – especially Sienna.

He kept picking on me to answer questions too, just because he could tell I was distracted. The lesson was about angles and he went, 'Being the captain of the girls' football team does not exonerate you from having to pull your weight in maths, young lady. You need maths as a footballer, as you have to score from various angles.'

Dear Diary, I have NEVER thought about calculating ANGLES while shooting for goal.

Anyway, the reason I was so distracted in maths – apart from the fact that Caiden and Sienna walked in linking arms – was because I realised that a journalist coming to tomorrow's match is the WORST thing that could happen since I won't be playing. The journalist won't see me in action. They'll be like, *why do I have to interview someone who was on the bench all match?* Let me *interview someone who scored goals!*

(I'll bet Lottie will score a million goals and the journalist will want to interview her instead 🖐)

Anyway, I'd better hurry. I'm running late for Kayleigh's lunchtime glow-up session.

But why does nothing EVER work out right for me!?!?

4.57 p.m.

Kayleigh said that a journalist coming to the match tomorrow is just what I need to be 'discovered'. She said the best football scouts in the country will hear about me and I might get SIGNED TO A PROFESSIONAL TEAM!! That was before I told her that Miss said I'm not playing.

I can't believe my bad luck. None of my friends knew what to say. Anaya eventually went, 'Don't worry. You can just say in the interview that you've been the league's top goal-scorer for two years. That should do the trick for any scouts who might read it.'

I suppose it might.

Scouts hardly ever come to watch our matches, which is why I wanted to go to that football camp over the summer. I heard they get lots of scouts from all over the country, including ones from the big teams in the Women's Super League.

Over the past two years, I've had interest from local clubs who play in the lower divisions of women's football. But each time, Mum and Dad said no. They say it won't be worth the distraction from my schoolwork unless I get interest from a really good club or a scout who's known to get their players into the top teams.

Personally, I'd rather play for any club, even an embarrassing, rubbish one. You just need to get your foot through the door, then bigger teams might notice you. Unfortunately, Mum and Dad don't agree.

Anyway, Kayleigh clapped her hands, like she was a teacher, and said, 'We're losing time and we have a glow-up session to get through.'

She clearly listened to our feedback yesterday because today she did better. She'd found us some make-up tutorials, one for each of us by girls who look a bit like us, and posted the links in our group chat. We sneaked into the music room and each watched our personal tutorial on our phones.

Mine was by a GORGEOUS woman called Patricia Bright. I can only hope to grow into such a goddess when I'm older. I don't have all the make-up she used, but I have the basics and I think I can recreate the look for bowling tomorrow.

My main concern is my hair 😩

After we'd finished watching our tutorials, I told my friends about Caiden and Sienna linking arms. 'What if they're boyfriend and girlfriend already?' I asked. 'Is there even any point in doing make-up tutorials and glowing up if they are?'

Kayleigh gave me an exasperated look, and I realised my mistake. 'Not that I'm glowing up for him,' I rushed to add.

'Were they linking each other, or was it just Sienna hanging on to his arm?' Anaya asked.

I shrugged. 'I don't know. Both those scenarios would look the same, right?'

Anaya wrinkled her nose. 'I'm getting pretty desperate vibes from Sienna. I don't think Caiden is into her, but she's latched on to him like a leech.'

I thought of how cosy they looked in maths. How cosy they *always* look walking through the hallways together, laughing at some private joke. Sienna seems to constantly be whispering in his ear too.

To be honest, I don't know what to think about it all.

I need to step up my game if I'm serious about Caiden asking me out before the party. My make-up tomorrow will have to be flawless!

Kayleigh had zero interest in discussing Caiden. She changed the subject by asking me how I'm getting on with planning my supermodel session.

I actually haven't planned anything yet, but there was no way I was telling Kayleigh that. 'It's going well,' I said vaguely.

'What have you planned so far?' she asked.

'Wait and see.'

Kayleigh's eyes narrowed with suspicion. 'You haven't planned anything, have you?'

'I have!'

Kayleigh pursed her lips. 'Football is no excuse to slack on the glow up, Lara.'

I didn't have the energy to defend myself. I feel like I'm being pulled in a million different directions. How am I supposed to be a good student, do chores at home, lead my football team to one hundred games unbeaten – and also have supermodel, queen, independent woman and goddess energy?

7.49 p.m.

I just asked Mum if I can relax my hair, and I gave her all the reasons why she should let me:

- The embarrassment of playing football in the rain and my hair going BERSERK (possibly in front of a journalist with a camera 📷)!

- The time I'll save – honestly, it will make my life much easier. I'll be able to get ready quicker in the mornings. Plus, spending less time on hair will free me up to do more chores. (I threw in the chores part because I thought that would definitely work.)
- I even said, *I'm now in Year 10 and need to focus on schoolwork, not hair.*

But she said no.

When I asked why, she went on and on about how damaging the chemicals are. How natural hair is best. How I should even stop straightening my hair so I don't get heat damage. When she finished, I told her about all the YouTubers with healthy relaxed hair and how I'll follow their advice.

She still said no.

It was so AGGRAVATING. She's deliberately trying to RUIN MY LIFE. I think Dad felt sorry for me because he came to check on me in my room a few minutes later. He even knocked first. He tried to get me talking about football, but I wasn't in the mood. I was glad when he left so I could mope and write about it in my diary.

Naomi Campbell, I NEED you. It's urgent now.

Please come and rescue me from my life.

Anyway, I guess I'd better straighten my hair now so that it doesn't take me too long in the morning.

On a happier note, tomorrow might be the day I've been waiting for. I'll be hanging out with Caiden with no Sienna in sight. It could be our chance to connect 😊😊😊😊😊!

And who knows, maybe he *will* ask me out before the school party!!!

8.32 p.m.
The last time I went bowling I was ten, and I DROPPED A BOWLING BALL ON MY FOOT. I almost DIED from the AGONY!!!

I've never been bowling again since.

Note to self:
- Be careful tomorrow.
- DO NOT MAKE A FOOL OF YOURSELF!

11

Girl in the Gutter

Saturday 15 September, 9.30 a.m.

Dear weather gods,

    Please don't let it rain today.

    Goddess Naomi Campbell,

    Lend me beauty and grace as I bowl.

    Queen Zendaya,

    Make me cool and calm like you.

    Amen.

    Let's GO!!!

9.53 a.m.

There's so much happening today:

- Bowling (Jay's arranged it for noon so that we finish in time for Match 99, which is at 3 p.m.)

- Match 99 (a journalist might be there, but I won't be playing ⚽)
- Kayleigh's goddess session (I'm not sure whether to be worried. I know FOR A FACT that she's going to try and get us to do something weird or silly).

11.26 a.m.

Mum just saw me putting on make-up for bowling and said, 'You're already beautiful, Lara. You don't need all that.'

I just ignored her. She likes to be 'au naturel', but that doesn't mean I have to be.

Then she said, 'Where did you even get ALL that make-up?'

Anyone would think I had a whole make-up counter or something. I have foundation, eyeliner, mascara and clear lip gloss. But it was a great opportunity to get Danny into trouble, so I said, 'Danny gave me the money to buy it. He supports me wearing make-up.'

Mum immediately stalked off to Danny's room to demand an explanation.

What I'm wearing:

- My favourite blue jeans
- A cute red tank top that's a little bit cropped
- Black flats

Hair: nice and straightened. I sprayed some of Mum's hair oil on it and it looks all shiny. It should hold up all day and still look nice after the match if the journalist wants to take a picture.

I've hugged Nala for good luck. Now it's time to go!

12.02 p.m.

I just walked into the bowling alley and the first person I saw was SIENNA! The SNEAKY THING!!

I had to walk away and pretend to be checking out a huge claw machine full of pink and blue teddy bears, just so I could quickly journal about it.

I do not for one minute believe that this is just a coincidence. She's with Paige and Molly (who else?). They're acting super-surprised to see us, but I can tell it's all LIES LIES LIES!

They must have found out, somehow, and decided to gate-crash the party.

Sienna must be pretty desperate for Caiden.

Speaking of Caiden, he just walked in. And he's looking very 'hot vampire' today in all black 😍. He seems to like wearing black.

My heart feels like it's doing jumping jacks!

Anyway, I'd better go. It's time to get our bowling shoes.

2.17 p.m.

Bowling was a DISASTER!!

Sienna, Molly and Paige joined us and said we should do girls against boys since there were equal numbers. That was a bit annoying. I would have preferred mixed teams 😬

Caiden was up first, and his ball knocked all the pins over. It was very impressive, but there was no need for Sienna to whoop the way she did, like some kind of unpaid cheerleader.

Then, of course, Sienna was first for the girls. She just barged to the front and started acting like we'd elected her our team captain or something. She got a strike too, and she had Paige and Molly filming her so she could post it on TikTok.

Anyway, I ended up going third for the girls. I grabbed a bright, multicoloured ball and rolled it with all the strength I could muster. But halfway down the lane, it skidded sideways and fell into the gutter.

The boys all cheered at my failure, while the girls looked unimpressed.

On my next turn, THE SAME THING HAPPENED.

AND THE THIRD TIME TOO!!! I even chose the biggest, heaviest ball, thinking it would be less likely to roll off in a random direction, but it still fell into the gutter.

That's when I started to get paranoid. I started wondering

if Sienna had done something to my balls, but there was no way for her to know which ball I would choose. Short of having MAGICAL POWERS, it wasn't her sabotaging me. I had to face the facts: I suck at bowling!

My excuse is that the music was too loud. It had this fast, thumping beat that was so distracting. I COULDN'T CONCENTRATE!

Plus, I haven't been bowling since I was ten!

Even more embarrassing than my ABYSMAL performance was the fact that Caiden disappeared during the fourth round. Then, just as I was gathering up the tatters of my confidence on my turn, he appeared beside me holding a blue slushy.

'This is for you,' he said, offering it to me. 'To help you calm down.'

Everyone laughed and my insides felt like they were being passed through a meat grinder. I accepted the slushy and took a long sip, savouring the icy sweetness.

It didn't help. I STILL couldn't get the ball to stay on the lane!

Everyone else was managing to hit the pins, and lots of people had got strikes. Why couldn't *I* do it?

Honestly, I think I'm cursed. Always falling over. Always embarrassing myself. Can't bowl 😫

Sienna was filming my failure and chortling loudly at how rubbish I was. Anaya and Becky told me to ignore her.

On my fifth attempt, Caiden accompanied me to the

lane. I HAVE NEVER BEEN SO MORTIFIED IN MY LIFE!! He tried to help me. Told me how to stand, told me to try doing a 'throwing roll' rather than a normal roll, told me to focus on the pins at the end of the aisle.

All the boys started yelling at him, asking why he was helping me, and calling him a traitor.

He didn't listen. He just patted my back. 'Go on,' he said. 'You've got this.'

I tried. Honestly, I REALLY tried. I followed all his instructions, but the ball still ended up in the gutter!

'Whoa!' Caiden exclaimed. 'Well, I suppose that was a *bit* of an improvement.'

Behind us, everyone was laughing, Sienna loudest of all.

I could only stand there, cringing. I looked at Caiden. His lips were twitching, like he was trying hard not to laugh.

'You must have zero hand-eye co-ordination,' he said.

I had to agree.

My cheeks were burning as I walked back to join the rest of the girls.

On Caiden's next turn, he got another strike. It'd been all strikes for him so far. He did a little jig as he returned to where the boys were standing.

'Show-off,' I muttered.

He turned. 'What was that?'

I quickly forced an innocent smile. 'Huh?'

He sauntered over, hands in his pockets, a look of mischief

in his eyes. 'You said something. Sounded like "show-off".'

'I would NEVER say such a thing,' I denied.

'I heard you.'

'Caiden, can you stop flirting with the enemy and get back over here?' Daz yelled.

Caiden bumped me with his shoulder then leaned close. WAY TOO CLOSE. 'Don't worry. I have a plan to help you on your next turn –'

Before he could say anything else, Jay came and dragged him away.

But my brain was still stuck on that one word that Daz had said: FLIRTING.

Was Caiden flirting with me? I wasn't sure.

On my next turn, he dragged over this frame and positioned it at the start of the aisle.

Everyone burst into laughter. Again.

'What's that?' I asked.

'A ramp,' he said. 'To help you roll the ball straight.'

I looked around the room at all the people bowling. Only two other people in the whole place were using ramps, and they were both LITTLE KIDS!

'Why are you helping her?' one of Jay's cousins said in exasperation. 'Do you want them to win?'

Caiden ignored him. 'Think of it this way,' he said to me. 'Bowling is just balls, just like football is balls.'

'This is *very* different to football,' I replied.

'True,' he acknowledged.

'You do have a point though. Maybe I should try kicking it. I'm good at kicking.'

Caiden grinned and it was REALLY cute. 'Uh, I don't think that's allowed.' He nodded at the ramp. 'Just put more power behind the roll. And focus on the pins.'

Even though it was highly embarrassing, I used the ramp. I selected a big red bowling ball, the type Caiden always selected. I figured that since they worked so well for him, one might work for me too. Then I looked at the pins at the end of the lane. I really needed to at least hit one of them. Just one would be enough.

I set the ball on the top of the ramp then pushed it off as hard as I could.

Anaya, Becky and Kayleigh started clapping and cheering, as if the ball could hear them and might decide to stay on the lane. It shot towards the pins. I held my breath. It looked like it was going to make it.

'Come on, come on!' Anaya yelled.

The ball flew on until it was almost at the end of the lane – almost at the pins – when it suddenly careened sideways and fell into the gutter. AGAIN!

There was a collective groan from my friends. I covered my face with my hands.

'At least it went a good distance before rolling off this time,' Caiden said.

'Yeah, you're getting closer,' Anaya called.

But I was done. I'd had enough of making a fool of

myself. I asked Anaya to take the rest of my turns then went to check out the burger place at the other end of the hall.

By then it had already been almost two hours. I was soooo ready to leave.

Twenty minutes later, everyone joined me in the restaurant, the boys gloating over their win. Sienna looked daggers at me. 'We would have won if we didn't have Lara on our team messing things up.'

And somehow, she managed to sound all sugary sweet like she wasn't being totally mean.

Everyone ordered food, then we piled into two booths. Unfortunately, I ended up with Sienna, Caiden and all the rest of the boys.

I couldn't believe it when Sienna complained that there wasn't enough room, then sat on Caiden's knee. Jay's two cousins got up and went to sit with the girls, so they made room, but Sienna remained perched right where she was. She even took a picture of her food, then a selfie of her and Caiden, and posted them on Instagram.

Jay plonked himself down beside me then gave me a little side hug. 'You can't be good at everything, you know?'

I didn't have the energy to reply.

'Why aren't you eating?' he asked.

'I don't feel like it.'

'Nervous about the match?'

Jay knows me too well.

I nodded, then glanced at my watch. I had to leave soon.

Jay slid his plate of food between us. 'Have some fries. And lighten up, please.'

I grabbed a handful of his sweet potato fries and tossed them in my mouth.

'Have you practised for your interview?' he asked.

'I was supposed to practise?'

'Yeah. You should have answers prepared. Stuff that makes you sound all profound.'

'But I don't know what they're going to ask.'

'You're supposed to try to guess. For example, they'll probably ask you how you got into football, what you like about it, what your goal is – as in do you want to go pro or is it just a fun hobby. Things like that.'

That's when I noticed Caiden watching us.

As Jay and I chatted, Caiden watched us LIKE A HAWK. He didn't look like he was listening to a word Sienna was saying, even though she was literally all up in his face talking at a million words a minute.

'You could get scouted after being in the papers,' he called when Sienna stepped away for a moment to go and get some sauce.

'Everyone keeps saying that,' I replied.

'Remember us when you're famous, eh?' He winked.

Heat scorched through my veins at that wink.

Just then, Sienna came back. Her lips were super-glossy and her skin looked all dewy and extra-smooth. I felt my eyes narrowing. Getting sauce had clearly been a cover for 'going to touch up my make-up'.

As she settled on Caiden's knee and forced his attention back to her, I wished I was at the next table, where Anaya and Becky were giggling over something on Becky's phone and Kayleigh was shamelessly flirting with one of Jay's cousins.

When we all left half an hour later, I was glad it was over. Outside, there was a fountain. The type where water sprays from grids in the ground. Children were running through it, laughing and squealing as they dodged the jets.

I was so preoccupied with Match 99, I didn't even realise that Caiden had sneaked up on me.

A sudden shove from him startled me. I let out a piercing scream as I went flying into the fountain. The water jets drenched me completely before I managed to catch myself and leap out. The water was FREEZING COLD! It soaked right through my cute red top and the top part of my jeans.

I glared at Caiden, water running down my face and into my eyes.

EVERYONE laughed except my friends. Caiden wasn't laughing either. He looked horrified. 'Lara . . .' he sputtered, 'that was just a little nudge. I didn't expect you to go flying like that!'

I barely heard him. I'd just realised I couldn't feel my hair lying in obedient sheets around my shoulders. I lifted my hands to my head, hoping to feel my silky, smooth, straightened hair. Instead, I felt the THICK PUFFINESS of my AFRO!!

'Lara, your hair!' Sienna cried, her cheeks red from how hard she was laughing. 'And your jeans. You look like you've wet yourself!'

I wanted to vanish into thin air.

Kayleigh shoved Caiden out of my way. 'Are you okay, Lara?'

I couldn't speak, but NO, I was NOT okay.

'I can't believe you did that!' Anaya growled at Caiden.

'I didn't mean to,' he protested. 'It was honestly just a nudge.'

'It's fine,' Sienna said. 'You're just stronger than you think, Caiden. You didn't mean it.'

Caiden stepped back in front of me. 'Lara, I'm sorry.'

'Don't apologise,' I replied. 'I'm plotting my revenge.'

'Hey, you can't take revenge on someone who's sorry,' Caiden said. Then he shucked off his top and held it out to me. 'Put this on.'

I hesitated for a moment, eyeing his top.

Anaya snatched it from him and handed it to me. Then she grabbed my arm and hurried me back into the bowling alley. We fled to the toilets, but it was too late. The water had already transformed my hair into a FRIZZ BOMB, and without any straighteners *nothing* was going to change that.

I also had PANDA EYES from my mascara getting all smudged and runny.

Images flashed through my mind of journalists taking pictures and me on the front page of the *Liverpool Echo* with my hair standing on end, like I'd been electrocuted.

Anaya helped me stuff it into a bun – a VERY PUFFY bun – then I removed my soaking wet top and pulled on Caiden's black sweatshirt. It completely swallowed me up. The sleeves were super-long too. I had to roll them up.

Kayleigh joined us as I was staring miserably at my reflection in the mirror.

'You can still have your picture taken,' she told me sternly. I don't know how she knew I was freaking out about that. 'Remember, this is how you usually wear your hair anyway. It looks fine.'

'Stop lying!' I said hotly. 'It *doesn't* look fine!'

Okay, the curls hadn't tightened as much as they had last week during the match in the rain. But this was still a disaster. I held my head in my hands. "This isn't how I wanted my hair to be for the pictures."

'Hey, calm down,' Kayleigh said, pulling me into a hug. 'Listen, maybe the universe wants it this way. Lots of girls with hair just like yours will see you rocking it proudly in the *Echo* and might start walking a little bit taller.'

'Plus, it really does look fine,' Anaya said.

'The curls suit you so much better than straight hair,' Kayleigh agreed.

I didn't believe her. My hair is a cocktail of different types of curls and frizz that make me look like walking chaos!

Anaya slipped some hairpins out of her bag and tried to slick down my bun with them. It looked a bit better, but I was still NOT HAPPY.

When we got back outside, nobody looked at my hair. It was like they were purposely ignoring it. Becky must have said something.

Poor Caiden was standing there in his vest, a sheepish look in his eyes.

'You're going to be cold,' I said.

He shrugged. 'I'll stop at home before the match.'

I didn't have time to stop at home and get changed or sort out my hair, but maybe my own top would have dried a bit by the end of the match. 'I'll give you your top back at the match,' I told Caiden.

He just nodded. Then his gaze slid up to my hair and he grinned. 'For what it's worth, your hair is –'

'Um, no,' Kayleigh cut in. 'You don't get to mess up someone's hair then have an opinion about it. Come on, Lara. Let's go.'

We're on a bus right now, on our way to the match.

Note to self:
- NEVER GO BOWLING AGAIN!

2.45 p.m.

My hair is what?

What was Caiden going to say???

2.58 p.m.

OMG! OMG! OMG!

I'm at the match now. It's going to start in TWO MINUTES. There are THREE journalists here. All with cameras! OMG!!!

3.50 p.m.

It's really nerve-racking having to watch from the sidelines, unable to do anything to help.

The other team has already scored. My teammates have been trying, especially Lottie and Bisi, but they haven't been able to score yet and it's half-time.

I begged Miss Simpson to let me play, but she said I have to rest my leg so that I can play in Match 100 on Wednesday. But we won't make it to Match 100 if we don't win today!

Imagine if they lose, after all our hard work to get this far. And in front of three journalists too!

This is all Angelica Locke's fault for fouling me on Wednesday.

I'm ABSOLUTELY FUMING!

4.50 p.m.

ARRRRRGHHH.

The last forty-five minutes have been the WORST. I could barely contain myself. I was so worried that we were going to lose, but we didn't.

Tasha scored in the eighty-seventh minute. Just three minutes until the end of the match.

Final score: 1–1.

PHEW!! We're still unbeaten!

5.11 p.m.

I'm still at the match. Everyone is celebrating like we've won the World Cup or something!

I was just looking for Caiden so I could give him back his top. (I changed back into mine in the locker room after the match.)

Caiden isn't here.

I asked Jay where he is, and he said he didn't come to the match. Instead, he went to the cinema with Sienna to watch the new Marvel movie. The movie *I* was supposed to watch with him.

Okay, he did say we should go with all our friends too, BUT IT STILL SUCKS!

5.24 p.m.

I had to leave the match and find a secluded place to journal. I'm in this dilapidated playground around the block from Stanley Park playing fields, where the match was held. And I'm freezing in my damp top.

Miss Simpson gave me a spare football kit, so I suppose I should change into that. She wants me to wear it for the interview, which is in an hour at school, as the journalists want to take pictures of us by our school sign. But I don't think I can be bothered going.

Life is so unfair.

Girls like Sienna just flutter around, adored by all, never a hair out of place, being mean but never getting called out on it, while girls like me get knocked into fountains, are injured when journalists come to watch their team and NO MATTER HOW HARD THEY TRY, no matter how hard they roll their bowling balls, they fall in the gutter and are ridiculed.

I'm the girl in the gutter.

5.36 p.m.

I just checked Sienna's TikTok.

It looks like she and Caiden went to the cinema right after bowling. Throughout the match she was posting snippets of them at the cinema: buying popcorn, her Coke exploding when she tried to open it, she and

Caiden laughing while they try to clean up the mess. It looks like a fun date.

5.47 p.m.

I suppose after a boy has seen you bleed all over your football shirt, no amount of glowing up can help you.

6.02 p.m.

Sienna just posted again. She and Caiden are now at some kind of festival in Sefton Park, and she's eating a ginormous pink candy floss.

I guess I finally have the answer to the question I posted on *Q&A: Do boys like girls who are good at football?*

The answer is no. Even if Caiden wanted to ask me to be his date for the party, or be his girlfriend, he hardly gets an opportunity since I'm always training or playing matches. I've hardly seen him all week. Football is getting me completely friend-zoned!

But I just had an idea. If Sienna can crash bowling, I can crash the festival and 'accidentally' run into her and Caiden.

Sefton Park is just a couple of streets away from Prince's Park. I can get there in twenty minutes if I leave immediately. It'll mean skipping the photo shoot, but they'll probably be more interested in Lottie since she actually played today, and Tasha because of her goal. I don't want to have my photo taken with my hair back in a puffy bun anyway. I wanted it in a sleek ponytail.

I've texted Lottie to let her know I'm not coming and she can do the interview.

I'm off to Sefton Park.

6.26 p.m.

I'm at Sefton Park now. There's an art festival on, and the place is packed. Finding Sienna and Caiden would be impossible – if Sienna hadn't just posted on TikTok again. I would say something about how sad it is that she's so obsessed with posting every second of her life, but since it's helping my quest she should TikTok away!

In the video she just posted, there's a sign in the background that says 'Goop Troop'.

I just need to find that sign.

6.48 p.m.

So, I found the sign.

But you'll nevewr beliebve what happenefd.

Sorry, I can'\t type.

I'm shaking.

7.04 p.m.

Okay, I've found somewhere to hide, and I've stopped shaking enough to type.

Arrrggh! Dear Diary, next time I have such a stupid idea, please come to life and tell me to stop. I never should have come to Sefton Park and tried to crash Caiden and Sienna's hangout, date or whatever it is – especially not when I actually had somewhere else to be.

I imagined this whole scenario going so differently. In my head, I show up and Caiden is delighted to see me. We dance to the bluesy festival music playing and he asks me to be his date for the Match 100 party.

But in reality it was very different.

Now we have a new contender for 'Most Embarrassing Moment of My Life!' – even more embarrassing than my fall at Anfield Stadium.

It took me about ten minutes to find the 'Goop Troop' sign. I finally spotted it poking up from the other side of a hill. I climbed up and there were Caiden and Sienna, among a crowd of people that had gathered on the slope.

Sienna spotted me first. Her eyes narrowed to tiny slits and her lips pressed into a thin little line. I was feeling all smug, thinking, 'What's wrong? You don't like a taste of your own medicine?'

Then Caiden noticed me. But instead of his face lighting up, he frowned.

I forced a shocked look. 'Caiden? Sienna?' I said. 'I didn't know *you* would be here!'

'What are you doing here?' Caiden called, still looking at me like I'd sprouted a nostril on my forehead. He didn't ask *Sienna* that when she crashed bowling. Instead, he welcomed her with open arms. (Literally. They hugged.)

Luckily, Sienna jumped in before I could reply. 'Come over here and watch this performance art with us,' she called, beaming. 'It's really good.'

I should have suspected something. Since when does Sienna ever invite me to do anything with her?

That's when I realised how slippery the ground was. The so-called 'art' was literally four men at the bottom of the hill covered in this greeny-brown gooey slime, standing stock still, up to their waists in it.

I slipped a little, but managed to catch myself. Then I tried to carefully pick my way back to a safe patch of ground, but at that exact moment a dog bolted away from its owner and started scampering around people's legs. I tried to get out of the way and slipped, landing flat on the ground.

It gets worse.

I could hear Sienna laughing, and I tried to stand up too quickly. My legs shot out from under me and I went sliding down the slope. I screamed and tried frantically to stop myself, but it was no use. I must have looked completely ridiculous as I thrashed around on the ground.

I didn't stop sliding until I landed in the goo and slammed into one of the men being a slime statue. He didn't even bother to help me. I began to sink in the goop, which was making all these gross squelching sounds, like some kind of beast feasting on me, but the man remained completely still, as if pretending to be a slime statue is more important than saving a girl from drowning in goop.

It was Caiden who rushed to the edge of the goo and reached out a hand to me. I grabbed it so hard that he fell in too! The shock on his face would have been hilarious at any other time, but at that moment I was just completely and utterly mortified. I might have lowered myself further into the goop and let it drown me if Caiden hadn't snapped out of his shock, clamped his arm around me and hauled us both out.

Nobody was watching the 'performance artists' any more. They were all staring at me and Caiden who were now COVERED in the thick goop.

'Are you okay, Caiden?' Sienna cried, completely ignoring me.

I don't know if Caiden heard her. He was busy frowning at me.

'Sorry,' I muttered, feeling completely ridiculous.

'Why are you even here?' he asked. 'Have you had your interview already?'

I wanted to lie, but I knew he would find out soon enough that I didn't do it. 'No,' I muttered.

He looked confused. 'Why?'

And that's when it hit me. I *really* should have gone to my interview instead of coming here.

'That's such a big deal, Lara,' Caiden said. 'This festival is on until ten, so you could have come after. You never know what opportunities you could get from being in the papers.'

'Did you not go because of your hair?' Sienna asked sweetly.

And then Caiden's face fell and he looked all guilty.

I couldn't speak. I just turned and ran away. I fell twice, but each time I got up and continued to run. My sore leg started to throb a bit from all the falling, but I didn't stop running until I couldn't hear the music from the festival any more and I'd found somewhere to hide.

Lottie's just texted me. She said they've finished the photoshoot and are about to be interviewed, so I can still make it if I hurry. But I can't go like this! I don't even know what this stuff is that I'm covered in. It's all sticky, but parts of it are starting to dry and get flaky.

How is standing in slime supposed to be 'art' anyway?

Ugh! Guess what: it's just started raining.

Could today get any worse?!

7.21 p.m.

I'm trying so hard not to cry. I'm walking home now, and it feels like a walk of *shame*. People are staring at me and I don't blame them. I'm the walking SLIME MONSTER.

It's raining quite heavily, so I've released my hair from the bobble Anaya shoved it into. I figured the curls are going to tighten and shrink and start escaping the bobble anyway.

I must be an absolute sight, covered in slime and hair all sticking up in a puffy RIOT!

I'm sooooo glowed up. Not!

8.12 p.m.

I'm alone in my room with Nala. Alone with my racing thoughts.

When I got home, Mum opened the door. She looked horrified. She didn't even know who I was at first until I let out a little whimper.

'Lara?' she asked, eyes widening.

I pushed into the house and ran up the stairs. She screamed at me not to get any mud on the carpet, but I was past caring.

Mud? If only I was simply covered in mud.

No. Whatever that disgusting slimy goop was, it was a nightmare to get off. I had to soak in the bath for thirty minutes, scrubbing myself. Mum said I might as well bin my clothes, as she didn't think she could get the slime off them.

That's my favourite jeans ruined!

As she ran a bath for me, she asked what happened, but I refused to talk until she threatened to follow me to school on Monday and demand answers from the headteacher. So I mumbled my way through what happened.

'Wait,' she interrupted as I was explaining about the Goop Troop. 'What were you doing at a festival in Sefton Park when you had an interview after the match?'

'I, uh, went to the festival instead,' I muttered.

'WHY??'

'B-because my friends were there.' It wasn't a total lie. Caiden is my friend, I suppose.

Mum went and told Dad, and Dad lectured me about 'focus' and 'determination' from the other side of the bathroom door while I scrubbed my skin.

You need to start making better decisions, Lara.

You can't pass up big opportunities just to hang out with friends who you see all the time anyway.

Your future is more important than dillydallying aimlessly around the city and getting covered in slime.

It was the last thing I needed after the nightmare that today has been. Finally, the tears I'd been holding back all the way home began to fall. Partly because I knew he was right, but mostly because I suddenly felt so disappointed in myself.

I love football.

Before Caiden, nothing could have stopped me from attending an interview about football. Worst of all, I stooped to Sienna's level, showing up uninvited to crash her and Caiden's date.

I feel completely and totally pathetic.

By the way, Sienna and Caiden are no longer at the art festival. I checked TikTok as soon as I got out of the bath, and saw that she walked him home. She made a video of him dancing in the rain, covered in goop.

Caiden can dance too. He was doing all these funny zombie-like moves and Sienna was laughing her heart out. Then she started dancing with him.

They're having so much fun, while I get only embarrassment at every turn!

Kayleigh: Namaste, divine sisters 🙏. Nightfall is at hand. You may now begin your pilgrimage to the temple (my house).

8.34 p.m.

Kayleigh just posted in the group chat, reminding us about the goddess session.

I replied that I'm not coming. I've had enough of glowing up and all the effort we've been making. All for what? It isn't working.

8.42 p.m.

Kayleigh just called me.

'Why aren't you coming?' she asked.

'It isn't working,' I muttered, burying my face in Nala's fur.

'It *is* working. You're taking better care of yourself, aren't you?'

'I suppose, but . . .' I trailed off, not sure how to explain without sounding pathetic.

'This is about Caiden going to the cinema with Sienna, isn't it?' Kayleigh asked.

Well, it's about so much more than that now, so I told her about the festival, even though it was really embarrassing.

Kayleigh sighed down the phone. 'This is why I keep saying you have to glow up for *you*, not for a boy. It's all well and good for boys to carry you through school and put you on a pedestal for a few minutes. But you know what's better? Putting yourself on a pedestal. You know what's even better than Caiden liking you? Liking yourself!'

'That's easy for you to say,' I mumbled.

'Like I've already told you a million times, glowing up is about YOU, and no one else,' Kayleigh said. 'Value YOUR strengths. Own YOUR identity. Forget about impressing anyone else.'

There was a long moment of silence then she asked, 'So, are you coming?'

'No.'

Kayleigh sighed. 'Okay. I'll check on you after.'

Self-knowledge Question
List three things you like about yourself.
I DON'T KNOW AND I DON'T CARE.

12

Build-A-Boy

Saturday 15 September, 11 p.m.

I went.

I don't have the time to care about Caiden and Sienna. I have football to focus on. GOALS TO SCORE.

At least, that's what I told my friends. But I'll be honest with you, dear Diary: deep down, I was still a bit down in the dumps.

'I hope you're not thinking about stopping football again,' Becky said.

I shook my head.

Kayleigh beamed. 'Of course she isn't. Lara is too busy glowing up to care any more. Caiden can have Sienna and her drama. Good riddance.'

Well, I do care, but I'm just rolling with the punches. What else can I do? Plus, I need to stay focused on Match 100.

'Caiden was helping you a lot at bowling today,' Anaya said.

'So?' I asked.

'Well, last week you were talking about him helping Sienna. Today he was helping you.'

True. But it didn't make me feel cute and girly. I just felt ridiculous.

I wonder if Sienna felt ridiculous last week. Maybe not, since she wasn't truly in need of help and was clearly pretending. I actually *needed* the help. And it didn't even make any difference. I was still unbelievably RUBBISH.

'Maybe Caiden is just one of those sweet people who likes to help other people,' I said, reaching for another gold doughnut from the spread of food on the coffee table. Everything was glazed with edible gold to make us feel goddessy. Kayleigh had also decorated the living room to make it look like a temple by hanging colourful sheets of material on the wall. When we arrived, she told us to imagine they were wall drapes made of pure silk. There were also rose petals on the floor (good thing her family has laminate flooring in the living room, not carpet) and she'd also hung a disco ball. It scattered colourful light over the room.

'He bought you a slushy,' Becky pointed out. 'That was totally unnecessary.'

'So?'

Becky shrugged. 'I don't know. You said Sienna *asked* him to help her at the arcade. You didn't ask for his help today. He just took it upon himself to help you.'

'And Kayleigh told us about the festival,' Anaya said. Her lips twitched like she was trying not to laugh. 'He didn't have to help you out of the slime.'

'D'you think it's funny?' I asked.

Anaya quickly shook her head. 'No.'

I took out my phone and showed them a picture I took of myself as I was walking home from Sefton Park. I hadn't yet looked at it myself, and I was shocked at how bad it was. Green-brown slime all over me. Hair standing on end, as though rejoicing in the rain.

Me and my friends were quiet for a moment, then we all burst into laughter. I was so glad I could laugh about something that I'd spent thirty minutes crying about in the bath.

'Caiden made a TikTok about it,' Becky said. 'I don't think he's annoyed that you dragged him into the slime. He said something like "a girl did this to me" and he was smiling. I think he found it funny.'

I waved a dismissive hand. The last thing I wanted was my friends giving me false hope. Caiden going to the cinema with Sienna to watch the Marvel movie that *we* were supposed to watch together tells me all I need to know. 'Can we change the subject now, please?'

Everyone was quiet for a moment, then Anaya started

telling us about Liam. She's seeing him tomorrow. He's adopting a puppy from the animal shelter and invited her along to help him pick. His mum and dad are going to be there and everything.

'Are you nervous?' I asked.

Anaya nodded.

'There's no need to be,' Becky told her. 'Just be yourself.'

'I can't wait to see all the cute puppies,' Anaya said.

'Make sure you take pictures,' I said. I've been wanting a dog for ages. I think Nala is sassy enough to handle a dog sibling. I won't be asking my parents any time soon though. Not after her weeing in Mum's shoe on Monday.

'Well, enough of all this chit-chat,' Kayleigh said. 'We can't do the main part of our goddess energy session yet because we need the moon, but we're going to be productive while we wait for the moon to come out.'

'We need the moon?' Becky asked.

'Is it going to be something weird again?' I asked.

'It's going to be fabulous,' Kayleigh drawled, clicking her fingers. 'Now, our first activity is called Build-A-Boy. You know, like Build-A-Bear? So get your phones out. You have ten seconds to list all the qualities of your perfect boy.'

'Ten seconds?' Anaya asked. 'That's too short.'

'Yeah, but it'll show what's most important to you. Ready, steady, Build-A-Boy!'

Ten seconds later we compared lists.

Kayleigh's list
- Doesn't stink
- Interested in self-improvement and stays 'glowed up'
- Kind and feminist

My list:
- Nice
- Funny
- Likes me back (otherwise there's really no point, is there?)

Becky's list:
- Can sing (playing guitar would be a nice bonus)
- Makes me happy

Anaya's list
- Six pack
- Rich
- Kind to animals and small children
- Good dancer
- Good-looking

I don't know how Anaya managed to type all that in ten seconds. And of course she put 'rich'. I should have put that too.

Next we went into more detail, mixing and matching attributes of real people:

Kayleigh
• Looks like Chris Hemsworth
• Doesn't take himself too seriously

Me
• Looks like Caiden
• Good football skills

Becky
• Justin Bieber's voice
• Everything else is Richard Skelley

Anaya
• Liam's face
• Dwayne Johnson's muscles and money
• Good dancer

We had a good laugh discussing the various celebrities we'd mentioned and googling to compare them.

As soon as it was completely dark outside, Kayleigh said it was time for the goddess session and yelled up the stairs to her sister Hailey.

Hailey is sixteen, Danny's age, but unlike Danny she's actually quite nice to her younger sister – most of the time.

'Hailey is going to be in our goddess session?' Anaya asked when Kayleigh returned.

'Yeah,' Kayleigh said. 'I've told her what to do. She

didn't want to, but I overheard Mum promising to pay her a tenner if she does it.'

Hailey appeared moments later with four blankets. She looks exactly like Kayleigh but taller and with jet-black hair. She also has a nose piercing.

'Sit on the floor,' Hailey ordered.

We did, and she proceeded to wrap us tightly in a blanket each. She explained that we were 'cocooning', like caterpillars do before they become beautiful butterflies.

My blanket was really tight, and I developed a newfound appreciation (and pity) for what caterpillars go through.

'It's moth caterpillars that form cocoons,' Anaya said. 'Butterfly ones form a chrysalis.'

Becky looked at Kayleigh and Hailey in horror. 'What? You're taking us through the motions of becoming moths?'

'It doesn't matter,' Hailey replied. She sounded bored. 'It's the same idea. One girl's cocoon is another girl's chrysalis.'

'Just focus on butterflies, not moths,' Kayleigh said, 'and it'll be fine.'

'What's this got to do with being a goddess though?' Becky asked.

'We're transforming from girls to goddesses the way a caterpillar transforms into a butterfly,' Kayleigh explained.

'Oh,' Becky said. 'Alright then.'

'Do you guys want to just ask questions all night?'

Hailey asked. 'I can just take a seat and listen, or I can, like, start the session?'

'Start the session,' Kayleigh said quickly.

Hailey connected the TV to YouTube and played meditation music with nature scenes. She talked over the music in a bored voice. 'Close your eyes and imagine yourselves as slimy caterpillars. Little girls with zero redeeming qualities. Mucky. Gross. Lots of legs. Sit with that image of yourself for a bit.'

I imagined myself with lots of little caterpillar legs, climbing up a tree. I saw a Caiden caterpillar at the top. He was still good-looking as a caterpillar.

'Now imagine yourselves all alone inside a cocoon. It's safe. It's dark. It's a bit lonely too. But sometimes you've got to be a lone wolf in order to become the top dog. Chickens peck around in packs. Eagles fly alone. D'you wanna be a chicken or an eagle? Chickens get cooked in barbecue sauce and eaten. They're prey. Eagles do the eating. They're predators. There's this quote by Seneca that says, "Throw me to the wolves and I'll come back leading the pack". In your cocoon, you think about these things, all alone, away from the distractions of the world. Take a deep breath and see yourself in your cocoon.'

I took a deep breath and saw myself. My cocoon was warm. A nice little shelter. A safe place where it never rains. And I was definitely a soaring eagle, not a chicken.

(But I do like chickens.)

'I'd like to be a chicken that lays golden eggs,' came Becky's voice over the meditation music.

'SHUT UP, CLOSE YOUR EYES, AND DON'T INTERRUPT THE MEDITATION,' Hailey scolded.

For a moment the only sound was the meditation music. It was all one boring note that made me feel a bit sleepy.

'Now imagine bursting out of your cocoon,' Hailey said in a much more animated voice. 'You've been a slimy caterpillar, you've paid the price of cocooning, and finally, nature has rewarded you with a TRANSFORMATION. You catch your reflection in a pond and you have wings. You're colourful. You even have antennae –'

'Caterpillars have antennae too,' Anaya began but Kayleigh and Hailey shouted at her to shut up.

'You go back to all your caterpillar friends and they can't believe how much you've changed. How beautiful you are. How talented. How glamorous!'

Suddenly, the meditation music changed to a thumping club dance remix of 'Don't Cha' by the Pussycat Dolls.

'Open your eyes and fly like a butterfly!' Hailey shouted, setting Anaya free from her blanket.

Then she came over and yanked my blanket off. 'Fly like a butterfly!'

My leg was feeling a bit better after all the slipping and falling in Sefton Park (I think the soak in the bath helped), so I jumped onto the sofa then jumped off, trying to stay in the air for as long as possible. Everyone laughed.

We all zoomed around the room, pretending to fly.

'Now walk like goddesses,' Hailey shouted over the music.

Anaya, Becky and Kayleigh sashayed around the room with their hands on their hips. I walked very slowly, so that I wouldn't trip.

Abruptly, the music stopped.

'Okay, that's enough,' Hailey said. 'Now it's time for goddess yoga.' She started a YouTube yoga video then sat down and started texting on her phone while we tried to twist our bodies into all kinds of ridiculous poses. It was twenty minutes of pure TORTURE.

After that, Hailey read from a script that Kayleigh had written for her, telling us that goddesses are creative. Apparently the whole point of being a god or goddess is to be a creator and make stuff.

We moved into the kitchen, where Kayleigh's mum was FaceTiming her sister in Australia, and we got to work creating our own worlds. Kayleigh and Hailey had already set out lots of art supplies on the dining table.

My world was called Laradom. The oceans were made of fire instead of water. And the people there had four arms (they can get more done than humans), loved football and worshipped me.

'Lakes and oceans of fire?' Anaya asked. 'Sounds like hell.'

'That would make Lara Satan,' Kayleigh said.

They all laughed like it was oh so funny.

'It can't really be hell if sweets and chocolate are a healthy diet and they're encouraged to eat them five times a day,' I informed them. I was pretty proud of the world I'd made.

'Yeah,' Becky agreed. 'That sounds more like heaven.'

When we all finished, we put our worlds side by side and decided that, together, they were a solar system. They all orbited a sun called KayAnaLarBeck.

In Kayleigh's world, women ruled. In Becky's, it rained marshmallows from cotton candy clouds and there were rivers of lemonade. In Anaya's, wild animals were tame and all the boys had Liam's face and Dwayne Johnson's muscles.

We decided that the people on each of our planets wouldn't consider each other aliens. They would love one another and allow interplanetary tourism.

After that, the moon was out, so we could do the main goddess activity. Kayleigh led us into the back garden.

'Ready?' Hailey yelled from inside the house.

'Yeah,' Kayleigh called back.

Suddenly, fairy lights flicked on all over the bushes. It was pretty magical.

Hailey came out and looked up at the moon. 'The moon is a charger,' she announced. 'Just like your phone charger. Mum charges her crystals in the moon, and all things are made of the same stuff: atoms, molecules and all that. If the moon can charge crystals, it can charge you gorgeous living jewels too. You're going to charge yourselves until you're chock-full of moon goddess energy. We chose the moon goddess mainly because there are too many goddesses and we had to pick one – but also because the moon has phases and cycles just like females do. Her name is Selene, by the way.'

'So how are we going to charge ourselves?' I asked warily, knowing that things were about to get weird.

'WE'RE GONNA HOWL AT THE MOON!' Kayleigh yelled, pumping a fist. Her voice echoed through the night.

Becky's brows lifted. 'Like wolves?'

'Yeah,' Kayleigh replied, like it was no big deal. Like stable, upstanding people regularly howl at the moon on a Saturday night.

'Cool!' Becky said.

I exchanged a look with Anaya. She shrugged. 'We've showered in milk and honey, we've said no to our parents and hung up on them. We can't stop now.'

'BRING IT ON!' Becky yelled. 'Owoooooo!!'

Kayleigh took a deep breath. 'Owoooooo! Owoooooo!'

So, just two weeks after burying my Cyclops chest in the mud under an oak tree in Kayleigh's front garden and vowing that I would never let her talk me into anything ridiculous again, I found myself howling at the moon with my friends in Kayleigh's back garden.

It helped that Kayleigh and Becky had zero shame about it. It meant Anaya and I could get into it too without feeling too ridiculous. Before long, it sounded like a pack of rabid wolves had laid siege to Kayleigh's street.

Later, when we got back inside, Kayleigh's mum told us that SEVEN neighbours had called to complain.

Note to self:
- Sleep with the curtains open so that the moon can shine on me and continue to charge me all night (Kayleigh's instruction).
- Kayleigh, Becky and Anaya are the best friends EVER. (Even if they do have their annoying moments.) I honestly don't know what I would do without them. Hanging out with them always lifts my mood and makes everything seem so much better. I think having good friends is one of the most important things in the world!

Self-knowledge Question
Which do you say more of, 'yes' or 'no'?
It depends who I'm talking to. If it's my parents it's mostly 'no', but it doesn't count for anything because they still end up making me do whatever I said 'no' to. If it's my friends it's mostly 'yes', which is why I end up doing outrageous things like HOWL AT THE MOON!!!

11.37 p.m.

I don't feel at all sleepy yet, so I'm going to answer some more self-knowledge questions.

My throat is a bit sore after all that howling. Mum made me a warm honey and lemon drink when I got back. I think she feels sorry for me about the goop incident and my hair getting wet again in the rain.

En Vogue is bumping through the walls. Sounds like Jay's mum is having a good night.

Self-knowledge Questions
If you could change your name, what would you change it to?
After tonight, Selene. Why wouldn't I want to be named after the goddess who draws the moon across the night sky in a chariot?

Sienna once said that my name, Omolara, means 'child of my body'. Apparently she used some online translator that was obviously incorrect. She said, in front of everybody, '"Omo" means "child" and "Lara" means "body". So I guess the equivalent English phrase is "fruit of my loins". So whenever we call her "Lara" we're basically saying "loins".' Everyone started laughing. I had to google 'loins' because I didn't know what it meant.

Apparently, 'loins' can mean GENITALS!

I tried to tell everyone it wasn't true. My name means 'my child is my kin', and is based on the concept that a person's child is their most valued and reliable relative. There is no universe in which it means FRUIT OF MY LOINS!!!

But did anyone listen? NO!

What do you want to be when you grow up?
I don't know. Is that bad? Does that mean I don't know myself enough?

11.49 p.m.

I asked Dad if I should be worried that I don't know what I want to be, and he said it just means I don't know enough about the world and the jobs available. I regret asking because he said he's going to have me speak to Uncle Tobi about it.

Uncle Tobi, Mum's brother, is a doctor. His wife, Aunt Maggie, is a doctor too. And they're obsessed with education and good grades and children growing up to become doctors.

On the bright side, Dad also said that when I go to their house tomorrow, my cousin, Kemi, can relax my hair for me.

Can you believe it, dear Diary?

OMG!!! I'm so excited I could die!!

Mum tried to burst my bubble by saying, 'I used to relax my hair but it never worked. I still had to straighten it with straighteners, and it would turn back into an

Afro if I even looked at a glass of water. Your hair is going to be the same.'

She also said the money she's paying Kemi to do my hair is my allowance for the next couple of months.

I couldn't care less.

Speaking of names, my cousins have such nice Yoruba names: Kemi, Sadé (pronounced with a 'sh' not a 's') and Yewandé.

Why didn't my parents call me Sadé? Or maybe Shola, which means 'wealth'?

Instead I get a name that can be mistaken for LOINS!!

This is why I need to be adopted. If Naomi Campbell was my mum, I wouldn't have had to beg to get my hair relaxed. She'd probably even let me dye it or wear weaves, which are amazing hair extensions that can totally transform your look.

Goddess Naomi, please help a fledgling goddess out!

13

Insta Star

Sunday 16 September, 8 a.m.
I texted Kemi last night asking what time I should come over and she said six. SIX PM!!

HOW AM I SUPPOSED TO CONTAIN MY EXCITEMENT UNTIL SIX PM???

I asked her why I couldn't come in the morning, and she said because she'll be doing her beauty routine. I asked why I couldn't come in the afternoon, and she said because she'll be braiding someone's hair. Someone who booked an appointment two months ago rather than springing themselves on her the day before.

That shut me up. Kemi is kind of in demand. She went to beauty school, much to her parents' horror. Yup, she refused to do a degree in medicine and now she does hair and make-up on TV shows and has had lots of celebrity clients. She has half a million followers on Instagram, where she posts pictures of her clients, and pouty, moody-looking pictures of herself. She's hardly ever in Liverpool. It's lucky for me that she has lots of hair bookings for clients in the north-west over the next week.

8.17 a.m.

I can't believe Match 100 is THIS WEDNESDAY.

If we win, the party will be on Friday. I would pick out clothes, but I don't want to jinx it. There's also my goal of Caiden asking me out by the party. I don't think that's going to happen.

But anyway . . . POSITIVE THOUGHTS ONLY, LARA!!

I can't wait for the party. I'll not just be the star of the football team, but I'll have gorgeous sleek hair and I'll be all glowed up. (And if, by some miracle, Caiden *does* ask me out, I could be the girlfriend of the cutest boy at school.)

Okay . . . I need to stop thinking about this.

8.29 a.m.

I CAN'T STOP THINKING ABOUT IT!

Argh!!!

Why don't brains come with 'off' buttons?

3.13 p.m.

Since I desperately needed a distraction, I decided I might as well do my supermodel energy session, and called my friends. I told them to bring their school uniforms.

They piled into my room at ten o'clock, all groggy and red-eyed.

'Please let this be a chilled session, Lara,' Anaya croaked, picking up Nala and stroking her. 'I'm tired this morning and I need to get home before two so I can make myself look less like a corpse before I meet up with Liam.'

It's all 'Liam, Liam, Liam' these days.

'There's not much we can get up to on a Sunday morning,' I said. 'There's no way my mum and dad are going to let us blast music at this time or shout or anything.'

'Good,' Becky croaked.

It seems all last night's howling has taken a toll on everyone's voices.

I went to make them cups of tea, and Dad said he would do it. He also brought us up some bacon, eggs and toast! Dad, who only makes breakfast for his wife on weekends. He and mum have got my friends convinced that they're never annoying, but I know better!

'Supermodels are not slaves to fashion,' I told my friends after we finished eating. 'They set the trends and the fashion slaves follow. To have that energy, we need to be trendsetters too. That's why we're going to come up with new, cool ways to wear our school uniform.'

I held my breath, suddenly realising how nerve-racking it is to run a session. I now regretted all the times I'd rolled my eyes or snorted during one of the other girls' sessions.

'Let's do it!' Kayleigh yelled.

'No yelling,' I reminded her, glancing at the door. My mum only got back from a night shift an hour before and I knew she'd be trying to sleep. The only thing scarier than DEATH ITSELF is my mum when she's tired.

'Let's do it!' Kayleigh whisper-yelled.

I grinned. 'Come on, then.'

They all got off my bed and we put on our uniforms. I made my skirt shorter on the left side and longer on the right side. Asymmetrical. Kayleigh rolled up her skirt until it was really short, then rolled her school socks over her knees to look like thigh-high boots. Becky tied her cardigan like a tie-front top instead of buttoning it, and rolled her school trousers up to look cropped. Anaya rolled up her cardigan like a belly top and said she was going to wear a petticoat under her skirt to make it poof out.

'We look ridiculous,' Kayleigh said, as we all stood before my mirror when we were done. 'Especially Anaya and Becky.'

'It's not about looking good,' Anaya told her. 'It's about being different and setting a trend. Imagine if people at school copy us?'

'I say we do Lara's asymmetrical skirt and Kayleigh's over-the-knee socks,' Becky said.

'So we're really going to do this?' I asked.

'Of course,' Kayleigh said. 'Isn't that the whole point of the activity?'

'Oh,' I said. 'Okay.'

We all did the asymmetrical skirt and over-the-knee socks look. We actually looked okay.

'Show up like this for school tomorrow,' Kayleigh told us all. 'Without fail.'

'Uh, whose session is this?' I asked. 'Yours or mine?'

'I'm just helping you enforce the rules,' Kayleigh told me.

'Right. Well, next we're going to practise supermodel walks,' I told them.

'Are you sure?' Anaya asked. 'Shouldn't you be resting your leg for Wednesday's match?'

'My leg is pretty much fine now,' I assured her.

I took them downstairs to the living room where I'd set up a makeshift runway. It was just some cardboard that I'd cut into strips then stuck together.

Danny was in there playing *Call of Duty* as usual, and he had the nerve to wink at Anaya.

'Hi, Danny,' Anaya said shyly.

'Hey, NayNay.'

UGH! I wanted to *puke*.

Except for a grunt here and there, I haven't heard my brother's voice all weekend.

I actually hadn't been sure if he was even capable of speaking any more. But my pretty friend walks in and suddenly he bothers to string a sentence together. And a silly one too.

Kayleigh knocked Danny's hat off his head then screamed when he stood up, tossed her over his shoulder and carried her out.

'Dad!' I called. He was on his laptop in the kitchen, watching the highlights from yesterday's Premier League matches. 'Can you tell Danny to leave Kayleigh alone?'

I heard a scuffling and giggling in the hallway. I went to drag Kayleigh back in, then I tried to get Danny to leave the living room because I knew he would make fun of us while we practised our walks.

Danny wasn't having it though. And he kept snorting, determined to embarrass us while we watched a clip from this TV modelling competition where the contestants were taught how to walk for the runway.

When we refused to engage with him and he realised that we weren't going to be distracted, he started videoing us.

That was the last straw. I grabbed his headphones and threatened to snap them. Dad came in while Danny and me were chasing each other around the room.

'What's all this modern stuff?' he asked, looking at the TV. 'In the old days, models practised walking with books on their heads.'

He made Danny put his phone away, then he grabbed some thick books from the shelf and gave us one each.

'Walking well starts with good posture,' Dad said. 'So stand tall.'

We obeyed. Then we balanced our books on our heads and began to walk down the runway in turn. My book fell off my head two steps down. Kayleigh's fell off halfway down.

Anaya and Becky, the horrible overachievers, made it all the way to the end with their books still balanced on their heads.

Then Dad and Danny did it too, strutting like models, and it was hilarious.

'You need to try again,' Kayleigh told me. 'You have to make it down the runway without the book falling off. Tackling your clumsiness was Step 3 of the Glow-Up Plan, remember? You haven't done that yet.'

So I dug my phone out of my pocket and shared my research with them. Clumsiness can be caused by any number of things, including anxiety, not paying attention or getting too little sleep.

'Are you anxious, love?' Dad asked.

I frowned. 'Dad, you're not supposed to be in here. Or you, Danny.'

Thankfully, they excused themselves and gave us some privacy.

'For me, I think it's not paying attention,' I told my friends. Sadly, I believe Dad is right.

'That explains why you're not clumsy when you play

football,' Anaya said. 'You're always paying attention during matches.'

'I have a joke,' Becky said. 'People who can't dance well have two left feet. What do people who can't walk well have?'

'Could it be two right feet?' I asked, unimpressed.

'Yes!' She laughed like it was hilarious.

'Well,' I retorted, 'now we know who *doesn't* have a future as a comedian.' I focused on Anaya and Kayleigh, who were taking this seriously. 'So all I need to do is pay attention, not assume that closed doors are open doors and smack into them, and watch my step so I don't trip over other people's feet and fall down a million steps.'

'You can do that, easy,' Anaya said encouragingly.

Kayleigh handed me my mum's human anatomy book. 'Do it.'

I balanced it on my head and stepped onto the runway. I made it halfway before it fell off. My friends cheered like it was a huge achievement. I was both embarrassed and grateful. I was also DETERMINED to make it to the end of the runway without it falling off.

It took me TWELVE tries, but I did it.

I balanced a big, fat book full of embarrassing pictures of human body parts on my head from one end of my makeshift runway to the other. I did walk really slowly. And the book did wobble precariously the whole time, but I, Lara Bloom, Goddess of Laradom, now have bona fide SUPERMODEL ENERGY!

After that it was time to do the final activity. I'd found a model on YouTube who had lots of 'What I Ate Today' videos. I skipped to the dinner recipe: chicken, brown rice and veggies. We cooked it together, following the supermodel step by step.

When we finished, I handed my friends a container each so that they could take some home.

'That's our dinner for tonight sorted,' I told them.

Before they left, I gave them my final supermodel energy tip: beauty sleep.

(Turns out Kayleigh was right when she recommended sleep.)

'Does that mean we have to go to bed early?' Becky asked warily.

'Only tonight,' I said.

'How early is early?' Kayleigh asked.

'Nine o'clock.'

They reluctantly agreed to it.

Self-knowledge Questions
Do you prefer morning, afternoon or night?
Night all the way!! Mornings are PAINFUL. They should be for sleeping in. Afternoons are okay. Evenings would be the best because of dinner (dinners are much better than breakfasts and lunches), but since evenings are also for homework, I have to say nights. Nights are for TikTok, YouTube and cuddling with Nala. Nights rock!

Which is your favourite season?
Summer, because it's warm and there's no school for most of it. Also autumn, because the school football season starts.

5.40 p.m.
Sooooo, something exciting just happened 🐌!

My phone buzzed a few minutes ago. Guess who'd texted me. CAIDEN!!

I didn't know it was Caiden since I don't have his number, so I was confused. The message just said: Hey. Did you manage to get all the goo off?

I replied: Who's this?

My phone buzzed with a response: Caiden.

Dear Diary, I nearly passed out!

I could hardly sit still as I typed a response: Yeah. It's all off. Did you get it all off too?

Caiden: Yeah.

After that, I was wondering if I needed to reply again, when he sent another message: So is there anything going on between you and Jay?

I immediately messaged Becky and Kayleigh to tell them about it, and Kayleigh did a group FaceTime right away. 'What does he mean?' she asked me.

'I'm not sure.'

'Maybe he thinks Jay is your boyfriend,' Becky said.

'Why would he think that?' I asked.

Becky shrugged. 'Uh, I don't know, maybe because Jay gives you piggybacks and hugs all the time.'

'Not *all* the time,' I protested.

But I finally had an explanation for why Caiden kept watching me and Jay during bowling. He must think I have a crush on Jay.

I tapped out a response: What do you mean? Do you mean like *something* something?

When I read it to Kayleigh and Becky, Kayleigh said it was 'incoherent'. But I'd already sent it. Caiden must have understood what I meant though because he replied: Yeah.

Crap! Mum is calling me. Uncle Tobi is outside. He's going to drive me to his house.

Anyway, I replied: No. Why?

Caiden: Just wondering.

I didn't know what to say after that so I guess the conversation is over. Kayleigh said maybe Jay tried too hard to defend me over that weird text that Paige sent from my phone, so Caiden thinks there must be something going on between us. And Becky asked. 'If there is, why does he care?'

That's the question *I* want answered.

Do I dare hope that Caiden is bothered by the thought of Jay and me together? If he isn't, why bother to ask?

Mum is shouting me again.

Off to my cousins'.

5.43 p.m.

In the car now. Kayleigh just texted me. She thinks I should try to carry on the conversation with Caiden, but I don't know what to say to him.

Anaya just posted a whole slew of ADORABLE PUPPIES in our group chat. But before my heart could melt she added a message that was really confusing:

Anaya: Liam ended up choosing the brown Labrador. We just left the shelter, and he asked me about Lara. He said Caiden said someone called Paige said that Lara has a crush on someone called Jay.

I had to read that last sentence twice to understand it.

Paige LIED to Caiden that I like Jay? Why???

I replied saying: Really???????

Anaya: Apparently she told him this last week at the arcade.

No wonder. Caiden has been watching me and Jay ever since. But why does he care?

Oops! Uncle Tobi just said, 'Put your phone away and let's talk about your future!'

This is about to be the most BORING car ride EVER!

5.55 p.m.

I was right, this *is* the most boring car ride ever! Thankfully,

Uncle Tobi just got out to buy some petrol, so I get a break from hearing about how fantastic his job as a doctor is and how I need to 'sit up and start paying attention in life' so that I can someday become a doctor too.

Anyway, I heard a *ping* a few minutes ago. I think it was from my journal app, but I didn't dare take my phone out to check while Uncle Tobi was talking. I checked just now and can't see any notifications.

Weird.

I just caught up on all the messages in the group chat:

Kayleigh: Lara, you need to have a word with Paige. She's out of order.

Becky: Yeah. She's deliberately trying to sabotage you. Talk to her tomorrow at school.

Anaya: I'll come with you. She can't keep spreading ridiculous lies about you like this.

Kayleigh: I still think Sienna is behind it.

Anaya: Of course she is. Paige hasn't got a mind of her own, so she does whatever Sienna says. Pathetic!

Kayleigh: When you talk to her, Lara, remember, this isn't a fight over a boy. It's just about standing up for yourself.

I think I *will* talk to Paige tomorrow.

I'm SICK AND TIRED of her.

8.30 p.m.

My cousin Kemi is the COOLEST! She's twenty-one and really fashionable. Like REALLY! Today her hair was in long, long cornrows, and she was wearing bright blue eyeshadow and an orange jumpsuit with lots of cleavage showing.

Sadé is eighteen, and was wearing just her knickers and a vest around the house. Uncle Tobi said to me in annoyance, 'She thinks this house is a NUDIST CAMP!'

Sadé ignored him.

Yewandé is fifteen and always tries to act like she's so much older and worldlier than me. She showed me a picture of her new boyfriend on her phone (blond hair, bright green eyes, not as gorgeous as Caiden). Before we could chat for long, Aunt Maggie (who was wearing a silk Chanel dressing gown) told her to go and finish her Kumon, which is extra maths and English lessons that she has to do.

'It's Sunday,' Yewandé protested. 'Even God rested on Sunday.'

'No, He rested on the Sabbath, which is Saturday. Now go and finish your work. You're behind.'

Yewandé groaned and stomped out of the living room, which has been newly decorated. It's cream and teal now (before it was pale grey with pops of yellow). Aunt Maggie has had a conservatory built too.

But you know what? Whenever I think about all the Kumon maths and extra science lessons Sadé and Yewandé have to have (Kemi too, before she escaped to beauty school), I feel grateful that my parents aren't as loaded as theirs. Dad would definitely have me going to extra maths and science if he could.

But before I feel too smug, Sadé or Yewandé'll probably become prime minister someday while I'll be sweeping the streets, or something, since I don't even know what I want to be when I grow up. Sweeping the streets is important too, though.

Kemi took me into the conservatory to relax my hair. Her girlfriend, Briana, who is just as stylish as Kemi, was lounging inside, reading *Vogue* magazine.

'I'm using a mild relaxer since it's your first time,' Kemi told me, tearing open a box of Dark and Lovely with a smiling Black girl on it.

'Look at you getting your hair done,' Sadé sang, padding into the conservatory, still in her knickers. 'What's the occasion?'

'There's no occasion,' I replied.

'Come on, spill the beans.'

Briana lowered her magazine. 'She's only fourteen. She can't really have many beans to spill.'

'Are you kidding?' Kemi asked. 'Teenagers are living their best lives these days. I bet we'd be surprised to hear what Lara gets up to in her private time.'

I snorted. If they found out that I spend my so-called 'private time' howling at the moon with my friends and dancing to 'She Wolf', they would probably laugh until they cried.

Kemi opened the tub of relaxer and I felt a bit giddy. FINALLY!

I held super-still while she coated my hair with it, and tried not to think about all the horror stories I've heard about people's hair getting chemically FRIED! People have had big-time disasters with hair relaxer, even having it burn bald patches into their head.

When I was seven, Mum told me that if I relaxed my hair I would wake up in the morning and when I sat up, my hair would still be on my pillow because I was too young for it. I believed her until one of my classmates came into school with relaxed hair that hadn't fallen out in the night. Even Yewandé got to relax her hair when she was eight.

'I don't know why you want straight hair,' Sadé said. 'Natural is best.'

I wished she would shut up so that Kemi could concentrate and make sure I didn't get any bald patches.

'People who relax their hair might as well announce to the world that they're ashamed of their natural hair and don't love themselves,' Sadé added.

'Tell her to shut up if you want,' Kemi told me.

'It's true,' Sadé said. She flicked her beaded braids then launched into the same monologue I've heard a thousand times. 'How come in every movie where there's an "ugly" character who needs a makeover, she has frizzy hair and glasses? And how come the makeover is straight hair and no glasses? Is that supposed to be the pinnacle of beauty?'

'I'm just trying something new,' I told her.

'You tell her, Lara,' Kemi said. 'What you want to do with your hair is nobody else's business.'

Kemi is always really nice.

After all my hair had been coated, Kemi set a timer for fifteen minutes on her phone. I set a timer on my phone too, just to be safe. Waiting too long before washing it out is how disasters happen.

Kemi left Sadé, Briana and me in the conservatory. Yewandé managed to sneak away from Kumon and came to tell me more about her boyfriend. His name is Jack and he's a rapper. He's in a band and everything, and Yewandé said he's even written some raps about her.

Kemi returned just as my timer went off and we went upstairs to the en-suite bathroom in her old bedroom. Now that she's left home, Aunt Maggie has taken over her wardrobe and filled it with her clothes. I could see floral dresses and conservative trouser suits that Kemi wouldn't be caught dead in poking out of it. I even spied a huge flowery bra. Aunt Maggie must be, like, an F cup!!

I prayed hard as Kemi washed the relaxer out of my hair.

When she finished, I glanced in the bathroom mirror and was glad to see all my hair still there. And it was STRAIGHT! Much straighter than when I use hair straighteners. *Woohoo!*

'I'm going to give you a blowout,' Kemi said, draping a towel around my shoulders.

Back in the conservatory, she put a load of protective oils in my hair then dried and styled it. When she finished, I looked in the living-room mirror and could only stare at my reflection in shock. I couldn't believe how long my hair was. I'm not Rapunzel or anything, but when your hair grows upward instead of downward, you can't really tell how long it is. At least, I've never tried to guess.

My hair was well past my shoulders! And it was shiny and midnight black and AMAZING! And Kemi had given it soft waves that looked so GLAM.

I squealed and hugged her, jumping up and down in pure joy. I was already imagining it in a sleek ponytail on Wednesday when we play Match 100. I've already checked the weather and it isn't supposed to rain that day, but you never know.

Since my hair turned out so well, Kemi took a picture of me and uploaded it to her Instagram. Caption: My little cousin, Lara. Relaxer and blowout xx 😙

Immediately, likes and comments flooded in. I refreshed her Instagram page over and over as Uncle Tobi drove me home, reading all the comments:

Your cousin is so cute ♥
What a QUEEN!!!
Kemi, your family has the pretty gene!

I didn't hear a word Uncle Tobi said as he talked about

preparing for a bright future by taking maths and science seriously and studying medicine at uni (I sat in the back seat this time so he couldn't see that I was on my phone). I think he told me something about the various branches of medicine that I could consider.

'Oh, gynaecology sounds interesting,' I muttered to humour him as I scrolled through comment after comment.

By the time I got home, there were THREE HUNDRED comments and counting!

'I'm a star,' I sang as I sauntered into the house. 'I'm Insta famous.'

'You look very nice, love,' Dad said.

Mum smiled. 'Are you happy now?'

'Yes!' I twirled through the living room, letting my hair float around me. Then I dashed up to Danny's room and slapped him with my hair – something you can't really do with an Afro since Afros don't move much and they're soft.

Then I noticed who else was in the room. Alex! I did feel mortified, but I didn't feel any butterflies (I didn't even feel a caterpillar). I'm well and truly over that crush.

'Hi, Lara,' Alex said as I ran out of the room.

'Hi,' I replied. 'Bye.'

I'm so happy with my hair. I texted Kemi to thank her again, then I checked if I had any new messages from Caiden, even though I already knew I didn't.

Now, I'm off to have my supermodel dinner!

14

A Doom Worse than Death

Monday 17 September, 7.15 a.m.
I'm feeling really confident about this week and I'm so excited for Match 100. It helps that my hair is rainproof, lol 😄 😄

Match 100 is against Westlake High at their terrible pitch, which always gets waterlogged with the slightest bit of rain. Well, whether it rains or not, I'm going to give that match my all and score a hat-trick.

We're going to win!

8.47 a.m.
When I got to school, my friends were waiting for me at the gates. Their eyes widened at the sight of me.

'You look amazing!' Becky said.

'Thanks,' I replied.

We were all wearing our over-the-knee socks and had rolled up our skirts so that they were asymmetrical.

EVERYONE stared at us as we walked through the gates.

EVERYONE stared at us as we walked through the hallways.

It was either my hair or our new way of wearing our uniforms. Or maybe even the fact that Match 100 is in JUST TWO DAYS!!!

As we made our way to our lockers, Anaya gushed about Liam's new puppy.

A piece of paper fell out of my locker when I opened it. On it was written:

Have a great day! ☺

I showed it to my friends, but they all said they hadn't put it there.

'Maybe you have a secret admirer,' Becky suggested.

I would have doubted that if not for the cold, hard evidence in my hand.

Interesting.

Self-knowledge Questions
What's the scariest dream you've ever had?
I once dreamed that Cruella De Vil, Captain Hook and Darth Vader were chasing me through Prince's Park.

All the trees in the park had eyes and mouths, and their branches were lots of arms. The trees kept reaching for me with their arms and I was TERRIFIED of them. In the end, one of the trees caught me and lifted me up in the air so that Cruella, Hook and Darth couldn't get me.

I was like, wow, they were trying to help me all along. But then the tree that saved me opened its mouth and started lowering me towards it! Frantically, I kicked it in the eye and it dropped me.

Wild, huh?

What's the best dream you've ever had?
It was this dream about me scoring a hat-trick for England in the World Cup. We were playing against Brazil. My England kit was all glittery and I was wearing high heels. For some reason I had a microphone, and I sang and danced after each goal like it was a concert.
I had backup dancers and everything. The whole stadium was chanting my name. *Lara! Lara! Lara!*

It was so amazing! I was devastated to wake up and find that it wasn't real, and that what *was* real was the fact that it was a rainy Monday morning and I had double maths.

11.45 a.m.
Dear Diary, I'm at home.

Why are you at home when you're supposed to be at school? I hear you ask.

Well, you know that ping I heard yesterday? That ping from my journaling app that I didn't pay any attention to? I SHOULD HAVE PAID ATTENTION because I somehow managed to PUBLISH MY JOURNAL!

I can't breathe. I'm going to be sick.

I'm going to DIE!

You have two options on my journaling app after you finish typing an entry. 'Publish' for people who want to share their entries, and 'save' for people who don't.

I don't know how I did it. Did I hit 'publish' by mistake when Mum was yelling at me that Uncle Tobi was waiting outside? Did it take a few minutes to publish, hence the delayed ping?

That would make sense, because when you click 'publish' it'll ask if you want to publish that one entry or the whole journal. It published MY WHOLE JOURNAL, which must have taken a while.

Or maybe it happened when I was in the car. Maybe I 'butt-published', the way people 'butt-dial' by accident and call random people?

I'm shaking so much, I can hardly type.

I BUTT-PUBLISHED MY JOURNAL while in Uncle Tobi's car, and released all my DEEPEST SECRETS in Cuckoo font for the WHOLE WORLD to read.

I unpublished it as soon as I got home, and I'm just using a notes app on my phone now, but the damage has been done.

Now I understand why people were staring at me when I got to school. It wasn't because of my hair or because me and my friends were trying to be trendsetters with our uniforms. It was because they'd read my innermost secrets.

This means EVERYONE knows about my flat-chestedness.

I'm going to throw up!

Everyone knew about my published journal except for me and my friends. I was just floating around feeling so good about my hair. Then I found out in the worst of ways when I was on my way to my locker after history first period.

There were all these strange printouts stuck to all the walls.

OMG! OMG!! OMG!!!

Everyone knows I like Caiden.

Caiden knows I like Caiden.

I need to lie down.

I'll be back in a bit.

12.01 p.m.

Okay, I'm back.

So, as I walked through the hallway, looking at the printouts on the walls, I saw snippets of familiar words here and there.

Flying monkeys . . .

Why did God create big brothers? They're horrible!

This evening, I told my friends that I might stop playing football . . .

I began to panic. I COULDN'T FIGURE OUT WHAT WAS GOING ON! Other people were staring at the printouts too.

Then my phone started buzzing off the hook. Anaya, Kayleigh and Becky were all calling me. That's when I realised I had a text from Anaya: Did you publish your journal? Someone has printed it out and stuck bits of it all over the school.

I nearly passed out right there in the hallway!!

When I got to the lockers, it seemed like there were HUNDREDS of people around.

'There she is!' someone yelled, and everyone stopped and turned in my direction. Many of them were holding printed pages from my journal. They'd been reading it.

I was going to hold my head high and flounce over to my locker like I was unbothered when I heard the opening music of 'Baby One More Time' by Britney Spears.

But instead of 'Oh baby, baby', the voice sang, 'Oh boobies, boobies', and I realised it wasn't 'Hit me baby one more time'. It was a spoof version called 'Make my boobies one more size'. I've heard it before. In the chorus, the singer croons about how her flat-chestedness is killing her.

And that's when it hit me. Someone was blasting that particular song from their phone because of *me*. Because they'd all found out about MY FLAT CHEST! I was wearing my three-sizes-bigger bra today so they were probably wondering why I thought I was flat-chested.

Then I realised they wouldn't be wondering. If they'd read my journal they would all *know* I was wearing a three-sizes-bigger bra!

Guess what happened next?

I BURST INTO TEARS. I actually CRIED in front of them all! I should have held my head high, acted like it didn't bother me, stuck up my middle finger . . . anything. But I started crying like a BIG BABY!

Then I ran home.

I didn't even duck down when I passed Mr Griffiths' office. I just ran past and he came out and yelled at me to get back on the school premises.

I didn't listen.

He can call my parents if he wants.

I'm NEVER going back to school again!

Thursday 20 September, 9.10 a.m.
Dear Diary,

I've missed you!!

I haven't been to school since I ran out on Monday. (Yes, it's taken me three days to summon the will to journal again.) Mum and Dad tried to make me go, but I refused.

I miss my friends, I've been wondering what Caiden thinks of the stuff in my journal (if he's read it), and I'm even slightly bothered about how much work I'll have to catch up on, but I still can't bring myself to go back.

Mr Griffiths visited yesterday to assure me that the situation will be dealt with, but I refused to go down to see him.

Nobody can make me return to school. Emotional distress is a very valid reason to stay off school or work. I googled it.

Mum slipped a letter under the door yesterday from the school. It said:

```
Due to the extreme nature of some of the
things Lara wrote in her journal, we advise
that you seek immediate professional help,
beginning with a psychological assessment,
which we have booked via our school's well-
being programme.
```

I was shocked. There's nothing 'extreme' in my journal – unless they mean trying to grow my boobs in the soil under an oak tree!! But that's *hardly* something to force me into counselling over.

9.28 a.m.

On Monday, Mum and Dad came home early from work and kept asking me what was wrong. I couldn't bring myself to tell them. In the end, Mum called Anaya and got the lowdown.

I haven't spoken to Anaya, Becky or Kayleigh since Monday. The only thing worse than your enemies reading your journal is your friends reading it. I hope they're not offended by anything I wrote. And I hope they don't hate me for being so careless as to publish my stupid thoughts and let the whole world in on our glow-up stuff and crushes.

I think I'm clinically depressed.

Nala has been my only ray of sunshine.

9.47 a.m.

I shouldn't be depressed. I've done nothing but hide in my room watching YouTube compilations of terrible contestants on talent shows who think they're amazing singers. Those are hilarious.

On Monday, I pushed my wardrobe against the door so that no one could come in. I only emerge for food. And only when everyone is out. I always make sure to get more food just before my family is due home so that I don't have to leave my room once everyone gets back.

Dad has been leaving three meals in the kitchen for me each day. On Monday, Mum kept texting me things like:

Lara, please reply to this text so that I know you're still alive in there.

Hi Lara, please tell me if you begin to have any dark thoughts.

I replied, assuring her that I was alive and physically well. Still, she threatened to call the police and have them break into my room if I didn't let her in to see me for herself. I agreed to a compromise: FaceTime.

We've been FaceTiming three times a day.

The downside of hiding from the world is that Nala's litter tray is full and my room stinks so bad I can hardly breathe.

I've opened the windows, but that means the room is pretty cold now too.

10.15 a.m.
Ugh! I feel so horrible, and I don't know how I'll ever stop feeling this way. If only there was a button I could push to switch off the constant stream of anxiety flowing through my brain.

This situation isn't only bad for me; it's bad for my friends too. Everything we did for our glow up has been read by everyone at school. How did our glow up blow up? When am I going to grow up? How can I ever show up . . . at school again?

This is what happens when you're deeply distressed. You ask yourself rhyming rhetorical questions.

(Hmm, I could have added 'throw up' somewhere in there. This situation certainly calls for vomit.)

10.40 a.m.

Yesterday morning, Mum called through the door to remind me about Match 100.

I feel sick thinking about it 😣 🫨 😭

OMG, the party.

Anaya and so many other people have put so much effort into planning that party, and the team might not even have won.

I didn't go to the match.

That's right. I chickened out on my goal. I stayed home instead of going out and doing my part to achieve the thing I want most in the world: one hundred matches unbeaten.

It rained all day yesterday too. Throughout the day raindrops pattered against my window, making me feel even worse about myself and my life in general.

The team must despise me. Especially if they lost.

OMG, if they lost I'll be public enemy number one at school. Everyone will blame it on me for not showing up.

Now I'm terrified to check the results online.

I'm not checking.

11.25 a.m.

I HATE my life!

The party was supposed to be a celebration of all the hard work the girls and I have put in to stay unbeaten. Sure, the thought of it was stressful, but I had so many high hopes. Well, now I won't be going (if they've won).

To think I thought I could crown it all with a hat-trick.

To think I even hoped that Caiden would be so impressed by my football skills that he would develop a huge crush on me and ask me out, and we would make our 'couple debut' at the party.

Now, DUE TO MY OWN STUPIDITY, I won't even be going!

Ugh!

12.05 p.m.

I bet the team won without me.

Don't get me wrong, I'd be THRILLED for them. But I bet I'll have the captain's badge taken away. Lottie has probably already been made the new captain. I'll just be the disgraced ex-captain who the whole school is better off without.

2.19 p.m.

OMG OMG OMG.

I really hope my friends are okay. I know I'm going round in circles now, but I can't help it. I'm so worried 😞. I wonder how they're dealing with things at school. Everyone now knows about their crushes and everything else.

They'll never forgive me for this.

They'll probably never speak to me again!

2.46 p.m.

I just checked our group chat. They haven't removed me from it, so that's a good sign. They must not have decided to form a separate group chat without me either as Kayleigh has been posting glow-up stuff every day.

On Tuesday it was fashion advice:

Kayleigh: Don't be a slave to trends, wear what you want.

On Wednesday it was about self-esteem and using positive affirmations to change how you talk to yourself. She even included one I could use as I prepared for Match 100:

Kayleigh: 'I, Lara Bloom, am just the girl to lead the girls' football team to one hundred matches unbeaten.'

Tears filled my eyes. I let the team down by not showing up. I let EVERYONE down. Including myself.

This morning it was about gratitude. At the end of her long post she put, as an example to the rest of us:

Kayleigh: Dear Universe, I am grateful to be alive, and to have good friends and a family.

Anaya: Dear goddesses, I'm grateful that Miss Simpson said we're going to have the party whether or not the girls win Match 100. I can't wait!

I'm glad she didn't put whether they won or lost. I'm not ready to find out.

Becky: Dear God, I'm grateful for the opportunity I just had to slam a door in Paige's face!

I couldn't help a cackle of laughter.
Does this mean they're still my friends?

3.04 p.m.
Caiden just texted me!!!

Caiden: Aldersfield beat us only 3-1 yesterday. You owe me an apology for your lack of faith in us.

I was impressed. I immediately went on the school website to see who had scored. It was Caiden. To get a goal against Aldersfield is FANTASTIC! And to stop Aldersfield from scoring more than three goals is even more amazing. The Prince's Park Academy boys must have played *well*.

Then I cringed. Surely Caiden has read my journal just like everyone else. Even if he decided not to be nosey and chose not to read it, everyone would have told him what was in it. There's no way he doesn't know about my big, fat, pathetic crush on him!

I didn't reply to his text.

3.55 p.m.

I emerged from my room today a few minutes after my last entry. Danny had just got home from school and he was nice to me, which shows just how worried my family has been about me.

He must have texted Mum, Dad and Jay because twenty minutes later Dad was home, which is *very* early for him, and he said he was going to order pizza. Dad never orders takeaway. He says it's a waste of money, and home-cooked food is better.

Dad and Danny let me choose the toppings. Gee whizz! Maybe I should have catastrophic disasters more often!!

Jay showed up a few minutes after Dad. I wasn't ready to see anybody except family, but I realised I didn't feel any more embarrassed at the sight of Jay than I did at the sight of Danny and Dad. We went up to my room to talk in private.

'What's this?' Dad called after us. 'Boys thinking they can prance into my only daughter's room?'

'It's just Jay,' I called back, rolling my eyes.

Jay gave me a funny look but didn't say anything. I shut the door.

Nala was all over Jay. I think she has cabin fever after being cooped up with just me for three days.

Jay picked her up and gave her a cuddle. 'It stinks in here,' he observed. His gaze found Nala's litter tray. Then he looked at me. 'Why're you off school?'

I stared at him. 'Is that a serious question?'

'Nobody cares about your journal. Seriously, what's the big deal? It wasn't that embarrassing.'

It's official: *Boys are a DIFFERENT SPECIES!*

'Just because *you* don't care doesn't mean *nobody* cares. You might not see me any differently but other people will.'

Jay sat on my bed. Nala purred loudly, stretching out on his lap.

'So you really like Caiden, huh?' he asked with a smirk.

I glared at him.

'Okay, okay, I won't bring up anything that was in the journal.'

'Um, how much of it did you read?'

'All of it.'

'WHY?'

'Well, everyone was making it sound all juicy. It took me two days to get through it. It's always interesting to know what's going on in the minds of girls.'

I slapped his shoulder. 'I can't believe you read it!'

'There were some parts of it that were a bit . . . odd . . .'

'We're not talking about this, Jay.'

'Okay, okay. Well, you should keep it up, but you shouldn't publish it on that website because then you don't get paid. Start a YouTube channel or something and at least make some money off your bizarreness.'

I slapped his shoulder again.

Jay looked at my hand on his shoulder.

I quickly snatched it away. For some reason I remembered Kayleigh saying the other day, *Jay is getting kind of cute.*

That's when I noticed his eyes. I've always known that Jay has light brown eyes. They're unusual since he's dark-skinned. But I've never cared about them before.

I blinked.

I still don't care, I told myself.

I looked at Nala. For some reason, it felt safer to look at her than Jay.

I frowned. Jay has always been, and always will be, 'safe'.

Suddenly I felt really confused. Is this what happens when you have a personal crisis? You start noticing stupid things about safe people?

Or maybe it's just because of what Paige said about me having a crush on him. WHICH I DO NOT!

'Anyway,' Jay said. 'The team –'

'Don't tell me the score!'

He shrugged. 'Okay. Well, the party's tomorrow in the school gym.'

I felt my shoulders slump. I can't believe I abandoned my teammates.

'Are you going to come?' Jay asked.

'No way. I don't deserve to go.'

Jay gave me an incredulous look. 'But you're the captain and the top goal-scorer.'

'You don't understand . . .'

'I do understand, Lara,' Jay said gently. 'You care too much about what other people think. Screw them and live your life.'

4.20 p.m.

A few minutes after Jay left, Danny burst into my room without knocking.

'Oops,' he said when I glared at him. 'I thought you might have shoved the wardrobe against the door again. I didn't expect to actually get in.'

'What do you want?' I asked dully.

'Your team –'

'DON'T TELL ME!' I shouted.

But he told me anyway, because, unlike Jay, Danny NEVER respects my wishes.

'They didn't win yesterday.'

I think my heart actually stopped. A numb horror washed over me.

Then Danny smirked and said, 'Luckily for you, the match was called off halfway through because the pitch was waterlogged. You have a chance to redeem yourself. Miss Simpson even called to ask if you'll come. Dad told her he wasn't going to ask you because he didn't want you feeling pressured into going.'

I just stared at him for a moment. Then relief shot through me like a shooting star, lighting up, ever so slightly, the darkness that has been living in my heart since Monday.

Then I frowned. 'Don't get my hopes up, Danny. If this isn't true –'

He held up his phone. He had the results up on the screen.

I looked.

We're down 2–1. Lottie scored a goal in the first few minutes, then Steph Gonzales scored an own goal (??? 🙈), then Westlake High scored just before half-time.

Under the goal information were the words 'Play suspended due to rain'.

For the first time in my life, I owe the rain my gratitude. It's given me a second chance. (Hey, it's about time I got some good luck.)

'When are they playing the rest of the match?' I asked.

'Four thirty today in Walton Park. I've already called a taxi for you.'

Walton Park is at least half an hour away, but I knew I had to try to make it. I jumped up from my bed and started looking for my kit and football boots.

I must have looked a bit nervous, because Danny said, 'And don't worry about anyone saying anything. If anyone tries to mess with you, they'll have me to deal with.'

'Why are you being so nice?' I asked.

Danny paused. Then he said, 'I guess I *am* being nice,' as if he hadn't realised. Then he ruined it by saying, 'Don't get used to it. You're good at football, and you deserve to be at that match. But as soon as it ends, everything goes back to normal.'

4.55 p.m.

OMG, I'm BAWLING!!!

We're in the taxi now, almost at Walton Park, and I can't believe I get a chance to play.

(I high-fived my poster of the Lionesses before leaving. I need all the luck I can get.)

7.13 p.m.

The whole school must have been at that match to support us.

The turnout was *in*credible.

I arrived with just fifteen minutes left until the end. It was still 2–1.

Miss Simpson's jaw actually dropped when she saw me. She didn't even say anything to me. She just yelled to the referee that she wanted to make a substitution.

The ref blew her whistle and I ran onto the pitch.

I was SO SHOCKED when the whole crowd started cheering and chanting my name.

Lara!

Lara!

Lara!

I blocked them out though. Stuff like that is nice, but it can be really distracting. I blocked out everything: the crowd, my published journal, the fact that I had just fifteen minutes to score. I didn't even bother to check if Caiden was there. I honestly didn't care. I'm done caring so much that I forget who *I* am.

I did notice all the cameras though. There had to be at least five of them. I'd totally forgotten about the media interest!

I almost teared up when all the Prince's Park Academy players rushed over. I couldn't look any of them in the eyes as they all gathered around me, asking if I was okay.

'I'm so sorry I wasn't there yesterday,' I forced out around a huge lump in my throat. 'You guys did great to hold them to 2–1. I should have been there –'

I was silenced by Lottie saying, 'Shut up, Lara!' and throwing her arms around my neck in a tight hug. 'You're here now, so let's get cracking. I've almost scored a few times so we're close, but that Westlake goalkeeper is really on form today.'

Then all the other girls joined us, and it was one ENORMOUS group hug. The only reason I didn't cry was because I REALLY needed to stay focused.

The match restarted and Westlake scored right away.

At that point, I figured it was over. It was 3–1, and we didn't have much time.

Then I heard a voice shout, 'Namaste, Lara. You can score!' Kayleigh!

I burst into laughter. Is 'namaste' her new word now?

For some reason, that snapped me out of my fear and completely took the pressure off me. I might be the team captain, which is a pretty serious duty. But I'm also just a girl with a whole bunch of insecurities who has spent the past few weeks trying to glow up with disastrous results. It really is a wonder that I, of all people, have been the league's top goal-scorer for two years and that my team and I have been unbeaten for ninety-nine matches.

So I yelled to the team to just have fun. I told them that ninety-nine matches unbeaten is still amazing.

And I said we're already record-breakers, no matter what happens.

Next thing I knew, I had the ball and I was within shooting distance of the goal. Lottie was closer though. I was about to pass to her, but she yelled at me to shoot. She did have two defenders marking her, so I figured she was right.

The Westlake goalkeeper, Sofia Harley, is a small, willowy girl with curly red hair, and she's the reason Westlake does so well. Their team is really good, but Sofia is *fantastic*. She's always stopping people from scoring. She was covering the right corner of the net so I kicked the ball as hard as I could to the left corner. She dived across the goal line and actually managed to get there in time 😳. She almost caught it, but then she fumbled. Next thing, the ball was in the back of the net.

3–2.

The crowd started screaming and cheering, but I felt like I was in my own private bubble, listening to it all as though from far away.

None of the team celebrated. Everyone just ran back into position. We needed one more goal.

As soon as the ball was back in play, we all charged the Westlake players. Bisi did an amazing sliding tackle and passed the ball to Jamila, who crossed it to Lottie.

I began to run. I covered, like, half the pitch in no time at all to help Lottie, who was surrounded by Westlake players but was still managing to stay on the ball. As soon as I was close enough, she passed to me and I kicked it to Heather. She's a defender, so she was way out of position, but I didn't care. Everyone had to try and score.

She blasted the ball towards the goal and Sofia punched it out (I told you she's good).

I jumped up and headed it, and it went flying into the back of the net.

3–3.

This time, the team lost it. Everyone surrounded me in another big group hug, and I realised how much it meant to them when I saw that most of them were crying.

As the captain, I sometimes feel like I'm the only one who really cares about our matches. And Lottie too. She's pretty much a co-captain, if I'm honest.

'We've done it!' Heather screamed. I could barely hear her over all the noise from the crowd.

Lottie started jumping up and down and we all followed suit, still in a group hug, clinging to each other in disbelief.

It took the referee blowing her whistle three times to get us out of our tangle and back into the game.

I would have been happy with 3–3. Over the moon, in fact. We'd achieved our goal. We didn't have to win. We just had to be unbeaten.

But when the match restarted, the Westlake defenders got stroppy with me. Kirsty had kicked the ball to me all the way from near the halfway line, but I didn't really care about scoring. I was just waiting for the final whistle to blow and end the match, so I was dribbling past the Westlake defenders, having fun. I passed to Lottie after getting past three defenders, and one of them had the AUDACITY to blatantly kick me in the shin when I didn't even have the ball any more!!

The referee blew and stabbed a finger at the penalty spot.

Our school friends and family members roared with pure joy. There was so much screaming and chanting that I could barely think straight. It was completely chaotic (but awesome too).

I nodded to Lottie to take the penalty – two goals each seemed fair. But fortune must really have been smiling on me today, because she threw the ball to me. 'You might as well go out with a hat-trick,' she called.

And that's when I remembered my daydream: scoring a hat-trick in Match 100. Caiden falling in love with me and asking me to be his girlfriend. Our first kiss.

It all seemed so silly now.

If I scored this penalty, it was for me, and for the team. *Not* to make Caiden like me.

I still didn't know if he was there watching, and I didn't care.

As I set the ball on the penalty spot, I vowed that I would never try so hard to impress anyone ever again.

I am a footballer, I told myself, walking away from the ball and picking the spot in the goal that I was going to aim for. *And if I ever decide not to be, it won't be because I'm trying to get someone to like me.*

Mental images of my last penalty flashed through my mind. Rain. Wild hair. Sienna's taunt. Me missing the penalty.

'So what?' I muttered, shrugging it off.

The referee blew and I kicked.

Sofia was a blur of red hair, flashing across the goal-mouth. She stretched out a hand and whacked the ball away, but I ran forward and kicked it past her into the net.

My teammates all jumped on me and I fell to the ground, winded, but happier than I'd ever been in my life.

The ref blew for the end of the match, and our friends and family swarmed onto the pitch. Thankfully, Dad and Danny got to me first.

'Our taxi is waiting,' Danny said, tugging me to my feet and away from everyone. 'Let's go.'

I was relieved because I wasn't ready to talk to anyone.

My phone buzzed all the way home. So many people from school were texting me. The only text I read was Jay's: Well done, Lara 👏 👏 👏. You and the team did great!

I replied: Thanks 😊

Then I checked to see if Anaya, Becky or Kayleigh had texted.

They hadn't.

When we got home Mum was waiting, and so were our pizzas. My family expected me to grab a few slices and take them up to my room, but I decided to sit with them at the table, and Mum hugged me really tight for ages before we started to eat.

I'm SO GLAD I was able to play today.

Random info:
I've found a couple of meanings for 'Namaste':
- Greetings to you
- The divine light in me bows to the divine light in you
- When you and I bow to our true nature, we are one
- I honour the place in you that is the same as it is in me

This ⇧ is all *so* Kayleigh!

8.28 p.m.
Anaya, Kayleigh and Becky showed up around seven forty-five. (By then I'd taken out Nala's litter tray and my room was less smelly.)

They all hugged me and didn't say anything about my journal. I supposed that meant I was forgiven for my carelessness – and anything not so nice that I might have written about them.

After the hug, they went on and on, gushing about the match. I didn't know what to say. I just sat there on my bed, feeling slightly awkward.

Then Anaya nudged Kayleigh and Becky, and they stopped talking about it.

'Well,' Kayleigh said after a short silence, 'are you coming to the party tomorrow?'

'You have to come,' Anaya said. 'This is your chance for a fierce comeback.'

'Yeah,' Becky agreed. 'You need to walk into that gym tomorrow evening looking like an independent goddess queen who's a supermodel!'

We all giggled.

It felt so GOOD to giggle.

Suddenly, I wondered if shutting out my friends and family had been the right thing to do. Maybe I would have overcome my shame much quicker if I hadn't. I'll never know. But I wanted to be alone and I did what I thought was best for me. I can't beat myself up for doing what I thought was best in the moment.

'There's a metaphor in this situation,' Kayleigh said. 'The party is for one hundred matches unbeaten. Well, you need to come and show the world that *you* are unbeaten, both on and off the pitch.'

I couldn't help a smile.

'So are you coming?' Anaya asked. 'There's something I made the school order that I really want you to see.'

'Yeah, this is your chance to show them that you're not going to let what happened break you,' Becky chimed in.

'Yeah,' Anaya agreed. 'Hold your head high and people will have no choice but to put some RESPECT on your name!'

They all laughed. I didn't this time. Since they were now kind of referring to the journal fiasco, I decided I had to address it.

'I'm really sorry I was so careless –' I began.

'It's fine,' Anaya cut in. 'We know it was a mistake. Just be more careful, please. By the way, we only read the bits that included us. We didn't read anything else. We did a search of our names and only read those entries.'

'Uh, I read all of it,' Kayleigh admitted.

'How did you search it?' I asked. 'I unpublished it on Monday.'

Kayleigh gave me a pitying look. 'Someone downloaded it to this website . . .'

I wanted to scream. My journal is STILL out there?

'People can highlight their favourite parts too,' she informed me, 'and add comments.'

'What?'

When Jay told me it'd taken him two days to read my journal, I'd assumed there must be a printed copy that people were passing around. This is MUCH worse than that.

'Everyone's been having a right laugh about some of the pretty dark stuff you wrote about Sienna,' Kayleigh said. 'I knew you didn't like her, but even I was surprised.'

I frowned. I was about to ask 'What dark stuff?' when Anaya said, 'Don't worry, we're going to figure out who made the website and make them delete it.'

'I asked Lottie if she can hack it and take it down,' Kayleigh added. 'She said she'll try.'

I wanted to ask her what part of my journal she considered 'dark', then I decided that I didn't want to talk about it. Mortification was rising in my throat like bile at the thought of people not only reading my private thoughts, but highlighting and commenting on them too.

I sighed. 'Everyone knows about our glow up and your crushes now. Not just mine. Has everyone been looking at you funny?'

'Yeah,' Becky said. 'But Kayleigh is used to that. It's a bit new for me and Anaya though.' She shrugged. 'Richard Skelley asked me to go to the arcade with him on Saturday.'

'What? My embarrassment is totally paying off for you guys. First I fall and pave the way for Liam and Anaya, then I publish my stupid journal and set up Becky and Richard.' I growled long and hard and Nala meowed in a way that sounded like a telling-off.

My friends laughed.

'Well,' Anaya said, 'we thought you might be interested to know that Paige was reading out portions of your journal in the lunch room on Tuesday, and Caiden told her to stop.'

She was right. That *was* interesting. But it only meant that Caiden still thought Paige was the one who hated me instead of seeing through Sienna's act.

But maybe Sienna is innocent. After all, everything she's done to traumatise me is historic. She hasn't done anything directly mean for ages. Okay, she's done petty things, like that 'peep' incident with Mr Savage, that taunt when I was about to take a penalty the other week, and what happened at the art festival. But my only real gripe against her at the moment is that she clearly likes Caiden. I can hardly blame her for that though. Caiden is so cute 🐾

'So, are you coming tomorrow?' Becky asked.

'We'll have your back if anyone tries to tease you,' Kayleigh promised. 'And I'm sure Jay and Caiden will too.'

I sighed. 'I'll think about it.'

Self-knowledge Questions
What is your biggest strength?
I don't know. Football?
What is your biggest weakness?
Recently, it's caring too much about what other people think. (Thanks, Jay, for pointing that out.)

15

That Takes the Cake

Friday 21 September, 5.43 p.m.
Dear Diary,

You'll never guess what is happening right now!

I'm having my hair and make-up done – by a PROFESSIONAL!

But before I get into all that, let me tell you everything that's happened today and how I got to this point.

Once again, I couldn't bring myself to go to school this morning. I know the match went well yesterday, but it doesn't change the fact that everyone has read my journal and probably thinks I'm completely pathetic. Thankfully, Mum said I can have one last day off then I have to go back on Monday. She also said going to the party tonight could be a good way of easing myself back into 'school life', so that going to school on Monday won't feel quite as scary.

I'd already decided that I should probably go to the party anyway. I don't have to stay long. I can just show my face then leave as soon as it feels like too much.

Mum asked if I'd like to 'work through what happened' with a therapist. She said, 'Mr Griffiths said you have a severe dislike of Sienna. It might help you deal with that.'

I don't have a 'severe dislike' of Sienna. I'm just wary of her after all the things she's done. I even said in my journal, a few days ago, that I WOULD LIKE TO BE FRIENDS WITH HER AGAIN, so why is everyone acting so weird? First the school tried to force me to get professional help, then Kayleigh called my journal 'dark', and now my parents have offered me therapy. My journal can't be any worse than anyone else's my age!!

Seriously, they should offer their psychological assessments to people like Angelica Locke, who carry out full-blown assassination attempts during football matches . . .

I told Mum I didn't want to 'work through what happened with a therapist,' but that I'd let her know if I changed my mind. She didn't go to work today. She said she's off tomorrow too and that she would like us to 'spend some time together'.

After school, Anaya, Becky and Kayleigh came over to get ready with me. I was shocked when Kemi showed up too. She said Mum asked her to come and do my hair and make-up.

My mum, who doesn't like me wearing lipstick, hired me a beautician for a school party?!

'Your mum doesn't get the fact that I have other clients,' Kemi moaned, unpacking a box of make-up. She winked at me. 'It's a good thing you're my favourite cousin.'

Mum has probably told her about the journal fiasco.

'What's that?' Anaya asked, pointing at something on the centre table.

It looked like some kind of scroll. It was secured with a pretty red ribbon. I went to have a look and saw that it had my name on it. 'Ha, ha, very funny,' I said. 'Which one of you put it there?'

'I didn't,' Anaya said.

Becky and Kayleigh denied it too. I can tell when my friends are up to something, and they weren't up to anything now. They were telling the truth.

I unscrolled the little roll.

It was a letter written in gorgeous cursive writing.

Dear Lara Bloom,

Thank you for your letter of Wednesday 5 September. I am writing to say that I'm not trying to embarrass you. You embarrass me by not letting me be myself. By trying to make me conform and be just like all the other hair types.

I stand on end instead of lying flat because who wants to lie down all day and be an obedient little goody two shoes? In a world where most hair grows downward, I point to the sky. I frizz and puff up because it's in the nature of my magical disulphide bonds.

I need so much time and attention because I'm precious, and I'm showing you that precious things require investment. You are precious, so you deserve time and attention too, but you don't need to depend on getting those things from a boy. Give them to yourself.

You and I are not supposed to conform. We are a formidable team, and together we're supposed to break down barriers and disrupt the status quo.

My dearest Lara, I'm the crown you can't take off, which means you're always and forever a queen.

Sincerely,

Your Afro hair

Mum wrote it. It had Mum written ALL OVER IT!

'That is *so* sweet!' Becky exclaimed. 'Oh my goodness, I'm going to cry.'

'It's the part about "the crown you can't take off" for me,' Kayleigh said. 'It must be from your mum.'

Anaya and Kemi took the letter from me and reread it silently.

Kemi smiled when she finished. 'Gosh, I love Aunt Rachel.'

I couldn't deny that it was sweet. But it means that Mum has read my journal.

No WONDER she wants us to spend time together!

Somebody just SHOOT ME NOW!!

It never occurred to me that Mum and Dad might figure out how to access my journal and see why I was so depressed, but of course they would. They're probably shocked that I want to be adopted by Naomi Campbell.

Before guilt could take me over, the doorbell rang. I turned to the window and saw my friends' mums at the door, all in wigs and brightly coloured sequined clothes.

'What in the world . . . ?!' Becky exclaimed.

'Did you know they were coming?' I asked.

'No!' my friends chorused.

I stepped out of the living room to answer the door, and stopped dead at the sight of Mum coming down the stairs in a huge Afro wig and a skimpy silver dress.

'Mum!' I cried. 'What are you doing? Please get changed!'

'Are you going out or something?' Anaya asked.

'Later,' Mum said, 'but first we have a job to do.' She opened the door for the other mums and they scuttled into the house on their high heels.

Kayleigh looked mortified by her mum's black leather hot pants.

'You girls forgot an important female stereotype,' Anaya's mum said.

'It's "archetype",' my mum corrected.

Anaya's mum giggled. 'Sorry, Rach. I've already had a few glasses of rosé.' Then she turned back to us. 'Girls, how can you have a glow up based on female archetypes without including THE DIVA?!'

'I love it!' Kemi said. 'You all look fabulous!'

Like I said, Kemi is TOO NICE!

'Give us a twirl and tell us who you are,' Kemi said.

Now she was just encouraging them.

Kemi pointed at my mum. 'Let me guess, you're Whitney Houston.'

'The queen of divas herself,' Mum confirmed with a nod.

'I'm Faye Wong,' Becky's mum said with a twirl.

Kayleigh's mum struck a pose. 'Madonna.'

We looked at Anaya's mum. 'Diana Ross,' we chorused.

'You bet!' she said.

My friends and I exchanged looks as our mums strutted into the living room. Soon they were playing 'I Wanna Dance With Somebody' and dancing in ways that mums should NEVER dance.

'Shall we go upstairs?' I asked.

My friends all nodded.

'So, how do you want your hair?' Kemi asked when we got to my room.

I considered it for a moment, then I showed her a picture I downloaded to my phone last night. I wasn't completely sure about it, but Kemi loved it and said she had everything we needed to recreate it.

'What if I don't like it?' I asked her. I glanced at the time on my phone. I had time for trying two hairstyles, but did Kemi?

She assured me that she did.

I decided to kick my friends out, in case I didn't like it. I didn't want any pressure from them about going 'au naturel'. After my mum's letter, I knew they would want me to.

Huffily, my friends grabbed their party clothes and stalked out to change downstairs. Once they'd gone, I sat down and decided I might as well journal about all this now, while Kemi worked. She took a spray bottle out of her very big bag of hair and make-up supplies, went to fill it with water, then got started. She sprayed so much water on my hair that I started getting worried, because I know what water does to it. Then she used a whole bunch of other products and teased it a whole lot. But I don't know what it looks like yet because she said I'm not allowed to look in the mirror until 'the transformation is complete'.

The whole time, we could hear my friends singing off-key with our 'diva' mums downstairs.

Right now, Kemi's doing my make-up. She said she doesn't mind me journaling while she works. Apparently, a lot of her clients work on their laptops or take business calls while she does their hair and make-up.

Ooh, she just finished.

I'm finally allowed to look in the mirror.

Wish me luck!!!

6.45 p.m.

I am in AWE of Kemi!

My hair is *exactly* like the picture I showed her. I felt practically giddy as I studied my reflection in the mirror, admiring her handiwork. She's stuck faux flowers throughout my big, bold mass of tight coils, and it looks so cool.

My make-up is amazing too. Not too heavy, except for the dramatic eyeliner and metallic blue eyeshadow. I even have lashes and contouring and highlighter!!! I have NEVER looked this good in my entire life. I can hardly even recognise myself.

Confession: I actually feel pretty!

After hugging Kemi tightly and gushing about what a fabulous job she's done, I slipped into my royal blue, off-the-shoulder mini-dress – my favourite for parties.

Then I stood before my mirror again and decided to really look at my hair. Over the past few days, I've been wondering why I feel so negatively about it and how to change that. I think I was frustrated by my hair for the same reason I wanted to give up football: I was trying to fit into a mould I was never intended for.

The funny thing is, until recently, I didn't care much about my hair. I hardly even thought about it at all, which is why a bun became my signature style.

I decided, as I looked in the mirror, that my hair is actually pretty cool. I'm only embarrassed when it shrinks in the rain or frizzes every which way because I've been worrying about what other people might think. But, like Jay said, I need to stop caring so much about that.

Kemi came to stand beside me, meeting my gaze in the mirror. "What are you thinking?"

I shrugged. "I've never really appreciated my hair."

Kemi smiled. "Our hair plays by a different set of rules."

"Tell me about it. I never know what to do with it."

"Then learn."

I stared at Kemi in the mirror. Two simple words, yet so profound.

I've been so stressed out by my hair, acting like it's the source of all my problems and is ruining my life, when all I had to do was LEARN!!

Learn how to take care of it and how to style it. Learn about what it needs to thrive.

"I can teach you, if you want," Kemi offered. "Check out my natural hair blog and call me any time you have questions. You have such gorgeous, thick hair, Lara. There's so much you can do with it."

"Thanks, Kemi."

"You're welcome." She took out her phone. "Now, smile."

I obeyed and she took a picture for Instagram. She captioned it: My gorgeous cousin again. Released her 'fro and adorned it with flowers xx 😜

Downstairs, the living room came to a standstill when I walked in.

My mum recovered first. 'Lara! You look AMAZING!'

'Your mum was right,' Becky said. 'It *is* a crown. You look like a queen.'

'She looks like a straight-up GODDESS!' Kayleigh gushed.

Anaya beamed. 'Lara Bloom's hair has bloomed.'

'Yes! What glorious hair!' Kayleigh's mum exclaimed. 'You go to that party, Lara Bloom, and knock 'em dead. Ignore anyone who isn't supportive of your glow up, and always remember that you have allies. We are your allies.'

I giggled. *Allies?* What was this? A war?

I suppose that, in a sense, life does feel more like a war than anything else sometimes. But after what Jay said yesterday, I'm not sure how much of the war is external and how much of it is against myself and my own thoughts.

I grinned at my friends. 'You all look gorgeous.' And

I meant it. Kayleigh's multicoloured dress is pretty zany and 'out there' but it's perfect for her and she looks amazing in it. Becky's yellow dress looks stunning on her and she's twisted her hair into a gorgeous messy updo. And Anaya looks incredible in a white dress with lacy sleeves.

Mum actually started to cry. 'You girls are all so beautiful,' she sobbed. 'No matter what kind of hair you have, and no matter if the boys you have crushes on like you back.'

I couldn't believe she was CRYING!

Becky's mum hugged her. Then 'Material Girl' by Madonna came on and they all started singing.

Kemi offered to drive us to the party, and we left them to it. My friends just told me that our mums are going to a karaoke bar while we're at the party. Ha! Whichever bar they go to won't know what hit them!

We're in Kemi's car now, on our way to the party. We're almost there. I'm SO EXCITED!!!

7.34 p.m.

As soon as we got to school, I was ushered backstage to where the rest of the team were waiting. I was just in time. The team were all hugging and I immediately joined them.

'How amazing was yesterday?' Tasha said.

'You mean, how amazing was the last two and a half years,' I said.

Lottie sighed heavily. 'We deserve this party. I'm going to gorge myself on profiteroles and drink a whole bowl of punch.'

Everyone laughed.

'GOOD EVENING, ZOMBIES!' a voice boomed, ruining our moment. It sounded like Richard Skelley. 'We are gathered here in honour of our girls' football team. But first, the teachers would like me to announce that anyone who misbehaves tonight will be escorted off the premises by Mr Griffiths. And now for our amazing football stars. SHOW THEM SOME LOVE!!!'

Applause broke out.

When we walked onto the stage, the first thing I saw was a humongous football cake positioned on a stand across the hall. It was three tiers of footballs and I knew immediately that that was what Anaya had wanted me to see. It was incredible!

The hall was also decorated really nicely. Mini footballs festooned the walls and there were balloon garlands everywhere. Unfortunately they were in our school colours, maroon and yellow, but they were still impressive.

There were footballs all around the stage, and the team and I began to kick them about and do tricks (in our pretty dresses and high heels).

Everyone clapped, then Richard Skelley approached

us with a microphone and began to interview us. We'd nominated one girl from each year to do the talking. Lottie was the nominee for Year 10.

I didn't want to speak, but after chatting with the nominees, Richard turned to me. 'Lara, first of all, love the hair. Now, you've been captain since May and have led the team to this amazing achievement of one hundred games unbeaten. Congratulations. How do you feel?'

My throat closed up with sudden nerves, but I managed to force out some words. 'I feel great.'

'To conclude this interview, do you have any words for your teammates?'

'Just well done, girls, and . . . here's to two hundred?'

The gym erupted with cheers.

After that, the party began and we could get off the stage, thank goodness!

My friends descended on me and we headed to the drinks table. I was thinking I would stay five minutes then leave. When I told my friends, they were not impressed.

'Don't be ridiculous,' Kayleigh scolded.

'That hair deserves much more than five minutes in the limelight,' Becky added.

'Well, if it isn't poor little Lara,' came a sugary-sweet voice behind me.

My friends and I spun around and came face to face with Sienna and her friends. It was Paige who'd said that.

The three of them looked flawless. Sienna was wearing

a red dress that fit her like it had been painted on. She looked incredible. Molly's auburn hair was in ringlets. Paige's gold eyeshadow matched her nails and stiletto heels.

Paige's eyes lowered to my chest. 'It seems Lara Bloom is far from *blooming*. In fact, she's been relying on external help.'

I was about to tell Paige to get out of my face when Sienna turned on her.

'Leave her alone, Paige,' Sienna snapped. 'She's been through enough.'

Paige looked shocked. But she wasn't as shocked as I was.

Sienna gave me a little smile then walked off. Paige and Molly followed.

I looked at my friends. 'Was that a hallucination?' I asked.

'No,' Anaya said. 'It was real. Sienna defended you.'

'Maybe she isn't that bad after all,' I said.

Kayleigh wrinkled her nose. 'Just be careful. I don't trust her.'

Lottie sidled up to me. 'I heard what Paige just said. That was body-shaming and it isn't right. We can form a resistance group. Flat-chested girls strike back!'

'You're not flat-chested,' Anaya pointed out.

'Yeah, well, you don't have to be flat-chested to fight for flat-chested people,' she replied.

I couldn't believe we were standing in the school gym at a party, DISCUSSING MY FLAT-CHESTEDNESS!!!

I noticed that quite a few people had gathered around us. All girls.

'Does it work?' one of them asked. I didn't know her name. I think she was from the year below.

'Does what work?' I asked.

'Planting your, uh, boobs.'

Weirdly, they all looked like they were genuinely interested in my answer.

I turned and walked away so fast I didn't even look where I was going . . . then I slammed right into something.

I realised, as it wobbled precariously and a few bits of icing sprinkled onto the floor, that it was the FOOTBALL CAKE!

Quickly, I tried to steady it, but I slipped on a bit of icing. I grabbed the stand to steady myself. BIG MISTAKE! All three tiers came crashing down, splatting icing and jammy sponge cake all over me, and I let out a hair-raising scream.

It must have all happened in about three seconds, but time seemed to STAND STILL, with everything moving in SLOW MOTION. I now know what it must be like to be stuck in an avalanche. I couldn't see a thing; I could hardly even breathe as the cake smothered me.

Who knew cake could kill?

I tried to drag myself to my feet, but the cake stand had fallen on me too and it was crushing me to the floor. Eventually two teachers picked their way through the mess and lifted the cake stand off me.

The hall was silent as I stood up. Dua Lipa was blasting from the speakers, but all chatter and laughter had ceased. Hundreds of pairs of eyes were fixed on me.

The first shocked face I saw was Caiden's.

I *hate* myself! 😫😫😫😫

16

Hack-Tricks

Friday 21 September, 7.53 p.m.
I'm a disaster, dear Diary. An ABSOLUTE DISASTER!
I don't know why I thought I could have a glow up.
Everything about it has been completely and utterly
DISASTROUS.

All the reasons why I'm rubbish:

- I'm clumsy.
- I'm stupid (only a stupid person publishes their own
  journal and walks into a three-tier football cake).
- I ALWAYS find a way to sabotage myself (proved
  once again by the journal fiasco. Not to mention that
  I got all dressed up tonight, only to almost commit
  suicide by cake!).
- I'm a lost cause. None of the female archetypes was
  enough to help me.

- I'm hiding in the girls' toilets at a school party, covered in cake. It's everywhere! I'll never get it all off. My friends are outside the cubicle, telling me to come out. Why do they even care about me any more? Haven't I proved to them enough times that I'm not worthy of friendship? I'm nothing more than a big, fat EMBARRASSMENT!!

9 p.m.

SO MUCH HAS HAPPENED!!!

I've sneaked into an empty classroom to tell you all about it, and I'm using the voice note function as that's much quicker.

So . . . I was in the toilets, trying to clean myself up a bit with the help of my friends, when Lottie came in and said Jay was standing outside the door and wanted to speak to me urgently. I didn't want to talk to him in the hallway where anyone passing could gawk at me and my ruined dress, so we went outside. It was almost completely dark, and I was thankful for that.

I didn't want to see Jay's eyes clearly in case I got that weird feeling again.

'I've been thinking about some of the stuff in your journal,' Jay said. 'Odd stuff that didn't really sound like you.'

I glared at him. 'I'd rather not talk about my journal, Jay.'

'Parts where you said you wanted Sienna to die, and that she's so beautiful you wish you were her.'

I frowned. 'What?'

'Exactly.'

'I've never wanted to be Sienna! I definitely haven't wished *death* on her.'

Jay paused, letting it all sink in for me. As if my journal wasn't already embarrassing enough, someone had added EXTRA STUFF to it. Terrible stuff that made me look evil and jealous. No wonder Mr Griffiths had offered me counselling. No wonder Mum and Dad had been so worried and horrified. No wonder Kayleigh had said she was surprised at some of the 'dark' things I'd written!

I didn't write them!

'That note in your locker from your secret admirer was weird too,' he said. 'Any guesses who it might be?'

The question startled me, because it made me realise something. SOMETHING SO INCREDIBLY OBVIOUS!!! I received that note from my 'secret admirer' the day my journal was posted all over the school. What if it wasn't from a secret admirer who'd truly wanted me to have a great day? What if it was from someone who was being sarcastic and taunting me?

'Sienna!' I screamed, remembering my chat with her about journaling.

I probably sounded like a movie villain. I clenched my fists and waved them at the sky, so I must have looked like one too. My dirty dress and messy hair no doubt added to the whole effect, but I didn't care.

'Arrrgghh,' I growled, pure liquid RAGE coursing through my blood. 'I'm so glad that Sienna couldn't help taunting me and had to blow her own cover by sending that note. It's made it mind-bogglingly easy to figure out the truth.'

'I suppose it's a good thing I read your journal after all,' Jay said.

Anaya popped her head around the door. 'What's going on?' she asked.

'Are they kissing?' I heard Kayleigh call from behind her.

I was so angry I didn't have the capacity to feel embarrassed. I told my friends what Jay and I had just figured out.

'It does seem possible,' Becky said.

'But that would make Sienna more than just mean. This is a whole new level of conniving, calculating, evil genius,' Anaya said.

'She can't be that much of a genius if we've figured it out. I mean, how obvious can she get? Adding stuff about herself that I didn't write? She should have added stuff about someone else, but she's just so desperate to convince people that I'm jealous of her.'

'Well, you need to prove your complete lack of jealousy,' Kayleigh said. 'If she somehow published your journal and added extra entries to it, everyone needs to know. It's our word against hers – unless we can make her admit it.'

'We'll also make her delete your journal from that website she downloaded it to,' Anaya said. 'If it was her.'

She seemed to be struggling to believe that Sienna was capable of going this far. I was struggling to believe it too. But if there was stuff in my journal that I didn't write, this was the only logical conclusion.

It's not me who needs a psychological assessment. It's Sienna!

'What's the website called?' I asked. I needed to read the fake entries for myself.

My friends exchanged looks.

'What's it called?' I asked again.

'Uh, www.patheticlarabloom.co.uk,' Becky said in a small voice.

Now I wished I hadn't asked. I decided not to go on the website. I refused to give it any more hits!!

'If Sienna really did this,' Anaya said, 'how come she left in all the entries where you talked about the mean things she's done to you over the years? Wouldn't she have taken them out?'

'Who knows?' Kayleigh said. 'Maybe she left them in so it all feels more authentic. I suppose the more entries about her in Lara's journal, the more she can prove that Lara is a jealous hater.'

'Plus,' Jay said, 'why would she take out the part where

Lara wrote about her accusing her of doping, when that could cast doubt on Lara's football abilities?'

I exhaled loudly. I was already getting a HEADACHE from thinking about it all and trying to get into Sienna's twisted mind.

'We shouldn't confront Sienna,' Kayleigh said. 'She'll only cover her tracks. Let's talk to Paige.'

'Why would Paige tell us anything?' Anaya asked. 'She's Sienna's flying monkey, remember?'

'Didn't you see the way Paige looked at Sienna before when she defended Lara?' Kayleigh asked. 'I'm willing to bet that Sienna told Paige to say what she said, then embarrassed her in front of everyone by sticking up for Lara. Paige might be willing to talk. I'll go and get her.'

I didn't know how Kayleigh was planning to get Paige to follow her outside, but she returned a few moments later with Paige in tow.

'This had better be good,' Paige snapped. She stopped short when she saw the rest of us. 'What's going on?'

'Did you publish Lara's journal?' Anaya demanded.

Paige frowned. 'No.'

'Yes, you did!' Anaya yelled. 'You snatched her phone the other day. We know you did something. We're telling Mr Griffiths, and we're also going to get the police involved because what you did was a CYBERCRIME!'

I was about to tell Anaya that she was accusing the wrong person, then I figured out what she was doing.

Paige would be more likely to tell on Sienna if she thought she was about to get the blame for something Sienna had done.

Paige totally cracked. Her face went a deep, dark purply-red, like a BEETROOT, and she opened her mouth and began to tell us everything. She was shaking too. Apparently, Sienna *did* publish my journal. She waited until a few days before Match 100, hoping I would be too upset to play, and she added some nasty entries to make it look like I hated her.

'But why?' Jay asked. He looked bewildered.

'And how?' Becky asked. 'How did she get into Lara's journal?'

Paige only answered Jay's question. 'She hates you,' she told me.

'Why does she hate me?' I demanded. 'What have I ever done to her?'

'You're always getting so much attention because of stupid football!' Paige snapped. Then she ran off, teetering on her stilettos, her hair and skirt billowing after her.

And that's when it dawned on me: FOOTBALL is why Sienna and I stopped being friends.

She was as excited as I was to join the team back in Year 7. Suddenly, she had friends for the first time. Team-mates. But she wasn't very good at football. In fact, Sienna was as bad at football as I am at bowling.

She once scored a hat-trick of OWN GOALS!!! It

was pretty incredible, actually – FOR ALL THE WRONG REASONS! Afterwards, when people teased her, I defended her. But I probably wasn't helping matters because people were praising me for scoring goals (in the right net).

After that REVERSE HAT-TRICK, Sienna was never chosen to play for the team again, much to most people's relief. I felt like she should have been given a chance – how else would she improve? – but she was constantly left on the bench, watching with the other subs, while the rest of us played. She left the team soon after.

Now that I think about it, we didn't 'drift apart'. She stopped speaking to me. I still tried to hang out with her, but she just ignored me. I was so hurt at the time, and so confused because I didn't understand why. I didn't realise it was just because of football – or, more specifically, the attention I was getting because of football. (I don't think she cared that much about football itself.)

'Do you think she'll warn Sienna that we're on to her?' Anaya asked.

Kayleigh snorted. 'No way. Not when she's the one who told us what Sienna did.'

'Well, what do we do now?' I asked.

'We lure Sienna,' Kayleigh supplied. 'We need a full confession from her.'

We all listened while Kayleigh outlined her plan. I hoped it would work.

Step 1 of the plan, 'Lure Sienna', was Jay's job.

'Get Caiden to text Sienna and ask her to meet him in Mr Savage's maths room.' Kayleigh grinned wickedly. 'She'll come running.'

Jay took out his phone and called Caiden. Caiden must have wanted to know why because Jay said, 'Just do it. I'm not setting you up for anything. It's something to do with Lara and her journal getting published. I'll explain later.' He hung up.

A second later, Caiden texted him: Done.

Step 2 of the plan, 'Get Confession from Sienna' was up to me and Anaya.

I was waiting in a shadowy part of the hallway when Sienna arrived for her rendezvous with Caiden. She entered the maths room. I slipped in after her and shut the door behind me.

Sienna spun around. She was holding her phone, and must have been texting Caiden to ask where he was. I couldn't believe how sweet and innocent she'd been acting recently when she had so many tricks up her sleeves. She looked perfectly innocent even now as she blinked her big, blue eyes at me.

Her red dress was immaculate, while my blue dress was a wet, jammy mess. Her make-up was flawless, while mine was all smudged. I guess Sienna needs to eat some make-up, not just wear it, so she can be beautiful on the inside as well. Seriously, how can someone so evil look so innocent?

'Uh, you need to leave,' Sienna told me, glancing over my head to see through the window in the door.

'Caiden isn't coming,' I told her. 'Did you publish my journal?'

Sienna stared at me for a long moment. I thought she was going to deny it.

Then she opened her mouth and screamed. It was long and loud and EAR-PIERCING.

'Let me out,' she said when she finished screaming, 'or I'll do it again.'

'Just tell me the truth. You added nasty entries about yourself to make me look bad, then you published my journal. You did, didn't you?'

Sienna tried to barge past me, but I blocked her. Unfortunately, Miss Simpson looked through the window in the door just then and saw us. She must have come in response to Sienna's scream.

'Leave me alone!' Sienna screamed. 'Miss Simpson! Help!'

I quickly locked the door before Miss Simpson could open it. Soon there were, like, five teachers out there, banging on the door. Now I really needed Sienna to confess or I was going to be in BIG TROUBLE.

'Just tell the truth, Sienna. At least own up to uploading my journal to another website where people could keep reading it even after I unpublished it.'

Sienna smirked and I knew there was no chance that she would ever own up.

It was a good thing Kayleigh had anticipated that and come up with a way to force the truth out of her.

Sienna was still holding her phone. I lunged at her. She probably thought I was going to rag her hair or something, because she lifted her hands in defence, making it easy for me to snatch her phone.

It was unlocked too, with Caiden's text on the screen.

'Give it back!' Sienna yelled.

I ran across the room, then tapped into her journaling app. 'Come any closer and I'm going to publish your journal,' I threatened.

There must have been some pretty juicy stuff in Sienna's journal because she went as white as the stark classroom walls around us.

I had her attention now.

'What did you do?' I asked. 'How did you get into my journal?'

Sienna was quiet. I could tell she was thinking hard, plotting her next move. She turned towards the door.

'Open that door and I'll publish it,' I sang.

She froze. Then she lifted her chin. 'You're going to publish it no matter what I do.'

'No. If you tell me everything, I won't publish it. I promise.'

'I don't believe you.'

'Isn't it worth the risk? All I want you to do is tell the teachers the truth.'

Sienna's gaze sharpened and I knew she'd spotted the loophole in my offer, just as Kayleigh had said she would. 'Deal,' she said.

We were each asking for the other's trust. I was saying I wouldn't publish her journal if she agreed to confess to the teachers. She was promising to confess if I didn't publish it.

'The day Paige snatched your phone, I reset the password of your journaling app then signed back in for you,' Sienna said.

Whoa! That was practically HACKING! She had UNAUTHORISED ACCESS TO MY PERSONAL DATA!! And she could get in ANY TIME SHE WANTED!!! It's a good thing I now use my notes app to journal instead.

'And you added some entries that made me look like I'm jealous of you?' I prompted.

Sienna smiled sweetly. 'Only six.'

'And you downloaded my journal then uploaded it to some website?'

'Yeah. I can take it down if you want.' Her blasé tone told me she was only saying that to get her phone back. 'That's all there is to confess,' Sienna said impatiently. 'Now stick to your end of the bargain.' She held her hand out for her phone.

Slowly, I walked towards her. 'Are you going to confess to the teachers too?'

'Of course,' she said, her gaze on her phone. 'I promised, didn't I?'

I handed over her phone.

Sienna snatched it and stalked to the door. She unlocked it and teachers flooded in, all shouting:

What's going on here, girls?

What on earth has got into you both?

Sienna, are you okay?

'Confession time,' I told Sienna.

Sienna touched a hand to her chest. 'Lara locked me in here. I don't know why. She hates me for *no reason!*'

She was exploiting the loophole.

Thankfully, my friends and I were ten steps ahead of her.

Anaya popped up from under a table at the back of the room, waving her phone. 'I got it all on camera!'

It was time for Step 3 of the plan, 'Expose Sienna'.

We did that right away by playing Anaya's video to the teachers.

Note to self:

• Kayleigh is an absolute genius.

17
SQuIDGE Squad

Friday 21 September, 11.57 p.m.
After my last entry, Anaya texted me saying that Mr
Griffiths wanted to see me. I spent the next twenty minutes
in his office. He wanted to know everything. So I told
him. I also played him Anaya's video. Then I had to wait
outside his office while he spoke to Sienna. Eventually, he
emerged and told me I could return to the party.

The old Lara would have gone home, too embarrassed
to stay after knocking over the cake. But then I realised I
wanted to stay. I wanted to hang out with my friends.
I wanted to dance. I wanted to forget all about the journal
drama and move on.

The new Lara chose to stay.

Kayleigh, who had decided to hang around Mr Griffiths'
office, came running into the party while me and Anaya

were dancing to 'Fight Song' by Rachel Platten (Becky was dancing with Richard Skelley).

'Sienna's mum and dad just picked her up,' Kayleigh told us, eyes wide. 'Mr Griffiths marched them off the premises.'

We danced harder in celebration, attracting lots of amused glances. I even saw Caiden looking our way, but he, thankfully, didn't come over.

When the party ended at eleven o'clock, I found that I'd had so much fun, I didn't want to leave.

Gratitude:
Dear Universe, I'm grateful for the opportunity I had to EXPOSE SIENNA!

Saturday 22 September, 2 p.m.
Me and Mum went for breakfast at this café in town this morning. I had American pancakes with bananas, blueberries and strawberries, drizzled with maple syrup, and with a side of clotted cream. YUM!! Mum had a full English.

Spending time together turned out to be okay. I told her all about the party last night and what happened with Sienna.

My friends said I should have published Sienna's journal after she confessed. Mum asked why I didn't. I told her it was because I can't inflict that kind of pain on someone else after I've been through it and know how it feels. I wouldn't wish it on anyone.

Sienna's mum called me this morning. She was all apologetic for 'bothering me', and said she got my number from Paige. She wanted to speak to Mum. I hovered, eavesdropping, while they chatted about what had happened. Mum was all like, 'Your daughter created a WHOLE WEBSITE to bully my daughter,' and Sienna's mum said she'd told Sienna that if she could use the internet to bully someone, she could use it to apologise too, and that Sienna was going to post an apology on her TikTok. She also asked Mum how I'm doing, which I thought was really sweet of her. I could tell she felt really bad about what Sienna did to me.

Anaya kept an eye on Sienna's TikTok all morning, and shared her apology as soon as it appeared. She also sent it to everyone at school that she had phone numbers for, and told them to share it.

Alex was at ours when me and Mum got back from the café, playing *Call of Duty* with Danny. He took off his headphones when I walked into the living room. 'I didn't know you had a crush on me, Lara,' he said. 'It's a shame that you don't any more. Are you sure you don't?'

#AWKWARD!

I walked away.

I checked this morning, and patheticlarabloom.co.uk has disappeared from the internet. But my journal still lives on in people's minds. You can delete stuff from the internet but you can't erase it from people's brains!!

I've considered starting a vlog, since so many people are so riveted by my life that they read my journal from BEGINNING TO END.

Anyway, the best thing that happened today (after pancakes at that café) is that Danny got into BIG TROUBLE with Mum and Dad for blackmailing me into doing his chores. He now has to do all the chores for TWO WEEKS!

I pointed out to Mum and Dad that I've been doing Danny's chores for almost a whole month, but they said that's my problem since I was so afraid of him telling them about me calling them dictators in my journal that I allowed him to blackmail me.

They have a point. I mean, they've found out now anyway.

Self-knowledge Question
What superpower do you wish you had?
Right now, memory manipulation, so I can make people forget everything they read in my journal!!

Sunday 23 September, 7 p.m.
Got my hair done today. Braids. When Kemi finished, she added little gold cuffs to some of the braids – hair

jewellery. Cool! It's nice and simple, but cute too. It's also rainproof. (We have a match on Wednesday.)

I just went next door to ask Jay if he knows whether Caiden read my journal. He said yes.

Note to self:
- Avoid Caiden like the PLAGUE!!

Monday 24 September, 11 a.m.

Sienna isn't in. She's been suspended for two days!

Mr Griffiths was in assembly this morning to give us all an important message about bullying. He didn't say anything directly about Sienna, but he did remind us that the school has a zero-tolerance policy on all forms of bullying, including cyberbullying.

Self-knowledge Questions
What brings you joy?
Eating yummy food.
Cuddling Nala.
Scoring goals.
What gets on your nerves?
Nosey people.
Nasty people.
Women's football not getting enough attention.
RAIN!

5.16 p.m.

Guess what, dear Diary. I'm in the papers ⚽ ⚽ ⚽

There's a shot of me scoring my header against Westlake High last Thursday, and a whole piece about us being unbeaten for one hundred matches. They called me 'the future of women's football' and said I have a 'stunning flair for the beautiful game' and 'incredible pace and ball control'.

Lottie's interview was included, as well as an interview with Miss Simpson, who they called 'an extraordinary coach'. I agree. She is.

After we'd all read the article, Mum said, 'Your father and I are very proud of you, Lara. But whether or not you're in the papers, we love you and we always will.'

Then Dad hugged me. I couldn't help grinning, but I also felt really embarrassed too.

Tuesday 25 September, 12.27 p.m.

I just got out of English lit. We had to write a free verse poem that doesn't follow any rules of structure or rhyme. I channelled my inner Amanda Gorman and got to work:

> *If you, my crowning hair, were a person,*
> *What would you think of me?*
> *I've talked about you behind your back and to your face.*
> *Said mean things that I didn't mean.*

Maybe I learned it from a beauty industry that exists
To make us feel unworthy.
Empty. Deficient.
They can't make as much money from happy,
    content people
With rock solid self-esteem who know that they rock.

I tried to relax you, but you weren't stressed.
I needed to relax me and rule out the possibility
Of you following any rules. Let you rule.

What if I just loved myself, quirks and all?
What if I didn't compare?
What if I vowed never to say
Any more messed up things about my hair –
Give it a break, before all the negativity breaks
    its spirit?

What if everyone else did the same?

I really wanted to write *'What if Sienna did the same'*, but I figured it was best to leave her out of my poetry.

Anyway, Miss Baldwin liked it. She got me to read it to the rest of the class. When I finished, Jay roared like I'd scored a goal or something and everyone started laughing. It was so funny!

Wednesday 26 September, 5 p.m.

Sienna was back in today. Somehow, she still has lots of friends. The fact that everyone now knows how evil and conniving she is apparently means NOTHING. In fact, she, Paige and Molly came to the match after school with a huge posse.

I ignored them – and the rest of the crowd, which, thankfully, has now dwindled since we've achieved our goal of one hundred matches unbeaten. It was a home match, so it was held in the playing fields behind our school, and it was AWESOME! I can't believe I ever considered quitting football just because of Caiden.

I love playing football!

It's fun. It's exhilarating.

FOOTBALL IS LIFE!

After the match, Caiden came over. I've been avoiding him so hard because I just can't face him, knowing that he knows about my crush on him. We've only seen each other in Mr Savage's maths lessons, and in those I sit at the front. I always come in at the last minute too, and dash away immediately after.

It's been ten days since the journal fiasco. I'm slowly getting over everyone reading it, but not Caiden. I don't know if I'll ever get over him reading my journal. Just the thought of him reading all those gushy entries I wrote about him . . . it makes my head hurt.

I looked around, wondering how to escape as he headed

in my direction, but I knew it would be way too obvious if I just legged it. So I didn't.

But I couldn't look at him.

'You were on fire, Lara,' Caiden said. 'You played really well.'

I forced myself to look at him. It was hard. A hollow feeling twisted through my chest. 'Thanks,' I muttered.

Caiden smiled, and I felt like I was going to melt into a puddle 😊. 'So . . .' He dug his hands into his pockets. 'Well . . . I'm not a vampire.'

I wanted to CEASE TO EXIST!

If goddess Selene had any mercy, she would have struck me down with a lightning bolt.

Come on, I pleaded inwardly. *I've howled at the moon and everything. The least you can do is SAVE ME FROM THIS CONVERSATION!*

My face was so burning hot that it felt extra-cold when the heat flashed out of it again.

I didn't have a clue what to say.

'I can play the piano though,' Caiden said. 'So that's one thing I have in common with Edward Cullen.'

When I still didn't say anything, Caiden took out his phone. 'I wanted you to know that I have a journal too. The counsellor at my old school in London recommended it after my mum and dad split up, because I was in a bad place.' His dark brows pulled together and he cast me a nervous little glance.

I was intrigued. I hadn't thought that someone like Caiden could ever feel nervous.

'I hardly write in it,' he said. 'But I can show you my entry from Sunday the second of September.'

He handed me his phone. I took it and looked at the screen:

I met this girl today. Well, I first met her yesterday, but today we got to talk a bit. She's really nice. Really pretty too. Her name is Lara Bloom and she goes to the school I'll be starting tomorrow. Maybe moving to Liverpool won't be so bad after all.

I looked up, shocked.

He'd liked the pre-glow-up version of me???

Caiden raked a hand through his hair, and I noticed that it was a bit longer than usual. It had grown out about an inch and was all curly and cute. 'I didn't watch that Marvel movie with Sienna, by the way. I was saving it for when we go. We watched this really bad comedy instead that wasn't even funny.'

His eye roll would have made me smile if I wasn't TOTALLY ON EDGE.

He cleared his throat. 'Do you, uh, still want to go to the cinema?'

'Yeah,' I said with a casual shrug, even though my heart was doing star jumps. 'Sure.'

'Just us,' Caiden said. 'Me and you.'

I nodded again.

'Cool.' He flashed me a relieved smile. 'Wow. I wasn't sure if you were going to say yes.'

I didn't know what to say, so I just stood there like a dork. Around us, people were running, shouting and messing around, but they began to fade into nothing. I was so caught up, thinking about Caiden's journal entry.

The silence between us began to stretch out a little long, so I gave him the side eye. 'There's no way you can play the piano.'

'Hey, why do you never believe a word I say?'

Caiden grabbed my hand and marched me off the football field, into the school building, and straight to the music room. I stumbled after him, laughing.

He sat at the piano and began to play 'Perfect' by Ed Sheeran.

I was impressed. 'You're good! You'll have to teach me.'

'It's easy,' he said. 'But you can't co-ordinate your feet unless you're on a football pitch, and you've got no hand–eye co-ordination, so you might not be any good at co-ordinating your fingers either.'

I slapped his shoulder and he laughed.

Then the door to the room banged open and a bunch of our friends trooped in. 'I told you I saw them slip in here,' Kayleigh said.

Caiden's friends teased him about playing the piano to me while Kayleigh dragged me to a table across the room. Anaya and Becky followed. Kayleigh produced a pen and notebook from her bag and began to write. 'We're the squidge girls,' she said.

'What?' Anaya asked.

'Squid girls?' Becky asked. 'What is it with your family and slimy stuff? First caterpillars, now squid.'

Kayleigh set down her pen then held up her notebook. She'd written *SQuIDGE* on it. 'Not squid,' she said. '*SQuIDGE*.'

'What does it mean?' I asked.

'It stands for Supermodel, Queen, Independent woman, Diva, Goddess Energy.'

Anaya giggled. 'We're the Squidge Squad.'

'I like it,' Becky said. 'We can call each other squidges.'

'Listen up, squidges,' Kayleigh said. 'We might have completed our Glow-Up Plan, but glow ups are forever.' She took some silver bracelets out of her bag and slipped one onto each of our wrists. They were all engraved with the word 'SQuIDGE'.

'These bracelets,' Kayleigh said, 'are a reminder of all the work we did to glow up, and how proud we should be of ourselves.'

'Ah, thanks, Kayleigh,' I said.

I'm not sure if I've actually had a glow up, but I'm much more comfortable about being myself now.

I'm *me*, and I'm not going to try to be something I'm not any more.

I'm less worried about what people think of me too. Because after my journal getting leaked I have only two options: drive myself to despair, or move on.

I've chosen to move on.

It's hard, and it'll take time, but I *will* get over it.

Sooo . . . if a glow up is about becoming more of who you are, then yes, I, Lara Bloom, have glowed up.

Note to self:
- I can straighten my hair *and* love my curls.
- I can accept who I am *and* seek improvement/growth.
- I can be both girly and sporty.
- I'm a giant bundle of contradictions, and that's okay.

Acknowledgements

I'm incredibly grateful to you, dear reader, for picking up this book and spending time with Lara and friends. Thank you so much! It means the world to me.

Glow Up, Lara Bloom would not exist without my spectacular agent, Hannah Sheppard, who took a chance on me when I wasn't sure anybody ever would. Thank you, Hannah, for believing in me and championing my work. Thank you for your support and advocacy. You are an absolute goddess of agenting, and I appreciate all that you do.

To the wonderful Ruth Bennett and Tia Albert, a million thank-yous for believing in this book so enthusiastically and giving Lara Bloom a home at Hot Key Books. Immeasurable gratitude to Ruth for being such a magnificent editor. You are nothing short of amazing. Thank you for all your hard work helping me make this story the best it can be. Your vision, insight and keen editorial eye have been invaluable. I'm so thrilled that I got to work with you!

I was absolutely blown away when I first saw the stunning cover for *Glow Up, Lara Bloom*. Enormous appreciation to the incredibly talented Sophie McDonnell and Amanda Quartey for doing such an amazing job creating it.

Massive thanks to all the wonderful people at Hot Key Books who helped to turn my manuscript into a published novel. I appreciate all your hard work. Jane Hammett for copyediting, Christina Webb and Talya Baker for proof-reading, Emma Quick, Molly Holt and Eleanor Rose for marketing and publicity; Graeme at Envy Design for typesetting, Marina Stavropoulou for the audiobook and the supremely talented Sandra Gayer for giving Lara Bloom a voice, and Louise Brown for sensitivity reading.

A huge thank you to my mentor, Holly Race, for giving me the chance I needed to showcase my work and break through. You were the first person in 'the industry' to believe in me and encourage me. Thank you for sharing your publication journey and giving me the chance to rub shoulders with an actual published author. Talking to you made me feel like my dream just might be within reach. You have been pivotal to my journey and I will always be grateful for that. Likewise Stuart White and the whole WriteMentor team. Thank you for all you do for authors: the mentoring, the competitions, and all the time and effort you so selflessly invest. You are making dreams come true. You have certainly helped with mine. May your dreams come true too.

To Brook Lane, my dear friend (although sister is more appropriate), thank you for the coffees, the lunches, the spa dates (our very own glow ups), the conversations, the friendship, the sisterhood and everything else. I'm so glad we crossed paths that day at the school gates, and I'm so glad you're here, walking the earth in the same place and the same era as me. Thank you for being you.

Immeasurable gratitude to my amazing father and mother-in-law who have been praying for me endlessly to find a publisher. Look how your prayers have been answered! I appreciate you very much.

To my queens and all-round squidges, Rhema and Esther, I love you both so much and I'm always so proud of you just because of who you are. You fill my life with light and goodness and beauty. Thank you for your enthusiasm about Lara Bloom at every stage of the process. You are my inspiration.

Yomi, my rock, I hit the jackpot with you and I'm forever grateful to have you in my life. Thank you for your unwavering support, for dreaming with me since day one and for always being there. Thank you for the words that spurred me on whenever I felt like giving up, and for continuing to believe in my dream when I began to doubt. Thank you for all the colour you bring to my world and the music you put in my soul. I love you more always.

To my younger self, thank you for loving kid lit and YA novels. Thank you for reading voraciously and for your obsession with words. You led me to today.

And to God who always makes a way, thank You

for everything. They say 'count your blessings' but that's an impossible task because You have blessed me beyond measure.

Author Note

I wrote *Glow Up, Lara Bloom* with three main groups of people in mind: anybody who has ever struggled with low self-esteem, experienced mental health issues such as depression, or been bullied. And guess what? That's most people. If you are experiencing any of these things, you don't have to struggle in silence. There are lots of ways you can build your self-esteem and improve your mental health, and you have the right to live free from bullies.

Self-Esteem
If you're feeling bad about yourself, I want you to know that you're awesome, even if you don't feel like it right now. Most people feel bad about themselves sometimes, for example if they make a mistake or fail a test. It's part of being human. But it might be time to do something about it if you feel this way most of the time.

First of all, see if you can start being a kind friend to yourself, including in the things you say to yourself and how you think about yourself. You could also talk to someone about how you're feeling, read books about building healthy self-esteem and find resources that might help you. This website could be a good starting point: https://www.mind.org.uk/information-support/for-children-and-young-people/confidence-and-self-esteem/

Some Black girls, and people with kinky hair textures, struggle to accept their hair. If you are one of them, I want you to know that your hair is special and unique and that you don't have to believe the myths about your hair (such as it can't grow long, or it's hard work). Your hair might simply need you to do things differently. I encourage you to get excited about your hair and to see learning how to take care of it like an adventure. You'll need to be patient, and you'll probably need support from other people with hair like yours, but this can be a rewarding journey that could help you to accept yourself in other ways too. This website is a good place to start if you would like some information about Afro hair: afrocks.com/blog/10-things-you-didnt-know-about-afro-hair/

Mental Health

Mental Health is very important. If you're struggling with yours, you don't have to face it alone. Please speak to someone you trust who will be able to support you. There are great charities that can also help, such as Young Minds youngminds.org.uk

youngminds.org.uk/young-person/find-help

Bullying

If you are being bullied, there is help available. If the bullying is happening outside of school, speak to a trusted adult as soon as possible. If the bullying is taking place at school, talk to a teacher or ask a trusted adult to speak on your behalf.

If there is nobody you feel comfortable speaking to, or if the issue is not dealt with satisfactorily, these organisations can offer advice and support:

- Anti-Bullying Alliance
  anti-bullyingalliance.org.uk
- Childline
  childline.org.uk 0800 1111
- Bullying UK (advice for parents and families)
  familylives.org.uk 0808 800 2222

Finally, if you know someone who is struggling in any of the above ways, listening to their experiences, being supportive and encouraging them as they seek help could make a huge difference. And remember to always take care of yourself too.

Lots of love and hugs,

Dee xx

See what Lara does next

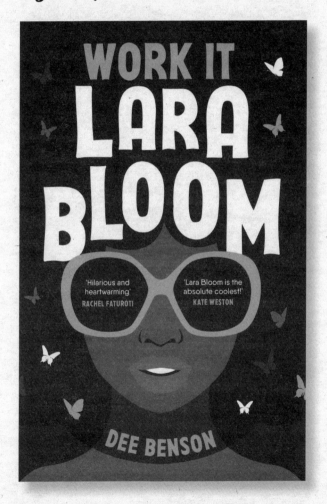

WORK IT

LARA BLOOM

'Hilarious and heartwarming'
RACHEL FATUROTI

'Lara Bloom is the absolute coolest!'
KATE WESTON

DEE BENSON

About the Author

Dee Benson has been obsessed with books since childhood. She finds it surreal that she now gets to create her own worlds and characters in books of her own. When she isn't writing, Dee enjoys long walks, good food and music that makes her wish she could sing. She lives in Liverpool with her husband and two daughters.

Thank you for choosing a Hot Key book!

For all the latest bookish news, freebies and exclusive
content, sign up to the Hot Key newsletter – scan the
QR code or visit lnk.to/HotKeyBooks

Follow us on social media:

bonnierbooks.co.uk/HotKeyBooks